WHAT WAS B
AND ROU

Beautiful scientist Dr. Nancy Derringer called
it an Apatosaurus, the most wondrous living
creature ever discovered in its unspoiled, natural habitat.

Skip King, the fat cat of fast foods, called it a
Thunder Lizard, and a meal ticket to a corporate feeding frenzy if he could bring it back
to America alive.

Chiun insisted it was a dragon whose essence,
when properly extracted, would assure him
of an extended reign as Master of Sinanju.

But to Remo, it was just a regular old dinosaur
. . . and he found himself on the side of this
monster who made King Kong look like a
monkey, against all the evil that money
could buy and a greed that could destroy a
creature who was fair game for foul play to
the very bloody finish. . . .

THE
LAST DRAGON

REMO LIVES ON

☐ **THE DESTROYER #67: LOOK INTO MY EYES by Warren Murphy and Richard Sapir.** A malevolent Mindmaster sends Remo and Chiun into battle—but against each other! They are on a collision course—and the world could end not with a bang, but with their crash . . .
(146468—$4.50)

☐ **THE DESTROYER #68: AN OLD FASHIONED WAR by Warren Murphy and Richard Sapir.** Something strange was happening all over the world. Chiun was the only one who knew what it was . . . but he wasn't telling. With Remo and Chiun divided humanity's ultimate nightmare was coming true by the hands of ancient evil. (147766—$4.50)

☐ **THE DESTROYER #69: BLOOD TIES by Warren Murphy and Richard Sapir.** Remo and Chiun are sent to stop a deadly assassin only to find out the mysterious hit man was Remo Williams—the one man the Destroyer could not destroy! (168135—$4.50)

☐ **THE DESTROYER #71: RETURN ENGAGEMENT by Warren Murphy and Richard Sapir.** Remo and Chiun battle a super-fiend who came back from the dead stronger than steel. They had to find the answer to the monstrous mystery of the man who called himself Herr Fuhrer Blutsturz and the antidote to his irresistible evil. But first they had to stay alive long enough to do it . . . (152441—$3.95)

☐ **THE DESTROYER #89: DARK HORSE.** Remo and Chiun vote for vengeance when death hits the campaign trail. (171160—$4.50)

Prices slightly higher in Canada.

The Destroyer

#92

THE LAST DRAGON

CREATED BY

WARREN MURPHY & RICHARD SAPIR

A SIGNET BOOK

SIGNET
Published by the Penguin Group
Penguin Books USA Inc., 375 Hudson Street,
New York, New York 10014, U.S.A.
Penguin Books Ltd, 27 Wrights Lane,
London W8 5TZ, England
Penguin Books Australia Ltd, Ringwood,
Victoria, Australia
Penguin Books Canada Ltd, 10 Alcorn Avenue,
Toronto, Ontario, Canada M4V 3B2
Penguin Books (N.Z.) Ltd, 182–190 Wairau Road,
Auckland 10, New Zealand

Penguin Books Ltd, Registered Offices:
Harmondsworth, Middlesex, England

First published by Signet, an imprint of New American Library,
a division of Penguin Books USA Inc.

First Printing, April, 1993
10 9 8 7 6 5 4 3 2 1

 REGISTERED TRADEMARK—MARCA REGISTRADA

PUBLISHER'S NOTE
This is a work of fiction. Names, characters, places, and incidents either
are the product of the author's imagination or are used fictitiously, and any
resemblance to actual persons, living or dead, events, or locales is entirely
coincidental.

For Joe DeVito, *Illustratosaurus Rex.*

And the Glorious House of Sinanju,
P.O. Box 2505, Quincy, MA 02269.

Prologue

On the first pass, they missed it.

The earthquake had opened up great red-brown holes in the green African veldt, and the imaging analysts thought it was one of those.

But a sharp-eyed photo enhancement analyst named Narvel Buckle saw the black blotches and bands dappling the elongated Halloween-pumpkin orange shape.

"I think it's alive," he muttered to himself. He told no one.

On the second pass, twelve hours later, it had moved three meters. Alive. Definitely.

His curiosity roused. Narvel made another search for it on the third pass. He told the satellite console operator that there were signs of volcanic activity. The government of Gondwanaland, he explained, would pay well for topographic photos of an emerging natural disaster like a volcano.

"They'll throw it into the package with our quake shots and they can double their foreign aid request," he said.

That was all he needed to say. The operator signaled the low-orbit Gaiasat camera to suppress all vegetation and bring up the warm end of the spectrum.

Luck was with Narvel on that third pass. The black-and-orange thing happened to be looking up as the satellite snapped a clear photograph that captured the upward-looking eyes. It was looking directly at the sun, which reflected as twin pinpoints of hot light.

"I know what that dadgum thing is!" he breathed, nearly dropping his jeweler's loupe.

And since he worked for a commercial satellite company which specialized in selling natural disaster damage assessment images to foreign countries—whose reputation could be ruined if they dared to put the photos on the international market—Narvel Buckle slipped the entire set into his briefcase, and set about peddling them out of his Chevy Chase apartment.

The *National Enquirer* laughed at him; they printed photos just like it every week. This week's issue was headlined BAT BOY FOUND LIVING IN CAVE! The managing editor's eight-year-old son had posed for it, and the computer graphics people had added the pointy ears and filed-to-chisels teeth.

Did Narvel have any shots of Liz or Madonna sunbathing in the nude? Preferably together? Maybe even kissing? No? Call when you do. Toodles.

The Smithsonian Institute in Washington kept shunting him back and forth between departments. The paleontology department couldn't have been less interested if he had been trying to sell them osteoporosis insurance.

"Our interests are restricted to old bones and fossils," a voice that sounded as if it had belonged to one of the latter said.

"But this is the real thing!" Narvel explained. "You can render it to the bone or something. Like they do with tired old horses to get glue."

"Try Natural History. I shall see if I can connect you."

The attempt was a magnificent one. Thirty-seven different people lifted department phones, ranging from anthropology to zoology, and tried to talk all at once.

Narvel Buckle finally hung up and asked the switchboard to connect him directly. After he explained what the satellite photos had disclosed, the chairman—or whatever he was—of the Smithsonian natural history department inhaled through his nose with a sound like a tiny elephant exhaling through his trunk.

"Impossible," he added.

"I got the photos," Narvel retorted. "And they're only two thousand dollars for the set of three."

"As I said, it is impossible. No such beast could be roaming the heart of Africa."

"Why the hell not?"

"For there to be one, there must be many."

"I don't follow."

"Follow this simple equation: One creature necessitates two parents. Two parents requires four grandparents. A quartet of grandparents implies a large sustaining population. No such population has ever been discovered on the African landmass."

"Hey, we're talking Africa here! It's not exactly Vegas."

"Africa has been satisfactorily explored. And certainly by now, an orbiting satelite would have snapped portraits of specimens such as you describe."

"That's what I got! High-resolution satellite images. In color. Nine by twelves. Glossies."

"Impossible. Sorry. Try the paleontology department. Let me connect you."

"I don't want to be—"

Narvel Buckle hung up just as the bone-dry voice of the head paleontologist was saying "Yes?"

No other museum seemed interested. Narvel thought he had a sale to the Harvard Museum of Comparative Zoology, but when they wanted the president of the Gaia Satellite Reconnaissance Company to personally vouch for the authenticity of the photos in question, Narvel had to admit that he was selling his photos under the table. The curator hung up without another word.

Then someone at the Royal Ontario Museum in Toronto told him to try the cryptozoologists.

"The what?"

"Try the International Colloquium of Cryptozoologists in Phoenix. This is exactly their sort of meat."

Narvel didn't know what a cryptozoologist was, but he called the number the Phoenix directory assistance gave him.

A woman answered. She had a pleasant voice that made him think of Michelle Pfeiffer, and as he told his story, he could hear her breathe into the receiver, at first in warm, measured intervals, and then with increasing excitement.

"We are very, very interested in your photographs," she told him.

"Five grand for the set of three," Narvel said instantly.

"Can you supply the longitude and latitude of the sighting?"

"That'll be $39.99 extra."

"Done."

"Deal."

"One question," Narvel asked.

"Yes."

"What the heck is a cryptozoologist?"

"Cryptozoology is the study of hidden animals," the blondish-sounding voice explained. "That's what crypto means: hidden. We are interested in creatures common zoologists dismiss as mythological, or which are mistakenly believed to be extinct."

"Oh. No wonder you want these photos."

Narvel faxed muddy photocopies of the photos that very day and patiently waited for a return call. It never came.

The check arrived the next day by UPS Express. Narvel waited until the check had cleared before fedexing the three high-resolution color photographs that the Smithsonian Institute had turned down, along with the exact longitude and latitude at which the satellite had snapped the shots. He never heard back from the International Colloquium of Cryptozoologists, and none of the photos ever appeared in print. But Narvel Buckle didn't care about that. He was thinking that he should have asked for ten grand. At least.

1

Dr. Nancy Derringer was starting to have second thoughts.

The heart of equatorial Africa was no place for second thoughts, never mind fear. But Nancy, blond as corn silk, willowy as bamboo, and tough as Arizona sagebrush, was experiencing both.

Those who knew her well claimed she was as fearless as the crocodiles she had spent her short adult life studying.

As the chief paleontologist and herpetologist for the International Colloquium of Cryptozoologists, Nancy Derringer had trudged through Himalayan snows for Yeti, plumbed deep-water lakes all over the Americas and the British Isles for surviving plesiosaurs, and penetrated abyssal depths in quest of garagantuan cephalopods.

Africa was a different matter. It was a hothouse for tropical diseases like river blindness and monkey pox, the reputed incubator for AIDS. A Caucasian had to undergo two months of inoculations before embarking on an expedition into the continent's humid heart.

They injected her twice against cholera, twice against typhoid, subjected her to a precautionary rabies injection that they warned might do no good if she were bitten in the wild, gave her a tetanus booster shot, and then sugar lumps impregnated with polio vaccine to take orally.

Nancy had been so anxious to get going she asked to be injected and inoculated all in one day. The doctors vetoed that. No less than four weeks between the yellow fever and hepatitis vaccines. And she would have to go to London for her yellow fever inoculation. It was unavailable in the U.S.

It had been painful and annoying, and she had taken it all without complaint, sustained by sheer adrenalin.

The flight from London had gone well. And the stopover in Port Chuma, capital of Gondwanaland, former European colony of Bamba del Oro, and now sovereign nation on the brink of social and economic catastrophe, was interminable.

Now, trudging through the Gondwanaland bush, popping her daily antimalaria tablets dry, Nancy was nervous.

She would have preferred a more politically palatable sponsor than the Burger Triumph hamburger chain. But the nature of the expedition was not exactly *National Geographic* cover material.

The major colleges had been too broke. She had been laughed out of corporate boardrooms from Manhattan to L.A. Even PBS had said no.

Until that day she met with Skip King, vice president in charge of marketing for the Burger Triumph Corporation, in his thirty-fourth floor office in their world headquarters in Dover, Delaware.

She had felt foolish even requesting the meeting. But a colleague had suggested it, and then faxed her one side of a Burger Triumph food bag that looked as if it had been designed by a precocious child. It showed the planet earth and boasted of Burger Triumph's new biodegradable packaging that conserved seven million tons of waste annually, not to mention the gasoline conserved and pollution cut by dispensing with the old cardboard containers.

"Planet-pleasing packaging" it was called.

A note scribbled on the fax said, "They're rich, they're environmentally conscious. Why not try?"

"They're trying to rehabilitate their reputation," Nancy snorted. But she made the call and got an appointment for the very next day.

There, she had made a short self-conscious presentation and laid the unmarked manila envelope on King's desk. Wordlessly, he had taken it up, unwound the flap-securing string, and shook out the three eight-by-ten glossies that had been taken from an earth observation satellite from a distance of over one hundred miles above Africa.

King had stared at them for five silent minutes, going through them briskly at first and then slowly the second time. At the end, he set the three photos side by side on his desk and stared at them a long while.

His face was too sharp to be called handsome. It had a foxy cast to it. Or maybe it was more wolfish, Nancy had thought. The nose, the thin-lipped mouth, even the high-tolerance cut of his jet black hair was too severe.

He looked up, and his eyes, black as volcanic glass, regarded her without any emotion she could read.

"You say they're alive?" he asked tonelessly.

"There is just one, as far as we know."

"How big?"

"Judging from the photos, forty feet from nose to tail."

King looked down and frowned. "Most of it is neck and tail," he muttered in a vaguely disappointed tone. "How big would you say the body is?"

"Oh, less than half of that."

"Fifteen feet, then?"

"At a rough estimate."

"Tall?"

"With the neck lifted, we estimate—"

He shook his head impatiently. "No—how tall from underbelly to the top of the spine?"

Nancy had frowned. "Possibly eight feet."

Skip King took up a pencil and began making calculations on a notepad. He crossed out columns of numbers instead of erasing them, and when he got an end figure, he looked up and said, very seriously, "Probably weighs eight tons, not counting head, neck, and tail. Ten tons in all."

"That sounds about right," Nancy had admitted, thinking, *This man is asking all the wrong questions.*

But King seemed so completely professional. Buttondown, no-nonsense, and thoroughly unruffled by the prospect of making zoological history.

"And you want Burger Triumph to fund your safari?" he had asked.

"Expedition. And we think it could be accomplished for less than two million dollars," Nancy told him.

"That include shipping costs?"

"Shipping?"

"Bringing the beast back alive."

"Back! How would we get it back? I mean, could we get it back. The government of—"

"Gondwanaland? Don't make me laugh. It's run by a tub of butter who's backpedaling away from Karl Marx so fast he's trampling his immediate ancestors. BT is a multinational company. We could buy Gondwanaland, if we wanted. Cheap. But it'll be a lot easier to grease a few official palms." He paused for breath, then said, "Miss Derringer, I believe I can get you an approval on this."

The suddenness of the statement had taken her breath away. Nancy had expected polite interest, and weeks—if not months—of corporate buck-passing until an answer was handed down.

"Are—are you sure? I mean, arrangements will have to be made about creating a suitable environment for the animal. And there is the question of a receptive zoo—"

Skip King raised a quieting hand. "Please calm down," he said. "All these things will be taken care of."

And they were. Within forty-eight hours, Skip King had called. His voice was smooth as champagne.

"It's set," he said, as if he were talking about a day trip to the Smokies.

"It is?"

"The CEO had sanctioned all the funding we need. A suitable transportation vessel is being chartered, and by the time we return with it, a climate-suitable habitation will be waiting."

"Where?"

"Somewhere near Burger Triumph World Headquarters. Maybe in it. We have a rather large basement."

"What!"

"We have a very large basement. It will be converted into a suitable temporary habitat."

"As long as it's temporary," Nancy had told him.

"We estimate we'll be able to leave in three to four weeks."

"Impossible."

"Not for us."

"Us?"

"I intend to lead this safari, Miss Derringer."

The statement floored her. But it had been delivered with such calm self-assurance that Nancy had been taken utterly off guard.

"Do—do you have any experience in this sort of project?" Nancy had stammered.

"Miss Derringer, special projects are my life."

"That's not what I mean. I meant field experience."

"Miss Derringer, I happen to be a graduate of the Wharton School of Business. I'm sure you've heard of it."

"Somewhere. And if you don't mind, it's *Dr.* Derringer."

King had sniffed thinly—the first hint of his true character, Nancy realized now. "And where did *you* go to school?"

"Oh, let's see. B.A. from Columbia—"

"A nice school, I hear. But no Wharton."

"—received my master's from Texas Technological University, and studied herpetology at the University of Colorado."

"You studied herpes?"

"Herpetology," Nancy said patiently, "is the study of reptiles. I've done extensive field work all over the globe for the Colloquium, and additionally I'm a member of the Crocodile Specialist Group of the International Union for the Conservation of Nature and Natural Resources."

"Oh," said Skip King in a tiny voice. "Well, I graduated magna cum laude."

Nancy suppressed a sigh. Two could play at this infantile game, she thought. "Summa cum laude."

"Second place is nice, too," King said smugly.

"Summa cum laude means *highest* honors, Mr. King. Magna cum laude happens to be *second* place. And unless you want to contract a wide variety of pernicious tropical diseases," Nancy added firmly, "we're not going until we've been thoroughly inoculated."

There was a protracted pause on the line. When his voice returned, it was almost a croak.

"Does that mean needles?"

"Yes. Long, sharp ones."

"I hate needles." And his voice was so dead that for a moment Nancy was afraid he would call the whole thing off.

He hadn't. But now, weeks later, Nancy was beginning to wish he had.

It had started when he had shown up at the departure point wearing a "Safari Til You Puke" T-shirt.

Nancy was able to overlook that. But when they reached Port Chuma, he had insisted the native bearers wear Burger Triumph T-shirts and pith helmets—and address him as B'wana King.

Ralph Thorpe, the British guide, had coaxed the Bantus into humoring King. Behind his back, they grinned and laughed. It was a big joke.

To Nancy, Thorpe had confided, "I've seen this happen before. Our Mr. King has gone 'bushy.' "

"Bushy?"

"Intoxicated by the African bush."

"But we aren't there yet."

"Let's hope it wears off by the time we do," said Thorpe.

It hadn't. It had only gotten worse. And they nearly lost their bearers when, on the first day out, they had broken out the provisions and King had insisted upon keeping the best food for the white expedition members and feeding the natives reheated Bongo Burgers, cheesefries, and flat soft drinks.

"Why are they spitting out their food?" King had complained. "Each Silly Meal is five bucks American. That's more than these guys make in a week."

"They are used to real food," Thorpe had warned. "And if they do not receive it, we shall all be fending for ourselves."

King had relented. And complained and complained.

That was when Nancy started to wonder if King was not "bushy" after all—just a few fries short of a Silly Meal.

Now they were walking single file through the bush. Ahead loomed the denseness of the rain forest, packed like green, leafy lettuce and cabled by hair-fine lianas and thick creepers. They were coming to the impenetrable Kanda Tract, where even the Bantus seldom ventured.

Nancy was walking in the rear, with the native porters. She had wanted to take a lead position, but Skip King had vetoed that, saying, "Your place is at the back of the pack."

She had let it go. There was some logic to it. If anything happened to her, there was no expedition. Simple as that.

Then he had made a remark that made Nancy want to strangle him. He had been thumbing through guide books, and calling out facts he found interesting. "Hey, Nancy! Do you know that among the Tswana tribe, they have only one noun for women?"

"That is not unusual among tribal cultures."

"Their word is *mosad*—and it means 'the one who remains behind and at home when men go to work.' You'd better hope we don't run into any Tswana, or you'll be in big trouble."

"I can handle myself, thank you," Nancy said tightly.

"Don't let it get to you. Remember, B'wana King is here to protect you."

"But who is going to protect B'wana King?" Nancy said through her clenched teeth.

Up ahead, King, flanked by the British guide, called, "Collluuumn, halt!"

The column halted. A misty haze was rising over the Kanda Tract. Sunbirds flashed through the air.

"Break out the videocams!" King called.

Nancy groaned to herself. "Oh, no. Not again."

The lead bearers unpacked the triple-wrapped videocams. Someone from the PR team lifted a light meter to the sky. Someone else took a makeup puff to Skip King's thrust-forward face.

Then King opened his eyes and said, "Where's the little lady herpes specialist?"

"Here," Nancy said in a voice that seemed to cool the surrounding by twelve degrees.

King waved her on. "C'mon up here. Let's get you into this shot."

"Coming," Nancy grumbled. She worked her way forward.

Skip King smiled broadly at the sight of her.

"Why don't you get in this shot?" he said. "I can't hog all the face time on this safari, now can I?"

"Very kind of you."

"Besides," he added as she took her place and submitted to a brief dusting of makeup powder, "we could use a little sex appeal, Nancy."

"Why don't you just call me Dr. Derringer, Mr. King?"

"Why don't you call me Skip? After all, how will it sound on TV? The expedition leader and his gal Friday not being chummy?"

"It will sound *professional,* Mr. King."

"Does that mean I can't chide you into unbuttoning your blouse a button or two?" King wheedled.

"Shall we just get this over with?"

"Okay, I'll wing it as usual."

Skip King cleared his throat and put the dead weight of one arm around Nancy's shoulders.

"We are standing at the edge of the fabled Kanda Tract," he began, "home of a creature not seen on this earth in a trillion years."

Nancy winced. The man had no conception of geologic time.

"Although incredible dangers await us, we have no fear. For we are corporate Americans, smart, savvy, and determined to fulfill our mission: to bring 'em back alive!"

He grinned into the camera lens like a Cadillac with an ivory grille and held the smile for twelve full seconds.

"Okay, cut! How was that?"

The PR man shot him an A-OK sign. "Super!"

"One-take King, that's me." He smiled down at Nancy and asked, "So—how was I?"

Nancy threw his arm off and stormed away.

"Must be that time of month," King muttered. And as the cameras were repacked, he turned to the expedition medic and said, "Okay. Prep me for the great adventure."

He unrolled the sleeves of his safari jacket as a native porter took off his leopard-striped bush hat. Someone wiped the makeup off his intent face.

They sprayed him down with insect repellent. The medic began affixing flesh-colored patches to his arms, neck, and cheeks.

"Antinausea wristbands," the medic announced.

"Check," said King, as they were adjusted.

"Antimalaria patch."

"Check."

"Nicotine patch."

"Roger."

"Vitamin A patch."

"Check."

"Vitamin C patch."

"Rickets and Scurvy are covered."

"Vitamin E patch."

"Just in case I get lucky." And King leered directly at Nancy. She turned her back.

The medic stepped back. "You're all set."

"Not yet. Where's the antileech shield?"

"There hasn't been a leech sighted since we got here," Nancy exploded.

"Take no chances, that's my motto."

Somebody handed him a furled black cloth rod.

And announcing to all within hearing, "Here's where we separate the men from the wusses," Skip King opened his black umbrella and walked into the Kanda Tract boldly and without fear.

"I don't believe this," Nancy muttered, falling in behind him.

The rain forest was like another world. The sky was a thing glimpsed from time to time through the cathedral-like canopy of overhanging branches and leaves. Sunlight, filtering through the green plant life, was a watery green hue. It was almost like walking through an underwater world of heavy, breathable air in which insects tweedled and cheeped and monkeys watched from branches with orbs wiser than human eyes.

Ralph Thorpe dropped back to walk beside her. He toted a big-game rifle on his muscular shoulder. His pith helmet was decorated front and sides with the big golden Burger Triumph corporate crown logo. He had scraped off the legend "Sponsored by Burger Triumph" and had made inroads on the crown itself.

"His back makes a tempting target, what?" Thorpe undertoned.

"Don't think it hasn't crossed my mind," Nancy said aridly.

"If we get what we're after, it'll all be worth it. Don't you forget that."

"Keep telling me that. I need it."

* * *

Three hours later, they broke into a clearing and Skip King immediately fell down.

"Quicksand!" he screamed.

They rushed to his aid.

"It's just a hole!" the PR chief said reassuringly.

"No, it's not," Nancy said in a squeezed-dry voice.

"Of course it's a hole," King was saying as they helped him to his feet. His sharp face hung slack and his dark eyes seemed on the verge of tears. He had smashed his antileech umbrella against a tulip tree. It was ruined.

"Everybody get away from the hole," Nancy said. The excitement in her voice made them all look at her.

"Get away from it!" she repeated. They jumped. Her voice was that loud.

Nancy paced around the deep depression in the earth, her features holding on to composure with twitching tentativeness.

"It's a hind foot," she decided aloud.

Skip King canted his head from side to side as if trying to get a crick out of his neck.

"It is?"

"The track of one."

King came closer. "Are you sure?"

"Rear tracks have five digits with claws on three. That's according to the fossil record. These are exactly the same."

She expected him to shout something macho. Instead, he gulped, "It's bigger than I thought."

She looked up. "Afraid?"

King squared his padded shoulders. "Honey, I'm fueled by testosterone. Fear isn't in me."

"Then you won't cry over your broken umbrella, will you?" And she pushed ahead.

Skip King went pale and started after her calling, "Hey! What are you doing taking the point? That's a man's job!"

* * *

The earthquake had felled trees all over the Kanda Tract.

Mighty kapok trees had toppled, so thick around that they flattened smaller saplings to juicy splinters. Here and there, thin-boled bamboo had splintered at their bases, their fall interrupted by the creeper-festooned forest canopy.

There were splits and fissures in the earth, great red-brown wounds that had already—two months after the quake—become green again with new plant life.

In some places the ground was as soft as peat moss poured from a plastic sack. The smell was about the same—heady, almost sweet.

The trail had petered out to a narrow path the rain forest was swiftly reclaiming. The hot air grew heavy in their lungs. The rain forest seemed to press in on them like a green, leafy stomach.

The first unusual event was the dragonflies.

Flying in arrow formation, they zipped across a break in the trees, their doubled wings flashing like iridescent vanes.

"Those can't be dragonflies," Skip muttered, freezing in his tracks.

Nancy had her Leica up and clicking.

"Fabulous."

King looked at her. "Dragonflies? Fabulous?"

"Modern dragonflies are not known to grow that big."

"Do African dragonflies behave like American dragonflies?"

"How do you mean?"

"Do they—do they sew up people's mouths?" King gulped.

"You must be joking!"

"This is my first time in Africa. You can't expect me to know every little thing."

"American dragonflies don't sew mouths. That's an old wives' tale."

"You sure?"

"Positive."

"Can't be too careful." He called over his shoulder. 'Who's got the Black Flag?"

"Don't you dare!"

"What's the problem? We're not here for dragonflies."

"If we can catch one, it will be just as important as capturing the beast."

"Not to Burger Triumph, Incorporated."

"Need I remind you that I'm the scientific leader on this mission?"

"Yeah, but I'm the bankroll. What I say goes. We push on."

King shoved past Nancy Derringer and took the lead. He walked with one hand rubbing his jaw absently, but Nancy knew that was a precaution. If the dragonflies got close, he was going to cover his big mouth. Nancy prayed for dragonflies in the thousands.

But the dragonflies flashed away in three different directions, like prehistoric helicopters.

The giant frogs were the next surprise.

They had been squatting, sides throbbing, in the rank grass of a small pond of standing water.

As one approached, it hopped once, landing in the middle of the road. It rotated nervously until it faced them with its unblinking bulgy eyes. Its throat pulsed like a great green heart torn out of a monster's chest.

"What the fuck is that!" King said hoarsely.

Ralph Thorpe came up, rifle in hand.

"Hah! It's an effing Goliath bullfrog!"

"It looks like the effing mother of all toads," King groaned.

"Aw, don't get your knickers tangled up, Mr. King. It's only a bleedin' frog."

"I don't like the way it's staring at me. Shoot it."

"No need to go to all that bother." Thorpe hefted a smooth flat stone in the frog's direction and it bounded away with a spastic kicking of its hind legs.

"See? There. Nothing to it, what?"

"I hope you'll be able to hold yourself together when we locate our quarry," Nancy said pointedly.

King said through his uplifted hand. "Hey, I had a bad experience with frogs when I was little."

"Oh? Did one eat your fly collection?"

King frowned. "The girls on my staff don't talk to me like that."

"Hire women next time."

King's frown deepened. They trudged on. Further along, he snapped his fingers and said, "PMS! Am I right?"

And it was all Nancy Derringer could do to keep from wheeling and slapping him silly.

The *hurrunk* cannonading through the green trees dispelled her anger like a breaking fever.

"What was that?" King muttered.

Nancy closed her eyes and seemed to be beseeching lurking jungle gods. "Oh, God! Could it be? Oh, please let it be what I think it is."

King's dark eyes went wide. "You think that's the sound *it* would make?"

"No one knows. There is no fossil record of natural sounds."

"Thorpe! Fetch that native guide."

The Bantu guide came padding up. He was tall and lean with a narrow wise face that looked ageless. Except for his Burger Triumph T-shirt, he might have been the genus loci of the rain forest.

"Ask Slim if that's the sound N'yamala makes," King demanded.

Thorpe addressed the native in his own tongue. The man gesticulated and ended up pointing at King, while spitting out a sparse sentence.

"What'd he say?" King asked excitedly.

"He asked that you not call him Slim," Thorpe translated.

"Why not? It's only a nickname."

"Slim is what the city blacks call in English, AIDS. Tyrone doesn't savvy American-style English very well, but he recognizes the word. He doesn't like it."

"Is everybody having a bad day?" King muttered

darkly. "Okay, tell him I'm sorry. Then get me my answer."

Thorpe and the native fell into a low exchange. At the end, the British guide said, "He says the sound we heard is the cry of N'yamala."

King cupped hands to his mouth. "Okay, look sharp everybody. This is it. We're going to make history. Somebody hand me a trank gun."

"I don't think that's wise, Mr. King," Thorpe warned. "These rifles are not toys."

King pulled the rifle out of Thorpe's hand and said, "You're in charge of policing this ragtag group of natives. I suggest you set the proper example for instant obedience."

And King turned on his heel, rifle at the ready.

Watching him tramp forward, Nancy told Thorpe, "Everything he knows about Africa, he learned from watching *Jungle Jim* reruns."

Thorpe scowled. "A wanker what would call a fine rifle a gun should be shot with an elephant gun."

The column resumed its march.

The undergrowth became thicker. There was no trail and no way to hack one out. They had to squeeze between boles and hand packs across the narrow passages by hand.

The smell of standing water came into the air and it was rank as dishwater in a heat wave.

"Watch him fall into the bleedin' water," Thorpe muttered for Nancy's benefit.

Then the cry went up. This time it seemed to shake the impossibly green leaves, and frightened monkeys flashed from treetops.

HARRUNK!

Skip King's voice volleyed back, high and excited. "It's just ahead!"

And he went plunging into the brush. They lost sight of him before anyone could react.

"That idiot!" Nancy hissed.

The boom of the rifle echoed back like a cannon blast.

"Oh no!"

King's voice seemed to be all round them in its exultant joy. "I nailed it! I nailed it!"

"That colossal idiot!"

They almost collided with him. King was threshing back the way he had gone. His foxy eyes were bright and wide.

"I bagged it! I bagged it!"

"Not bloody likely," Thorpe spat.

"Did it go down?" Nancy demanded.

"I didn't wait to see," King said excitedly. "Isn't this great? I'm the first man ever to bring down a dinosaur."

They pushed past him.

The ground became mushy. The bush grew thicker, more impenetrable, and rank as swamp grass.

Ralph Thorpe went right up to the edge of the great lake. There was no bank or shore. The trees just stopped and there was water and open sky.

And in the center of the pool, a vast shape loomed.

It was orange and black and glossy as a wet seal. But no seal ever grew so big. The neck was banded in black, and along the ridged back it was dappled in orange blotches as large as fry pans.

And as they stood looking at it, it swung its undersized serpent's head around like a crane and looked at them with goatlike eyes that were as big as their own heads.

The eyes were dull and incurious. the mouth was moving. Some leafy greenage was in its jaws and the jaws were working, lizard fashion, up and down.

The leafage quickly disappeared down its gullet and the black-and-orange bands of the neck began pulsing in time with the long bands of throat muscles.

King was shouting, "I hit it! I hit it dead center! Why is it still on its feet?"

"It doesn't even know it's hit," muttered Thorpe, the British nonchalance in his voice evaporating like the morning rain.

"Bring the cameras," Nancy whispered. "Hurry!"

Skip King stumbled back, his face flushed. He paled when he saw the great beast looking back at him, unfazed.

"What's with that thing?" he complained. "Doesn't it know enough to lie down when its been tranked."

"Evidently not," Thorpe said dryly.

"Well, I'll fix that!"

And before anyone could do anything to stop him, Skip King brought the rifle up to the leather-padded shoulder of his safari jacket and began pumping out rounds, deafening everyone around him.

"You unmitigated cretin!" Nancy screamed.

"It isn't going down!" King shouted. "More guns! We need more firepower!"

The beast in the jungle pool began to advance. The ground shook. Water sloshed on their boots.

And the Bantus began lining the pool.

Thorpe took command. "All right, lads. Make the best of a bad situation, now. Let's bag the brute!"

Rifle stocks dug into sweaty shoulders. Fingers crooked around triggers.

And the rifles began to spit thunder.

2

His name was Remo and he was explaining to the assorted rapists, cannibals, and serial killers on Utah State Prison's death row that he was from the American Civil Liberties Union.

"I already got me a lawyer," snorted Orvis Boggs, who had been scheduled to die of lethal injection on October 28, 1979 for eating a three-year-old girl raw because his refrigerator had broken down in a heat wave, spoiling three porterhouse steaks he had shoplifted from the local supermarket.

"I'm not a lawyer," Remo told him.

"You an advocate, then?" called DeWayne Tubble from the adjoining cell.

"You might call me that," Remo agreed. Agreeing would be faster. He would tell the quartet of human refuse anything they wanted to hear.

"Yeah? Well, advocate us out of this hellhole. My TV's been busted for a damn week. This is cruel."

"Reason I'm here," Remo said.

"Huh?" The huh was an explosive grunt. It exploded out of the mouth of Sonny Smoot, along with a yellowish red spittle, because when he felt uneasy Sonny liked to gnaw on the toilet bowl despite the fact that his tooth enamel always came out second best. Sonny had been educated in assorted juvenile detention centers, and somehow proper dental hygiene had not been inculcated in him.

"I'm with the ACLU's new Dynamic Extraction Unit," explained Remo with a straight face.

"You a dentist?" asked Sonny.

"No, I'm not a dentist."

"What's that in real talk? Dyna—"

"It means that in our infinite wisdom, we've decided that your complaints are not without merit," Remo said, choosing his words with Raymond Burr in mind.

"Not without merit. That means what?"

"That means, yes, the 247 appeals we've filed on your behalf claiming that 15 years on death row constitutes cruel and unusual punishment have been deemed sound, and we have decided to take emergency measures to remedy your plight."

"Plight? We got plights?"

"Situation. Or whatever Perry Mason would say."

"Our situation is that we're stuck in stir," Orvis grunted. "Hah!"

"And I'm the remedy," said Remo.

"What's that?"

"The CURE," said Remo.

"They letting us go?" wondered DeWayne.

"No, I'm pulling you out of here."

"ACLU can do that?"

"If the four of you will kindly keep your voices down long enough for me to get your cell doors open," Remo said.

Immediately everyone shut up. Except Sonny, who grunted like a pig and asked, "You got the key?"

Remo held up his index finger. "Right here."

"That's a finger. And this here's an electronic lock. You gotta have one of them magnetic credit card things."

"Pass cards," Remo corrected. "And I don't need one because I got a specially trained finger."

And Remo began tapping the lock housing. At first tentatively, then with increasing rhythm.

There was a red light on the lock. It winked out, and immediately below it a green light came on. Remo knew he had exactly five seconds to open the door, before the electronic mechanism automatically shut down.

Remo yanked open the door and said, "Hurry it up!"

Sonny Smoot came out in a cloud of body odor.

Remo went to the next door. Boggs's. Smoot crowded close, his eyes intent upon Remo's finger.

"You're in my light," Remo told him, breathing through his mouth so Smoot's microscopic scent particles would not enter his sensitive nostrils, to lodge there for the next seventy-two hours like petrified snot.

"Ain't no light. It's lights out."

"Don't argue with a trained professional," Remo said.

Sonny Smoot obligingly went around to Remo's opposite side and hovered there like an upright turd.

Remo worked the lock. He had the rhythm now, so the red light was replaced by green in jig time.

Orvis Boggs came out.

"I can't believe it! Free!"

"Not until we get past the guards," said Remo, attacking DeWayne Tubble's cell door now. It came open and Tubble came out.

Last to exit was Roy Shortsleeve, the last person on death row. He had been a participant in the lawsuit against the state of Utah, citing their lengthy sojourn on death row as cruel and unusual punishment, and contrary to the eighth amendment of the Constitution.

He had one question. "Is this legal?"

"Only if we don't get caught," Remo told him.

"Then I'm staying."

"You are?"

"Breaking jail won't clear my name. I'm innocent."

"Me, too!' said Sonny Smoot.

"Innocent, that's me."

"Likewise."

"But I'm really, really innocent," Roy Shortsleeve said quietly.

Remo looked into the man's soft eyes. They were

dark and wide-pupiled as a cat's, and his long, haggard face was sincere.

"Okay," Remo said. "You get to stay. But only because you're innocent."

"Wait a minute," said Sonny Smoot. "ACLU will bust *us* out of stir, but not an innocent guy?"

"That's the ACLU way," Remo said. "Innocent guys aren't that much of a challenge. Besides, I thought you were innocent, too."

"We are," said Orvis Boggs. "We just ain't innocent the way Roy's innocent."

"Yeah," DeWayne added. "We were born innocent and got a little lost, is all. Roy stayed innocent clear through to today." He grinned in the gloom. "That's why he's gonna eat needle, and we're gonna sleep with whores tonight."

"Only if you follow me, and do exactly what I say," Remo said flatly.

"Can that finger get us past the guards?" Orvis asked.

"It got me in, didn't it?" Remo countered.

"Oh."

As Remo led them away, Sonny had a question.

"Where can I get a finger like that?"

"This is an ACLU-issue finger. You can't just go into a Walmart and buy it."

"Can a guy boost it, then?"

"No."

In the darkness, the faces of Orvis, DeWayne, and Sonny grew long with disappointment.

"Well, maybe I won't ever be back this way again," Orvis allowed.

"Guarantee it," said Remo, pausing at an area-control door.

There was a guard seated beside it. On the floor. His head was lolling to one side and he looked peaceful and contented sitting there on the shiny floor.

Sonny grunted. "Hey, I know that screw. He done me a bad turn once. Think I'll cut his face."

"You cut his face," Remo warned, "and my finger will turn off the red light in your eyes."

"Can your finger do that?"

"My finger can do whatever I want it to," Remo told the man.

The three dead men exchanged looks in the dark as Remo went to work on the lock.

As he tapped in the darkness, Orvis whispered to DeWayne. "Maybe we should just jug this guy and bite his finger off."

"What if it won't work after it's off?" asked DeWayne.

Orvis grinned broadly. "Then I'll swallow it down. That way it won't go to waste."

"You'd eat a man's finger?"

"Sure."

"Thought you only ate little girls."

Sonny backed away. "Yeah. You queer, or something?"

"No, I ain't no queer. You know that."

"I can hear every word you say," Remo called back.

"Your ears magic, too?" Orvis demanded.

"I can hear you fart before you do."

This impressed the trio. "Forget what we said about that finger, man," DeWayne said quickly. "That your finger. You just let it do its stuff and don't worry about us none."

"Much obliged," said Remo, and the green pinpoint light came on. They passed through.

Remo took point. In the gloom, he did something that would have astonished and frightened the three trailing convicts. He closed his eyes.

Remo could see fairly well in the darkness. But for what he had to do, his eyes would be less useful than the magnets in his brain.

For over twenty years now, Remo had been aware of the magnets. He never thought of them as magnets, but as pointers. Since learning to breathe properly through his entire body and not just his lungs, he had been able to find his way in complete darkness by paying attention to the pointers in his head.

Remo wanted to go north. By closing his eyes, he knew exactly where north was. He was walking north.

It wasn't until recently, after he had read a magazine article claiming scientists had discovered that the human brain was riddled with tiny crystalline biological magnets, that Remo realized the pointers were magnets. If he had thought about it at all, he would have realized they had to be magnets.

According to the scientists, the magnets were present in the brains of many mammalian species, including man. They explained salmon returning to their spawning places, bird migrations, and even how the lost family cat could find its owners, who had moved clear across the country. Remo couldn't quite make the leap of faith that last example required, but he could accept natural magnets, which the scientists had said also explained how people got brain tumors from living too close to high-tension wires and other electromagnetic sources. The magnetic fields screwed up the delicate balance of the magnetic webs, causing the tumors.

Remo had no tumors. He didn't need a CAT scan or an X-ray to tell him that. His own brain told him it was tumorless. And that the magnets were guiding him unerringly north.

Other things guided him, too.

He felt a faint breeze on his cruel face and exposed hands that told of air currents coming from under doors. Remo had memorized every door on the way in. And every twist in the path. He knew exactly where he was. All he had to do was escort the three suffering butchers to the garbage disposal area.

"This ain't the way to the front door," said Orvis Boggs, a trace of suspicion darkening his voice.

"We're not going out the front," Remo said.

"It ain't the way out back, either," DeWayne muttered uneasily.

"The front and the back are always the best-

guarded places in a prison," Remo explained with
more patience than he felt. "My ACLU bosses made
a careful study of this before sanctioning a dynamic
extraction."

Sonny winced at the word extraction, and felt his
bicuspids.

"You do this before?" he asked.

"Actually, this is my first time," Remo said.

"What if we get caught?" Sonny wondered.

"We blame my superiors, and throw ourselves on
the mercy of the guards."

"We do?" said DeWayne.

"The ACLU isn't exactly the CIA," Remo said
pointedly. "It's every man for himself."

"I like that philosophy," said Orvis.

"I knew you would," said Remo, suddenly opening
his eyes.

They were on the threshold of the central crossroads
of the prison. Most prisons had central crossroads,
much like traffic interchanges and performing the
same function.

Remo knew this well. He had twice found himself
on death row, once in his earlier life as patrolman
Remo Williams, when he had been framed for the
murder of a lowlife pusher, and the second time, when
he had been warehoused in a Florida prison, his memory wiped clean, because of a screwup in the organization that had framed him in the first place.

That organization was not, and never had been, the
ACLU.

Oh, there were some letters in common between
the ACLU and CURE. But a world of difference lay
between. The ACLU stood for some self-appointed
mandate to meddle in an already muddled judical system, such as taking up the cause of a knot of death
row inmates first by helping them stave off their lawful
punishment—dragging the appeals process on ad
nauseum—and then using the extended period as a
justification to let them off the hook, citing the consti-

tutional guarantee against "cruel and unusual punishment" as an argument.

CURE had been set up to deal with situations like those caused by the ACLU. CURE was no anagram, but a prescription for America's ills. Conceived by a president who died in office too young, his promise unfulfilled, it was set up to balance out the often imbalanced scales of blind justice.

Remo was CURE's enforcement arm—judge, jury, and executioner if need be. Today, he was just executioner, thank you. The judge and jury had done their job long ago. Remo's task was to see to it their hard work and sacrifice had not been in vain.

At the crossroad, Remo looked through the square glass window in the door. On the other side was a guard in a glass-enclosed booth. He was preoccupied with a copy of *Playboy*.

Remo went to work on the door lock, using the same technique that had opened the other locks. He couldn't explain it, any more than he could have explained the magnets in his head, but his sensitive fingers detected the current that flowed through the lock mechanism. Once found, it was a matter of tapping in harmony until the current did what Remo wanted.

Soon, the door surrendered. Remo slipped it open. No alarm sounded. It had not sounded when he had entered, either.

"Stay close behind me and no sudden moves," Remo warned.

"Got it," said Orvis.

"You the man with the magic digit," added DeWayne.

"So far," muttered Sonny.

They crept out. The crossroads were well lit.

That was when the others got a good look at Remo.

He was a tall, lean man, with dark eyes under dark hair and cheekbones as pronounced as those on a skull. His age was indeterminate, and even looking at his face the three dead men could tell there wasn't an ounce of unnecessary fat on his catlike body. He wore a gray-blue uniform with the words *Sanitation Dept.* over the blouse pocket.

"Hey! How come he's dressed like a garbageman?" Sonny Smoot grunted.

"Sanitation engineer," Remo corrected. "And it's a disguise."

"How come you didn't bring no disguises for us?"

"Yeah," Orvis chimed in. "I want a drum majorette's outfit—preferably with the bitch still in it."

The others decided they wanted the same. Their metallic laughter made Remo want to fuse their empty skulls together right then and there. But if he did that, no way would the ACLU get the credit they so richly deserved.

"Great!" said Remo, seeing the guard start. Remo crossed the space to the guard booth like a shot.

The door was locked, but the guard solved that problem. He buzzed himself out, dragging a riot gun.

Remo met him at the door. To the guard, it seemed as if Remo had just sprouted up from the bare door like some gray-blue weed.

Remo relieved the man of his weapon and his consciousness, using one hand for each task. Holding the guard by the back of his neck, where Remo's hard fingers had found and squeezed down nerve centers, he lowered him to the hard floor.

Sonny and the others came up, and looked down at the slumbering guard.

"That's some finger," Sonny breathed.

"Can we kill this one?" asked DeWayne.

"No," said Remo.

"Can we boost his fingers?" Orvis asked. "You know, to practice what you just done."

"Practice with your own fingers," said Remo. "We gotta shake a leg, if we're going to make it out by dawn."

"So how come you're dressed ike a garbageman?" Sonny wondered.

"You'll see when we get there," said Remo, growing tired of questions.

"What will we see?"

"You'll see."

"When will we get there?"

"You'll know it by the smell," said Remo, coming to the conclusion that if the educational system had taught these losers to think with their brains, maybe they wouldn't be sitting on death row. Then again, maybe not, noticing Sonny gnawing on a whetstone he had brought along.

They came at last to an out-of-the-way corridor area that smelled sour and maggoty.

"This here's the garbage room," Orvis pointed out.

"You got it," said Remo.

"It smells," said Sonny.

"You should talk."

"Huh?"

Remo had been forced to lock the door behind him, and it was still locked. He opened it the hard way. It required a real key of the insert-and-turn variety, so he couldn't manipulate any electrical timer. He punched it. The door jumped inward, taking the lock-set and part of the jamb with it.

They slipped inside.

The place was a welter of sealed garbage cans and trash bags, and there was an old dumpster by the single loading door.

The back of a filthy garbage truck had been backed into the dock. The black maw of its cold steel belly gaped, the slablike sweep blade in the up position, like a fat guillotine.

"In you go," invited Remo, gesturing to the truck. His deep-set eyes, flat as river-bottom stones, were unreadable.

Orvis made a disgusted face. "What, you mean crawl in with the garbage?"

"Look," Remo said impatiently, "The ACLU went to a lot of trouble to set this up. We had to steal a garbage truck and a uniform for me to wear, work out timetables, and drill for weeks. Everything has been worked out to the tiniest detail. This is Thursday morning. The truck comes every Thursday morning to haul trash. Okay, we're hauling trash."

"But there's garbage in there," Orvis said unhappily.

"I have to make it look good, don't I?" Remo said. "I already emptied half the barrels into the back so the screws would see that I was working."

"I ain't sittin' in no garbage," Sonny said. "I want to sit up front with you."

"The gate guards know only one driver drove the freaking truck in. Don't you think he'll get suspicious if two of us drive out?"

"Tell him I'm your brother."

"He'll know I'm not because we don't smell like brothers," Remo said.

Sonny frowned. "What's that supposed to mean?"

Eventually, Remo convinced the trio to enter the truck. They clambered in gingerly and squatted down on their haunches, holding their noses and looking unhappy—except Sonny, who seemed either to enjoy the smell or not to notice it.

"Hold that pose," Remo said and, knocking off an aluminum lid, lifted up one of the still-full cans. He brought it to the truck's maw.

Three pairs of hands went whoa.

"Hey, what are you doing?" DeWayne hissed.

"Putting in the rest of the garbage," Remo said reasonably.

"But we're in here!"

"Look, if I only take half of the garbage, the guards will catch on."

"Okay, let us out and *then* put in the stupid garbage. After that, we'll get back in."

"You don't understand. What if they look in the back of the truck and see you guys?"

"Tell him we're your cousins," Sonny suggested.

"It's like this, I throw the garbage in or we call the whole thing off. You guys don't know how many

Mission: Impossible reruns my superiors had to sit through to come up with a plan as foolproof as this."

"You say this is foolproof?" Orvis said.

"Guaranteed not to fail."

"Okay. But watch the clothes. I didn't take time to pack."

"Did I mention all dry cleaning bills are on the ACLU?" Remo asked.

The three immediately brightened.

And Remo threw the contents of the can in their beaming faces. He had deliberately saved the worst, smelliest cans for this moment.

As he flung refuse, inundating the trio, Remo mentally called off the names of their victims, adding after each, "This is for you."

Eventually, the three were buried in rotting cafeteria leftovers.

Remo called into the malodorous pile. "That's the last of it. You guys still with me "

A knot of rancid cabbage seemed to say, "Yeah."

"Okay, I gotta close the sweep blade now."

"You mean the hydraulic thing?" DeWayne asked.

"That's it."

"Isn't that kinda dangerous?"

"Only to garbage," said Remo, climbing to the side and giving the lever a yank.

He couldn't quite remember which way it worked. Up for close. Up and down for close and compress. Maybe it was down and up. He yanked the lever up.

With a grinding of the mechanism, the hydraulics started toiling. The great slab of a sweep blade dropped and closed like a vault door. And stopped.

Remo frowned. He tried yanking the lever another way. Nothing.

Then a guard was shouting through the open door, "Hey, you!"

"Yeah?"

"You about done in there?"

"Almost."

"The guard captain wants to know what's taking you so long."

"Sweep blade is stuck."

"Well, get that smelly rig out of here and fix it on your own time."

"You got it," said Remo, giving the ridged truck body a reassuring tap.

Remo slid behind the wheel and trundled out toward the yard. He stopped at the gate and handed over a clipboard with a lot of unreadable signatures.

"They don't pay you guys enough," said the guard, holding his nose against the smell while trying to sign the clipboard with one hand.

"Working toward a cleaner planet is reward enough for me," Remo said airily.

The gates rolled aside electronically, and Remo drove through without a problem. He ran the heavy truck a quarter mile down the road, just fast enough to outpace the trailing smell, and pulled over to the side.

Getting out, Remo walked around to the back, tapping the side with a knuckle that actually left a small dent.

"We did it! We're out!"

The "Yay" coming from inside lacked enthusiasm.

"I'm having trouble breathing in here with all this slop," Orvis complained.

"Be with you in a second," Remo promised.

Remo took hold of the lever. There was a little light coming up now. It was dawn. The start of a new day. And in the light he found the metal plate that explained the proper way to work the hydraulic sweep blade. It was covered with grime. Remo swiped it clear with the sleeve of his gray-blue uniform.

" 'Push up and then down to compress load,' " Remo read.

So he pushed up and then down.

The sweep blade was already closed. Now it behaved like a monster steel tongue the truck was trying to swallow whole. The blade went deeper and deeper, and the three convicts inside began to panic.

"Hey! This slop's bunching up!"

"What goin' on?"

"My mistake," called Remo. "I think I yanked the lever wrong."

"What happened to your great training?"

"I had to rush through the lever part. I tried cramming for it, but you know how that sometimes goes."

"I'm feeling crammed right about now," Orvis complained.

"Do tell," said Remo.

"Do somethin'!"

"I'm open to suggestions," Remo said, casually leaning against the truck body and mentally counting off the seconds.

"Use your magic finger."

"Great suggestion." Remo counted five more seconds and said, "Oh-oh!"

"What was that uh-oh?"

"My magic finger isn't working."

"What! What happened?"

"Battery must have gone dead."

They were screaming now.

"You got fresh ones?"

"Sorry. Fresh finger batteries would have set off the metal detector."

"Oh, Mother of God," DeWayne groaned. "He's right!"

"The best laid plans gang aft a-gley," Remo said sympathetically.

"What was that last part?"

"If you ever find out, let me know."

Then they were screaming and their arm and leg bones were snapping. Howls came. Rib cages began splintering. Skulls were compressed and internal organs ruptured, merged, and became red masses of jelly.

Finally, the only sound was that of the hydraulics completing their inexorable cycle.

Satisfied, Remo drove the truck to the local office of the ACLU and after only an hour of trying, finally succeeded in getting the Leach Body to disgorge the truck's contents into the dumpster behind the office building.

Then he returned the truck and borrowed uniform to the Department of Sanitation yard, where he called the local police.

"Police Emergency."

"I got a hot tip for you," Remo told the police operator. "The ACLU just broke three death row convicts out of prison, and when they refused to pay their legal fees, killed them and dumped the bodies."

"Sir, there is a stiff fine for filing a false police report."

"I'm calling, not filing. And if you don't believe me, check the prison. Then go talk to the ACLU. And here's a major clue: look in their dumpster."

Remo hung up, knowing that even if the police followed through, the ACLU would probably weasel their way off the hook in the end. He only wished he could stick around to hear them explain away the dead bodies.

It was not an entirely happy ending, but in an imperfect world, it was as good as Remo sometimes got.

He walked away whistling.

3

Nancy Derringer was overcome by the urge to commit murder.

She had never wanted to kill a living thing in her entire previous twenty-eight years on earth. She loved all living things. The stinger of the desert scorpion filled her with the same wonder as the delicate mechanism of a butterfly's wing. The beauty and terror of biology were two sides of the same wondrous coin to her. All life was sacred.

Today, standing on the sloppy edge of a primordial pool, her nostrils filled with the fecund stench of swamp water, she wanted to throttle Skip King with her bare hands. Except that she was using them to cover her ringing ears. She had been standing directly beside him when he had unloosed the first volley of tranquilizer darts. That had pretty much paralyzed her left eardrum.

Nancy barely heard the call to open fire. But she heard the rest of the guns opening up through her remaining good ear. It was one great blast of concussive noise, and then she was down on her knees in the muck trying to hold the sound out with both hands while screaming, "Stop it! Stop it! Stop it!"

No one heard her. Not even herself.

The rifles had long fallen silent when she felt it was safe to unblock her ears. They rang. Quasimodo seemed to be busy in either inner ear chamber, ringing his discordant bells.

When she opened her eyes, Nancy saw the creature whose discovery was the culmination of her career slowly slip into the swamp water.

The head was looking directly at her. The face, seen full on, was a bright dayglo orange paint splatter that shaded to black just behind the brow ridges. It looked as if it were wearing some abstract Halloween mask. The face was dull, but the eyes were growing sleepy.

They were goat eyes, the pupils squared. The pupils were squeezing into vertical slits as the orange lids slowly dropped over them.

The head was swaying snakelike from side to side, like a sleepy cobra trying to match the snake charmer's rhythm.

It went *haroooo,* in a low, sick voice. Its tongue was green and forked, the dentition gray and worn from eating jungle roughage.

Then, dimly, although he was standing at her elbow, Skip King yelled, "Skip King, king of the jungle, bags another brute!"

Nancy jumped to her feet and slapped him so hard he lost his balance and his bush hat.

"You jerk!" she screamed. "Look what you've done."

King lay there, holding his face. "My job. I did my job."

The beast's head was dropping by stages.

"Your job! You agreed to be a corporate observer. Nothing more!"

"I didn't see *you* take up arms when we were in danger."

"The idea was to film it in the wild first. Document its habits. Now we've lost the opportunity forever."

"Skip that biology crap. This is bring 'em back alive. Frank Buck time. Man stuff."

The saurian head came up, wavered, and sank anew.

"Not unless we do something fast," Nancy said in a lower register.

"What do you mean?"

"Look at the poor thing. He's passing out on his feet."

"That *is* the idea," King said stiffly.

"In the middle of the swamp? If his head goes under, he'll drown. And all because you had to draw first blood!"

Skip King got to his feet. He wiped his sweaty brow and squinted through the bright afternoon air at the beast's slow struggles.

"Maybe it's amphibious," he murmured.

"Those are nostrils at the tip of its snout, not gills," Nancy spat. "It's no more amphibious than you are."

"You sure?"

"Yes!"

King's mouth dropped open. "Oh God."

"Now do you understand?"

"Understand? If that thing dies, it'll be my job! We gotta do something!"

"Wonderful. Now you're getting it." Nancy swung on Ralph. "Thorpe, any help you might render would be appreciated."

"Right." He turned to the natives and shouted out Bantu orders. Instantly, the natives dropped their rifles and pulled short machetelike swords out of their native clothing.

They went to work on the trees on either side of the creature. The boles were thin. They surrendered quickly. It was lucky for the expedition that they did.

Soon, the long thin boles were in the water, floating. The natives jumped in, completely without fear, and pushed the logs toward the wavering head.

"Magnificent!" Nancy said. "It could work."

The PR officer hovered close. "Should we be filming this, Mr. King?"

"And film my career going up in flames?" King spat. "I'll fire the first man who uncaps his lens."

The videocams remained capped.

More trees crashed down. Soon, there was a logjam, and slowly, the great beast known to the Bantu as N'yamala surrendered to the powerful narcotic coursing through his massive system.

The eyes closed completely before the chin settled onto the logjam. There was a breathless moment before they knew if the logs would support its weight.

Nancy closed her eyes and clasped her hands together. She was praying.

Everyone else held their breath.

"Somebody tell me to open my eyes if it's good news," Nancy said earnestly.

"Just a mo, Dr. Derringer."

Then Skip King made a guttural throat noise that almost brought hot tears to Nancy's eyes.

It was followed by him saying, "Yes! Yes! Yes! Yes!"

"You can look now, Dr. Derringer," Thorpe said quietly.

Nancy opened her blue eyes. The beast stood in the middle of the pool, still on his feet, like a preposterous elephant, but with his long serpentine neck undulating along the scattering of logs, where it had come to rest.

The head had plopped on a thickest part of the logs. Swamp water lapped at the lower part of the upper lips, but the nostrils rode high above the water, where they quivered and blew out air that smelled faintly of mushrooms.

"Thank goodness," Nancy breathed. And she was so relieved her knees began shaking and she let herself down onto the muck to give her legs time to calm down.

She was in no position to stop what happened next.

Skip King turned to the team and said, "Okay, cameras out. Get the banner into position."

"Banner?" Nancy said blankly.

The cameras came out. There were three in all. Two zoomed in on Skip King, who had recovered his hat and his rifle and was striking a kneeling pose at the swamp's edge, the rifle stock set in the muck. Almost as an afterthought, the third cameraman was shooting the slumbering reptile.

Two natives finished unpacking a long object and brought it up to King. It resembled two short rugs rolled together.

"Open it up." The natives separated, walking backward, and slowly a white banner unfurled between two rolling masts.

Nancy eyed it with growing horror.

BROUGHT TO YOU BY
BURGER TRIUMPH
KING OF CHEESEBURGERS

Above the banner was Skip King's lean face, and over his shoulder the dappled orange shape of the reptile was distinctly visible.

"I don't believe this," Nancy said in a sick voice.

King cleared his throat and began speaking in a deep unnatural baritone. "This is an historic day in the glorious annals of corporate history. Only a fast food giant like Burger Triumph, Inc. could have done it. Only its marketing chief, namely me—could have conceived it."

"King!"

"Cut!" King shouted. His face was red as a beet. "What's the matter with you? We're rolling here!"

"Our agreement was that there would be no overt commercialization of the expedition," Nancy reminded him.

"These are home movies."

"Then why do you sound like a commercial announcer?"

"A copy will go into the corporate vaults, of course," King said in an injured voice. He turned his attention to the others. "Okay, from the top."

As Nancy watched, she could feel the steam rise from under her collar. King repeated his spiel, and then picked up where he had left off.

"For over a hundred years explorers have returned from the Dark Continent with rumors of dinosaur survivals in the far reaches of the legendary Kanda Tract. White men scoffed at these native tales, but still the stories came out. Until the day Skip King, visionary

adventurer, public relations genius, heard the tales—
and believed."

He puffed out his chest like a proud adder.

"Behind me, ladies and gentlemen, lies the first
known Brontosaurus ever to be—"

"Apatosaurus," Nancy shouted.

"Not again! Nancy, what do you want now? I gave
you your fifteen minutes of fame at that last recording
stop."

Nancy folded her arms. "You said Brontosaurus.
It's an Apatosaurus. I explained that to you back in
the States."

"Not now!"

"My professional reputation is riding on this expedition, too. It's an Apatosaurus. Nothing but."

"Glory hound," King muttered. To his camera
team, he said, "Okay, we'll take it from the point
where I say, 'Behind me, ladies and gentlemen.' Got
that?"

The cameras rolled. The native bearers looked
bored. They had turned their Burger Triumph T-shirts
inside out as a form of silent protest.

Nancy felt her legs again and struggled to her feet.

And Skip King doggedly resumed his spiel.

"Behind me, ladies and gentlemen: Thunder Lizard!
Twenty tons of Halloween-colored monster."

"Thunder Lizard is incorrect," Nancy called, en-
joying the way King's sharp features turned red as a
fox when she interrupted him.

"What is it with you! Didn't I give you enough face
time back on the trail?"

Nancy folded her arms. "I'm not interested in face
time," she said distinctly. "You said Thunder Lizard.
You should have said Deceptive Lizard. Apatosaurus
means 'Deceptive Lizard,' not Thunder Lizard. Actually, Deceptive Reptile is the preferred term."

"Maybe you'd like to make up a bunch of cue
cards," King said acidly.

"Not really."

"If you had been on the moon when Neil Armstrong stepped off the *Eagle,* he'd never have got to say, 'One small step for man, one giant leap for mankind.' "

"Actually, he said, 'One giant leap for *a* man,' " Nancy corrected.

"He did not."

"I say he did."

"I imagine Dr. Derringer is right," Thorpe said.

"Who asked you?" King snarled.

"No bloody body." Thorpe undertoned in a voice that was edged with steel. "But you might start giving some thought to what we're going to do when the beast wakes up," he added in a more polite tone.

"There's plenty of time."

"We don't know that."

"That's right," Nancy added. "We're dealing with an animal whose metabolism has never been studied. No one knows how long he'll stay tranked."

"Long enough to get him to the railhead at M'nolo Ki-Gor," King snapped. "Where suitable transportation has been arranged."

"And how do you propose to do that?"

"Actually, the idea was to coax him to walk that far himself. But I guess I got carried away when I saw him."

"*That* was your plan? To lure him!"

"Don't have a platypus. We've haven't tried it yet. It could work."

"Except how did you envision getting him to walk? By leaving a trail of jungle chocolate for him to follow?" Some of the natives understood English. They laughed among themselves at the white woman's words.

King's face froze. Nancy met his glare with one of her own.

"Actually, I had figured on setting fire to the jungle behind it," King said. "The flames would have stampeded him in any direction we wanted."

The natives suddenly stopped laughing. Now it was their turn to glare.

"Burning a virgin rain forest!" Nancy shrieked. "Are you mad!"

"You have a better way?"

"You can't burn forest like this," Thorpe said laconically. "Not so soon after a hard rain. So let's all put any thought of burning out of our minds, shall we?"

"We can try," King said stubbornly.

"You can try," Thorpe answered. "But I rather doubt the native boys will cotton to the idea."

"Who asked them?"

"It's their country."

"Like hell it is. I have permission from President Oburu to do whatever I have to to fulfill the mission."

At the sound of the name of Oburu, the Bantus grew narrow of eye. Some spat into the ground. A few hissed through perfect teeth.

"Guess they voted for the other guy," King muttered uneasily.

"In Gondwanaland," Thorpe said, "there is no other guy."

"Okay, I'll find another way."

He stomped off into the bush.

"Think he'll come up with anything?" Thorpe asked Nancy.

"Not in a million years."

But only a few minutes later he was shouting frantically for them to come running. They came upon Skip King standing in the flank of one of the misty rises that from a distance resembled small hills, but which they now realized were great escarpments swallowed by low-hanging jungle mists. There was an opening in the foot of the biggest of these. It was huge. And it had fallen in. The mouth was choked with red earth.

Leading in and out of the mouth were great saurian prints.

"I think I found its lair," King whispered.

Nancy knelt to examine the prints. When she stood up, her features were pale.

"These prints are fresh," she said.

"Of course," King said. "Made since the last rain."

"And there are three distinct sets," Nancy added. "Larger than the one we found."

"You mean the one I got isn't full grown?" King gulped.

Nancy nodded soberly.

Everyone carrying rifles clenched them more tightly, and those who had no weapons crowded closer to those who did.

"Let's keep our heads, shall we?" Skip suggested.

"What do you think, Thorpe?" Nancy asked.

"Why do you ask him and not me?" King demanded. "I'm expedition leader."

He was ignored.

Thorpe was looking at the tracks now. He motioned to Tyrone, who joined him. They exchanged short words in Bantu and Thorpe looked up.

"The freshest tracks are those going in. I'd say there are at least three more of the brutes in that cave, trapped."

"No!"

" 'Fraid so, Dr. Derringer."

"Is there anything we can do to get them out?"

"Doubtful. You're looking at tons of dirt and rock that came down all at once. And there's no guarantee that the beggers inside survived the cave-in."

"Then our beast might be the last survivor!" King said.

"It's likely," Thorpe admitted glumly.

"That makes him worth a fortune!"

"That makes him an endangered species," Nancy said fiercely, "and I will not have him endangered any further by your irresponsible macho bull."

"I resent that!"

"Resent it all you want, about from now on, I'm calling the shots."

"My ass," King snarled.

"All in favor of doing things my way," Nancy announced to everyone within hearing, "raise their hands."

The natives immediately lifted their hands. First,

those who spoke English, and then the others when the first ones nudged them into following suit. Thorpe lifted one hand. As did two of the camera crew.

"All in favor of doing what Mr. King demands may now raise their hands," Nancy said.

Skip King raised his hand defiantly. His was the only one aloft.

"What about you clowns?" he yelled at the remaining members of the Burger Triumph observation team.

"We're abstaining," said one.

"In the interest of our long-term career prospects," said another.

"And our short-term survival," added the third man.

"Now that the new pecking order has been established," Nancy said. "Let's look around."

"For what?" King wanted to know.

"Anything that might be useful."

Circling the great lake, they found more dinosaur trails. The creatures seemed to have dwelt close to the cave and the pool, where fruit-bearing lianas grew thickest.

Nancy stopped to examine one. The creeper was thick and dotted with broad white flowers. At intervals, the great fruit sprouted like oversized green-skinned footballs.

"Jungle chocolate?" Nancy asked Thorpe.

"Likely. Recognize it?"

"Botanically, no. Earlier researchers have theorized it's probably a species of Landolphia—some unknown wild mango."

Thorpe took a knife to one of the big melons and hacked out a piece. It smelled like a green apple and had a vaguely nutty taste, like avocado.

They spit out their pieces and washed their mouths clean with canteen water.

The dinosaur trails ended at the line of hills that seemed to cut the Kanda Tract in two.

They found, on the other side of the great escarpment, a long stretch where the earth was flat and tawny grass grew around sparse, wind-slanted baobab trees. Savannah. Mixed in the grass were fields and fields of toadstools, every one a glossy orange color, like crouching elves who had pulled their caps down protectively.

"Odd," Nancy said, fingering one of them.

"Yes?" asked Thorpe.

"These are the same orange coloration as the Apatosaur's markings."

"You imagine a connection?"

"We know from old stories that N'yamala is reputed to eat so-called jungle chocolate. And we saw him eating fronds."

"We did."

"But his markings are all wrong for a jungle dweller. He's black and orange, like a salamander. If he had natural jungle camouflage, he should be green or brown or gray. Not orange and black."

"What are you suggesting?"

"Remember a year or so ago, they found the largest living creature in a Washington state forest? A behemoth underground fungus ten miles long, which had been feeding off dead tree roots?"

"Vaguely."

"They estimated it was thousands of years old. And it was entirely underground. Except for the mushrooms."

"Mushrooms?"

"They sprouted up all along the ground that covered it," Nancy said distantly as she crumbled the toadstool to fragments and watched the spongy bits cling to her fingers. "According to our best knowledge, Apatosaurs ate ginkgo trees, conifers, and other roughage."

"No pine cones hereabouts," Thorpe snorted.

"But there might have been prior to the period of continental drift that dispersed its populations to the newly created continents," she returned. "When flowering plants came along in the Cretaceous, Apatosaur would have suffered from a severe food shortage, but could have survived in small numbers on a modified diet."

"I fear I do not follow."

"Suppose the Apatosaur population went underground with the onset of the Lower Cretaceous period, induced by climactic changes and the rise of unfamiliar and unappetizing fauna?" Nancy mused. "Not excusively underground. But feeding on great subterranean expanses of fungi, and only occasionally emerging to forage for palatable food, like lianas and jungle chocolate."

"Would that turn the beasts orange?"

"It might. Or the coloration might be an adaptive response to cave living."

"A kind of underground camouflage, eh?"

Nancy shook off the last bits of toadstool and her voice cleared. "It's a theory," she said. "Let's find the others. We have to do something about our young Apatosaur."

"Such as?"

"If it *is* the last one, then we have no choice but do exactly what that idiot King wants if it is to survive."

"How are we going to move a brute that size, Dr. Derringer?"

"We'll ask B'wana King."

Ralph Thorpe looked skeptical.

"And then we do the opposite," Nancy said archly.

4

At the Salt Lake City Airport payphone, Remo reported in.

He lifted the receiver and depressed the *One* button until the automated switching relays clicked into place and a distant phone rang once.

A thin, lemony voice said, "Yes, Remo?"

"Chalk up another triumph for the ACLU," Remo said airly.

"I beg your pardon?"

"I told my targets I was with the ACLU. It cut through a lot of unnecessary bull."

"I trust these individuals are—um—no longer . . ."

"You can say it, Smitty. Go ahead. Say, 'dead.' "

Remo could almost hear his superior wince over two thousand miles away.

"Remo, please."

"Okay, they're landfill. Happy now?"

"That is satisfactory."

"All except Roy Shortsleeve."

"He did not get away?"

"No. I left him where he sat."

"Why, Remo?"

"Because he's innocent. I could tell, having been an innocent on death row once myself. I think someone should reopen his case."

"That is not our mission," Smith said flatly.

"And I say it is."

The line hummed in the silence that followed.

Remo shifted his feet. He had reverted to his habitual wardrobe, a T-shirt and chinos. Today the T-shirt was white and the chinos tan. Loafers of Italian leather covered his feet. They looked brand new. They were. When they lost their original shine or got scuffed, he just ashcanned them and bought a fresh pair. This was his third pair this week.

"Very well, Remo," Smith said in his eternally bitter voice. "I will make inquiries. But I do not expect miracles. It is very difficult to overturn such convictions."

"Tell that to the ACLU—who are going to have a lot of explaining to do after Roy Shortsleeve tells his story."

Smith groaned audibly. In the phone booth, Remo smiled to himself. The hand holding the receiver was of average size, but the attached wrist was freakishly thick.

"Anything else I can do?" Remo asked. "How about Dr. Gregorian? I sent you a bunch of clippings on that dried-up old ghoul. I can be in Milwaukee by sundown."

"Do not go to Milwaukee."

"No?"

"Fly to Boston."

"What's there?"

"I will be there," said Smith. "With Master Chiun."

"Yeah? What's up?"

"I have concluded purchase negotiations on the new residence Chiun has requested—"

"You mean extorted."

"—as a part of the latest contract negotiations," Smith finished.

"Boston, huh? I guess you talked Chiun out of living in a castle."

"No, I did not," said Smith.

Remo gripped the receiver so tightly he left fingerprints. Fingerprints that could never be traced because Remo had been declared dead, his identity files pulled. "You got him a castle! In Boston?"

"Outside Boston, actually. Try to catch the nine o'clock plane, and we will rendezvous at the airport."

"On my way," Remo said, not sounding at all happy about it.

Remo wore a long face as he cabbed to the airport. It was not a face that was at its best when it was long. Remo's face—resculpted over the twenty years he had worked for CURE—had been turned pretty much back to its original contours. Twenty years of faces. Twenty years of changing identities. Twenty years of assignments. And twenty years—minus a four-year period in which he had actually lived in a home in the New York suburbs—of living out of suitcases in hotels and motels all over the world.

And now, thanks to the Master of Sinanju's insistence, CURE was going to provide them with a permanent place to live.

It should have been something Remo would look forward to. But there were problems. For one thing, Chiun had insisted on a castle. Remo had no desire to live in a castle.

For another, Chiun was about to become a father. And it was his stated intention to prepare his new domicile for the baby and its mother.

For weeks now, in anticipation of this joyous occasion—dreaded by Remo—Chiun had been preparing.

And ignoring Remo. Remo had started to feel left out and between that and boredom, he had taken to calling up Smith and asking for missions. At first, Smith had little for Remo to do. A crooked judge in Buffalo. A gang leader in Detroit. Piecework. Nothing big. Definitely nothing challenging. Mostly it was fly to the hit's city, locate the hit, say hello to the hit and hit the hit. Wham, bang, thank you, hit. Have a nice death.

After a while, Remo had taken to cutting out newspaper articles about people worthy of being hastened to the boneyard and sending them to Folcroft Sanitarium by Federal Express. Always making sure to check off the "bill recipient" box on the airbill to give the penurious Smith added incentive.

An article on the ACLU's attempt to win reprieves for four death row inmates had been one of the latest. Remo was hoping Smith would send him after Dr. Mordaunt Gregorian next. Maybe tomorrow, Remo reflected. After they had gotten settled in.

The flight across the U.S. seemed longer than it should be because the stewardess kept trying to sit in Remo's lap.

Remo was not in the mood for stewardesses who wanted to sit in his lap, and he told the woman so.

This did not dissuade her. "How about I just kneel at your feet and massage them lovingly?" she countered.

"Won't they fire you?" Remo wondered.

"If they do, will you make it worth my while?"

"Not on this leg."

The stewardess looked ready to burst into tears. Remo, to avoid a scene, tried to head off the cloudburst.

"You know, you don't really love me," he pointed out.

"I do! I do! Since forever."

"Since exactly twenty minutes ago when I got on this plane," Remo said. "Before that you never saw my face."

"It just seems like forever," she said, brushing at his dark hair.

"It's only pheromones," Remo said.

"Huh?"

"I read about them in a magazine. Pheromones are personal odors. Sexual scents. People give them off. Some give off stronger pheromones than others. Me, I got pheromones that won't quit. Which is why I can't take naps during long flights because of the stewardess factor."

"Don't I give off pheromones, too?" she asked in a pouty voice.

"Sure you do."

She bent forward, giving Remo a dose of some

fruity perfume and an intimate look at her freckled cleavage.

"Aren't my pheromones good, too?"

"They're okay. It's just that I give better than I get."

Which was the wrong thing to say, Remo saw immediately, because the stewardess fell to her knees and said in a very, very earnest voice, "I give good pheromones, too. I swear."

She lay one hand over her heart.

Remo read her nametag: Stephanie.

"Listen, Stephanie—"

The hand came off her heart to Remo's hand, still warm. "Oh, you spoke my name!"

"Only in passing. Look, I can't help being the way I am."

She took his hand in both of hers now. They were sweating. She looked him dead in the eye and said, "I understand. Truly, I do."

"I was trained to be this way. It's not something I can control."

"I have absolutely no use for control, right now," Stephanie said, making her voice breathy.

The other passengers were staring now. Their expressions broke down into gender-specific categories. The men were envious and the women disgusted.

"You're making a scene," Remo pointed out.

"We can go into the galley. It's private there."

"What about the other stewardesses?"

"I'll stick plastic knives in their backs. We can use them for pillows after we're done. I give great afterglow, too."

"Sorry," Remo said.

"I'll hold my breath."

"Let me hold it for you," said Remo, reaching out for her throat. He found her throbbing carotid artery and squeezed until the blood stopped flowing to her brain. After twenty-two seconds, she was out like a light.

Remo hit the stewardess call button and explained

to the new stewardess that Stephanie had fainted, "or something."

She was carried to a first-class chair, checked for signs of injury, and allowed to sleep the rest of the flight away.

In Boston, Remo made a point of being the first one off the plane.

He was not surprised when Harold W. Smith met him at the gate. Smith was seated in an uncomfortable plastic chair looking uncomfortable. Harold Smith always looked uncomfortable. He probably looked uncomfortable sleeping in his own bed.

It was early spring, but Smith wore the same ensemble he wore summer or winter, rain or sun. A gray three-piece suit. The only splash of color was his hunter green Dartmouth tie.

He was a tall, thin man of Ichabod Crane proportions. His hair, thin as the first dusting of autumn snow, was grayish white. His skin was actually grayish, as were his weak eyes.

He might have been an accountant or a college professor or a retired undertaker. He was none of those things. He was Harold W. Smith, ostensibly head of Folcroft Sanitarium in Rye, New York, secretly the director for CURE, the supersecret government agency that didn't exist—officially.

Smith was reading *The Wall Street Journal*.

Remo padded up to him on silent Italian loafers.

"Uncle Smitty!" Remo cried. "It's been—what?—years. Am I still in the family will?"

Smith looked up from his paper with genuine horror on his patrician features. "Remo. Please. Do not make a scene."

Smith got up, folding his paper. He pushed back on the bridge of his rimless glasses, restoring them to correctness.

"You old softie," Remo said. "Still shy in public." Then, in a quieter voice he asked, "Where's Chiun?"

"He will be along shortly." Smith was tucking the

newspaper under his arm. He clutched a worn leather briefcase in one bloodless hand. It was so scuffed that no self-respecting thief would lower himself to steal it. It contained the computer link to the hidden CURE mainframes in Folcroft's basement.

They started walking.

"So, tell me about this castle," Remo prompted.

"It might be better if you see it without any prejudicial preconceptions."

"Has Chiun seen it?"

"No."

"You pass papers yet?"

"Yes." Smith avoided Remo's eyes.

"Which means if Chiun doesn't like it, you eat the mortgage, right?"

Smith actually paled. Although he had at his disposal a vast black-budget superfund of taxpayer dollars, he spent it as if the copper in every penny came out of his own bloodstream.

"Master Chiun stipulated a castle," Smith said. "Castles are not exactly plentiful in America. I have found him a perfectly good equivalent. Please do not spoil it."

Remo eyed Smith doubtfully. "You trying to pull something here, Smitty?"

"No," Smith said hastily.

"We'll see," Remo said slowly. "Let's find Chiun."

"He is coming in on Kiwi Airlines."

"Wonderful," Remo said. "That means either he'll be six hours late or he went down in flames over Pittsburgh."

"It was the most reasonable flight I was able to book for him on short notice."

"And they have the most wonderful frequent flier program in the air," Remo added. "Right?"

"Er, that is true."

"Which no one has ever managed to collect on, because they either ate tarmac or couldn't stomach flying Kiwi a second time."

"Those stories are exaggerated," Smith said
defensively.

They found the Master of Sinanju in the baggage
area, patiently waiting for his luggage.

He stood regarding the unmoving baggage conveyer
belt like a tiny Asian idol carved from amber and
dressed in scarlet silk. His face, in repose, might have
worn the accumulated lines of his combined ancestors,
the previous Masters of Sinanju, heirs to the House
of Sinanju, the oldest line of professional assassins in
human history and discoverers of the sun source of all
the martial arts, which was also known as Sinanju.

"Hey, Little Father," Remo called. "I see you made
it in one piece."

Chiun, Reigning Master of Sinanju, turned. At the
sight of Remo his wrinkled little face broke out in a
beaming smile. His wise hazel eyes brightened.

"Remo! I am so happy to see you!" he squeaked.

"Great," said Remo, quickening his pace. It was
true what they said. Absence does make the heart
grow fonder.

"For now I have someone to carry my trunks,"
Chiun added.

Remo's face fell. He struggled to keep his voice
light. "How many'd you bring this time?"

"All."

Remo's eye went wide.

"All fourteen!"

Chiun brought a yellow hand like an eagle's claw to
the wisp of beard that straggled down from his chin.
"Of course. For it is moving day. No more will I have
to bear them hither and yon, like a vagabond."

"Vagabonds usually settle for a change of clothes,
knotted in a ball and hanging off a stick. Not fourteen
freaking trunks."

And before the Master of Sinanju could reply to
that, the trunks began bumping through the hanging
leather straps.

The first was a gray lacquer monstrosity in which scarlet dragons vied with golden phoenixes for hegemony.

Chiun gestured with a hand whose long fingernails were like pale blades, and said, "Remo."

Unhappily, Remo took hold of the trunk and lifted it free of the conveyor belt. He set it to the floor, and at once the Master of Sinanju drifted up and began examining the lacquer and brass trim for nicks and other blemishes.

"It has survived unscathed," he announced sagely. The overhead lights shone on the amber eggshell that was his skull. Tiny puffs of cloudy white hair enveloped the tops of his ears.

"Only thirteen more to go," Remo muttered.

Then next trunk was mostly mother-of-pearl. It had collected no scratches.

And the others began coming, in a colorful sequence like a toy train.

One by one, Remo hefted them off the belt to join the growing pile. In a corner, Harold Smith buried his long nose in his newspaper and gave off a studied "I'm not with them" air.

"Smith tell you anything about this castle?" Remo asked Chiun.

"Only that it is in an exclusive area in an historical town."

"It would have to be if there's a castle involved."

"This is a good area, Remo," Chiun whispered.

"Since when?"

"It is one of the older provinces in this young country. It is very British."

"Since when are we Anglophiles?"

"The House has worked for Great Britain," Chiun pointed out.

"And sometimes against them."

"But more for them," said Chiun, dismissing the unimportant detour in historical truth.

The thirteenth trunk was green and gold, and after Remo set it down, the conveyor belt came to a dead stop.

"Hey? Is that all of them?" he asked.

Chiun's wrinkled features stiffened. "No. There is one missing."

Remo snagged a skycap.

"My friend here is missing a piece of luggage," he explained.

The skycap looked at the preposterous pile of trunks and commented, "How can you tell?"

"Because we can count. Why did the belt stop?"

"Because they finished unloading all the luggage."

"You're not saying it's lost," Remo said in as low a voice as possible.

"I'm not saying anything, but you better file a lost luggage claim before you leave the airport otherwise its your tough luck."

"Lost!" Chiun squeaked, flouncing up. "My precious trunk cannot be lost!"

"I didn't say lost," the skycap repeated.

"He didn't say lost," Remo said quickly. "It's probably misplaced."

"The lackey who misplaced my trunk would do better to misplace his head," Chiun said in a stentorian voice.

"He talks that way sometimes," Remo told the skycap. "Let me handle this."

"Remo, I will not countenence this," Chiun warned.

"And you won't have to."

"And if my trunk is truly lost?"

"We'll get it back. Come on, let's find a way into the luggage loading area."

"Follow me," Chiun said, and stepped into the dead conveyor belt. He passed through the fall of leather straps and as Harold Smith called his name in a frightened voice, Remo ducked in after the Master of Sinanju.

The other side was a maze of chutes, tunnels, and self-propelled luggage trucks.

Chiun looked around, his clear hazel eyes cold.

"Uh-oh," Remo said. For one man was driving one

of the trucks away from the area. A glossy blue trunk sat in back. Unmistakably Chiun's.

"Thief!" Chiun called. And flashed after the truck in a flurry of scarlet silk.

"We don't know that," Remo said, hurrying after him.

But they knew it for the truth a moment later. The man stopped the truck beside an open van. Two other luggage handlers were shoving stuff into the back of the van. Shoulder bags. Cameras. Videocams. Even a boxed VCR.

The man with Chiun's trunk got off and motioned for the others to give him a hand.

They noticed Chiun at that point.

"Hey!" one shouted. "This is a restricted area. Get out of here!"

"Thief!" Chiun cried. "To touch that trunk is to die!"

"And he means every word," Remo called.

The Master of Sinanju looked like a harmless wisp attired in his silk robes. His age could have been anything from eighty to a hundred and twenty, but in fact he had passed the century mark some time back.

The three luggage pilferers ranged from perhaps twenty-five to thirty-eight years. They were tall, and muscular from hoisting heavy luggage forty hours a week.

But the Master of Sinanju fell among them like a crimson typhoon hitting a palm oasis.

The man who had frozen with his hands on the trunk suddenly took his hands into his mouth. Not by choice. Choice had nothing to do with it.

From his personal perspective, his own hands had acquired a life of their own. Like frightened pink tarantulas they leapt into his own mouth for protection against the crimson typhoon.

The man had a big mouth. But his hands were bigger. Still, they went down his gullet as if the bones had melted—where they clogged his windpipe so completely that his last ninety seconds of life consisted of hopping about in circles trying to yank his hands out of his mouth and trying to breathe through nostrils that no longer functioned.

In a way, he was lucky. He lived longer than the others, who made the mistake of drawing personal weapons.

Remo and Chiun gave them no time to use them.

"In for a penny, in for a pound," Remo muttered and took the nearest man by his head. Remo simply grasped and began shaking the man's head as if it were a milkshake container. He got about the same result. The man's brain, having the natural consistency of yogurt, was pureed in the receptacle of his skull.

He dropped his box cutter, never having gotten the blade extended.

It was quick, silent, and actually painless to the victim. Remo dropped the limp-boned man to the oil-stained concrete and caught the last few seconds of the third man's death throes.

The man had producted a switchblade. He used it with great skill. The blade darted toward the Master of Sinanju—and abruptly changed direction to carve out a flowing script on the wielder's own forehead.

Then it split his nose clear to the brain pan.

The man was on his back, dead, before the word *THIEF* began oozing blood off his forehead.

"Now you did it," Remo said, looking around at the carnage.

Chiun's hands clasped his wrists. Interlocked, they retreated into the joined sleeves of his kimono. "I did nothing. It was their fault. These carrion started it."

"Smith is gonna to have a shit fit."

"I will reason with Smith. Come."

And the Master of Sinanju floated away.

Grumbling, Remo brought the trunk up on his shoulder and hurried after him.

"This whole trip had better be worth it," he muttered.

* * *

When Remo emerged from the baggage area, Harold Smith's complexion looked as gray as a battleship. And as lifeless. His eyes were staring.

"All is well, Emperor Smith," Chiun said in a loud voice, and went on to recount the other thirteen piled trunks.

"We gotta move fast, Smitty," Remo said, adding the blue trunk to the stack.

"What happened?"

"Luggage thieves."

"They're not—"

"Alive? No. Definitely not."

"Oh, God."

"Just hold your water. We gotta get outta here before anything breaks. Where's the rental car?"

"I had planned on taking the subway into town."

"With fourteen freaking trunks!" Remo shouted.

Smith adjusted his tie. "Actually, I had not expected this."

"Okay, I'll rustle us up some transportation."

There was a rental agency that provided vans, and Remo soon had one parked in front of the terminal.

After Remo had got the last of the trunks into the back of the van, he slipped behind the wheel and tried fighting his way out of the stubborn traffic congestion.

"Maybe the subway wasn't so bad an idea, after all," he muttered darkly.

He took the Callahan Tunnel and emerged near the North End, Boston's Italian district.

"I know this place," Chiun muttered.

"We were here about a year ago. That Mafia thing, remember?"

"Pah!"

"Where to, Smitty?"

"South. To Quincy."

"We were there, too. That was where the Mafia don had his headquarters. Come to think of it, weren't you interested in a condo there, Little Father?"

"I will settle for nothing less than a castle, as befits

my station as the royal assassin in residence," Chiun sniffed.

Remo took the Southeast Expressway to the Quincy exit, where they pulled three G's holding a curved ramp that took them up over a bridge.

"Go straight," said Smith. Remo ignored the left-hand fork of the bridge.

They passed condos, office buildings, and a pagoda-like structure that made Remo grip the wheel with sudden queasiness, but to this relief it turned out to be only a Chinese restaurant, and continued on.

At an intersection dominated by a high school, Smith said, "Take this left."

Remo drove left.

"Stop," said Smith, just as the high school fell behind.

"Where?"

"There!" said Chiun.

Remo stopped and looked out the window. And he saw it.

"You've gotta be kidding," Remo said.

"It is magnificent!" Chiun said rapturously.

5

The plan was simple, as Nancy Derringer explained it.

"We block all the jungle trails except the one we hacked out of the Kanda Tract. Are you with me so far?"

Everyone said yes.

"We know the reptile eats fronds and creepers. Probably he prefers so-called jungle chocolate. We'll harvest some and leave a trail."

"Ha!" King scoffed. "What happens when he gets his fill?"

"It takes a lot of jungle chocolate to fill a belly the size of a cement truck," Nancy told him coolly.

The Bantus smiled among themselves to see the *mzungu* woman who was smarter than the *mzungu* man.

"But to keep him moving we will intersperse toadstools whenever he seems to be losing interest."

"What makes you think he eats toadstools?" King wanted to know.

"A deep knowledge of sauropod dietary habits and a brain I'm not afraid to use."

Even taciturn Ralph Thorpe laughed out loud at that one.

They got to work. The Bantus, who had earlier been easygoing if not torpid when Skip King had been giving the orders, now found their enthusiasm.

They hacked down trees all along the jungle paths, blocking them so that even a ten-ton dinosaur would find them daunting.

The Kanda Tract was full of the wild mangos known as jungle chocolate. Much of it was untouched because the forest had been too thick for the Apatosaur to do much more than snake his long neck between the trees to bite off pieces of the scrumptious melon.

They harvested only as much as would stay fresh for a four-hour interval. And placed them in quickly woven baskets.

Every hand was needed to make baskets, because they had to carry as many toadstools as they would need.

"I'm not weaving baskets," King snarled when the subject was broached. "That's woman's work."

The Bantus all looked as him with their smiles on automatic pilot and their soft eyes steady as buttons on a coat.

King failed to notice. "I didn't go to Wharton to weave baskets, and that's final."

"Fine," Nancy told him thinly. "Then you may go toadstooling."

The Bantus formed a circle around him, leaving a space in the direction of the escarpment.

Angrily, King nested stacks of baskets together and went off to fill them.

It was approaching sundown when the great Apatosaurus began to stir.

Its leathery, black-rimmed nostrils twitched and blew out a snort. Slowly, the orange eyelids picked themselves up.

Lifting its long banded neck, it craned its masked head about in a semicircle as if seeking an explanation.

The goatlike eyes fell upon a fallen melon.

It made a sound. *Harruunukk.* It was a questioning sound.

Then on great round legs, it waded toward the morsel. Logs were bumped out of the way. Waves crashed and slopped on the shore of the great pool.

And the head came down, seized the melon, and gobbled it up after biting through it once with a pulpy sound.

It stood calmly as the neck muscles worked the fragments down into its stomach.

Then, it spied a second mango a little further inland.

From a leafy point high on the escarpment, Nancy watched through field glasses she held in crossed fingers.

"Please, please, see it," she murmured.

The beast seemed to hesitate. It made its curious sound again. Then slowly it stirred out of the pool, coming up onto the mucky ground and sinking its great padded feet deep with squishing-sucking noises.

The head came down and quickly gobbled up the second melon.

In the bush, Ralph Thorpe triggered his flashlight. It spotlighted the third melon.

Through the green gloom, the reptile saw it. He strode forward. And now the high ground shook with each lumbering step.

The Kanda Tract shook for the remainder of the night and far into the dawn of the next day.

They stayed out of sight of it. The natives were especially careful. They told stories of how N'yamala loved to upset river dugouts with his mighty tail.

"Has he ever eaten anyone?" King asked nervously.

"No."

"Good."

"He has never eaten a black man. We do not know if he might enjoy a white man."

And the Bantus smiled their fixed smiles.

The first trouble came just before dawn.

After lumbering along, pausing to snatch up melons and the occasional pile of sodden fronds, the Apatosaur suddenly stopped. It looked around. Its eyes grew rounder.

"What is the blighter up to, Dr. Derringer?" Thorpe asked.

"I don't know," Nancy said slowly. They were crouching in the bush, flat on their stomachs.

A *hruuu* sound filtered through the stationary predawn air.

"Beggar sounds forlorn."

"It may miss its family. Poor thing."

Slowly, the reptile began to back up. It tried to turn around. But the jungle path was too narrow. Its great tail lifted, swept about, and with a terrible sound, a stand of cedar was reduced to kindling.

The forlorn cry came again.

"It's trying to turn back!" King howled, horror in his voice.

"I'm not letting that happen," Nancy said grimly and disappeared into the bush.

Moments later she was creeping up the trail toward the reptile, a basket of orange toadstools balanced on her head, native fashion.

She dumped them onto the trail, not a dozen yards ahead of the creature. Stamping her foot into them to release their musty fungal scent, she retreated into the bush.

The scent did the trick.

The paint-splatter snout swept back, nostrils quivering.

Then it lurched forward. It fell on the piled toadstools with relish, snatching them up and ingesting them with up and down chewing motions. The pile quickly disappeared.

And up around the next bend in the trail, Nancy upended a smaller pile, stamped hard, and vanished into the bush.

After three basketfuls, they switched back to melons. And the melons got them to the first light and their next crisis. The outer edge of the Kanda Tract.

"Now comes the hard part," Nancy was saying in a hastily convened roadside conference. Thorpe, King, and Tyrone had joined her. The others were working through the bush, out of sight and sowing enticements along the trail.

"The beast will be prone to meander once he gets out into open savanna," Thorpe said. "Might even turn back, if he doesn't take to open spaces."

"Will the grass burn?" King asked.

"We are not igniting the savanna," Nancy fumed. "Even if it is dry enough to take flame, it would burn too quickly. We'd only end up with roast Apatosaurus."

"You have an answer for everything, don't you?"

"Everything except how you ever got beyond the 'Do you want fries with that?' phase of your career."

Skip King did a slow burn and said nothing.

Nancy turned to Thorpe.

Thorpe shrugged. "Nothing for it but to let old Jack run."

Nancy blinked. "Old Jack?"

"Reminds one of a bloody jack-o'-lantern, doesn't it?"

"You can't call him Jack," King burst out.

"And why bloody not?"

"I wanted to call him Skip."

"Skip?"

"King Skip, actually."

They looked at him.

"You know, like King Kong."

"Jack it is," Nancy said flatly. She looked to Thorpe. "You think he'll follow our trail of goodies through open savanna?"

"Haven't the foggiest," Thorpe admitted. "But it's either let Jack run or give up."

"I'm in no mood to give up. Get the men deployed."

"Righto." Thorpe crashed off.

"What about me?" King asked.

"It's morning," Nancy said, turning away. "Make yourself useful and brew up some coffee."

"You wouldn't talk to me that way if this weren't Africa!"

*　　　*　　　*

The Apatosaur emerged from the Kanda Tract like the final collapse of the burning house. The splintering of brush and nettles was tremendous. Then as if it had lost all substance, it padded serenely into open grassland.

From points of concealment at the edge of the tract, they watched it pause, look around, and swing its long serpentine head in undulant arcs.

It stared back at the sheltering rain forest lovingly, as if homesick.

"Now!" Nancy shouted.

The Bantus had rigged up slingshots large enough to launch the melons. They let fly. Three of the green globes arced high and came crashing down several feet ahead of the creature's path.

The pulpy smell immediately attracted its attention. The head swung back. And like a locomotive building up a head of steam, it started forward.

The melons vanished quickly. The head came up, eyes inquisitive.

And there in its path lay a single golden toadstool. It started toward it. And the toadstool retreated ever so slightly.

Undeterred, the reptile kept moving.

"What's going on?" King muttered.

Nancy looked around. "Where's Thorpe?"

"B'wana Thorpe in bush. Play trick on N'yamala."

"He didn't!"

"He did, Missy Derringer."

"That is one smart limey," Skip King said. "I may not dock him after all."

"You were going to dock him? For what?"

"For mutiny," said King.

"Your superiors are going to hear about every screwup you committed since we left the States."

"I'm going to have some choice words for them, too, Miss Masculine. Or should I say, *Dr.* Masculine?"

In the grass, the reptile was doggedly pursuing the elusive toadstool. Every time he got close enough to lower his head for the prize, it slipped away.

"He's pushing it," King said.

As if reading King's mind, the toadstool lay waiting when the great saurian head plunged down again. This time it succeeded. The toadstool went into the mouth as the head lifted up like a triumphant crane.

Then another toadstool appeared not far from it. The Apatosaur started for that one. And the stop-and-start game of cat-and-mouse began again.

By this time, it seemed safe to emerge from the rain forest and they filtered out.

They crept forward cautiously, keeping low. Most of the packs had been left behind.

One of the cameramen was creeping ahead of the rest and using his videocam to record a shot of the beast's undulating rump.

Nancy had a microcassette recorder out and was talking into it.

"Locomotion undulant, flexure resembling that of a pachyderm. Tail held off the ground in accordance with current theories. Skin appears semimoist and leathery but smooth in general appearance."

Then, the cameraman came back holding his nose in one hand and the camera in the other.

"What's wrong?" Nancy hissed.

"It dumped a load. Christ. It stinks!"

"That was inevitable. It's been feeding for six hours straight."

The stagnant air made the smell worse. The others walked around the steaming lump of matter. But Nancy, wearing a filter mask, crept up to it and using a twig, poked a sample loose and into a glass jar, which she quickly capped. There was a blank label on which she inscribed the date and the words *Specimen #1*.

For the better part of the day, they kept moving. The Bantus took turns spelling Thorpe. At one point, the beast let out a blood-chilling roar and they thought it was about to turn ugly.

A miasmic cloud enveloped those in the rear and it

was Skip King who figured it first. "The damn thing farted!"

After that, no one was willing to walk directly in the creature's tramped-down wake.

By evening, it did something they should have expected but didn't.

It stopped, looked around as if casing the area, and dropped its belly to the grass. The tail curled close to its body and the head settled flat on the grass.

"Oh my God, it's dead!" King wailed.

"Don't jump to conclusions! Who wants to investigate?"

"I'll take the trick," Thorpe said, motioning for two Bantus to follow him.

Together, they crept up on the creature. He walked around to the head, his body language indicating he was ready to shoot or run if the creature made a sudden move, and probably both.

Thorpe crept back.

"It's asleep," he reported.

"What do we do now?" King complained. "He's going to throw us all off schedule."

"You're right."

"I am?"

"Yes. We can't let him sleep away the night."

"Right."

"It was your idea," Nancy said. "Go wake him."

Skip King had his mouth open. He shut it. His eyes closed. "I am not in my element here," he muttered to no one in particular and went off to sit in the shade of a tulip tree and talk to himself in a low angry voice.

"Good," said Nancy. "This is the perfect opportunity for me to do something important."

Thorpe asked, "What?"

"I'm going to be the first zoologist to sex a dinosaur."

Nancy approached the reptile. They shone a light all over its tail, under the curve of his hind legs and generally poked around.

She came back with a disappointed look on her face.

"No luck?"

"Whatever he or she's got, it's well hidden."

"At least you didn't wake the brute."

It was while the Apatosaur slumbered that the Land Rovers were heard.

"Now who could that be?" Thorpe muttered aloud, peering into the hot twilight.

"Government men, maybe," Nancy ventured.

"Could be. Why don't I take a look?"

Taking two Bantus, Thorpe went toward the sound. The three were lost to sight in a matter of moments.

The first shot was not loud. But the ones that followed were. They cracked in the distance like firecrackers.

Then there was silence. The Apatosaur slumbered on.

Thorpe turned up twenty minutes later. Only one of the Bantus was with him and he clutched a wounded right shoulder.

"What happened?"

"Bandits."

"Bandits?"

"Blokes in camouflage outfits driving Land Rovers."

"Not government men?"

"Government men wear khaki, not fatigues. These lads had green berets. Very French. There's nothing French about the Gondwanaland Army. They did for poor Tyrone, though. He's dead."

Nancy bandaged the other native as she asked questions.

"Poachers?"

"Poachers don't wear matching berets. These lads dressed all of a type. Can't rightly make it out, actually."

"What do you think they want?"

"There's a lot of famine west of these parts. Fresh meat can fetch a pretty farthing on the black market."

Nancy looked up. Thorpe was staring at the slumbering dinosaur, his leathery features grim.

"You can't mean Jack?" she said. "He's the last of his kind. Worth more alive than butchered!"

Thorpe shrugged. "Out here meat is meat. I fancy even a few of these Bantus may be willing to try human flesh if things got desperate enough for them. I'm not sure I'd pass it up if the situation was sufficently sticky."

Grimly, Nancy finished what she was doing. She stood up.

"Will they be back?"

"Hard to tell. But we're sitting ducks as long as Old Jack is disposed to count sheep."

Nancy Derringer made a hard face. "I want a rifle."

"You ever handle a big-game rifle before?"

"No, but you're going to teach me. If those bastards so much as show their faces, I'm going to put them all to sleep!"

"You know," Skip King said slowly, "I think Africa's gone to your head."

"Better than it going to my gonads, like some people I know."

6

Remo was staring at the sprawling fieldstone structure that occupied a corner lot on a busy residential street.

It was not as big as he had expected. There were only two stories. Or was it three? It was hard to tell from the outside. Rows of dormer windows had been built into the sloping roof, turning attic space into a possible third floor.

At first glance, it did look like a castle. Also, like a Gothic church. Parts of it reminded Remo of a Swiss chalet, although it actually had Tudor features.

"It's hideous," Remo croaked.

"It is magnificent," said Chiun gliding across the street to the low wrought-iron gate.

"Oh no," Remo groaned. "He loves it."

"I thought he might," said Smith, relief in his voice. "I had better give him the key."

"Not so fast," Remo said. "What is this thing?"

"Why, Chiun's castle."

"Castle, my foot. It looks like a freaking church on steroids. You expect me to live there?"

"If you do not like it, Remo, I will be glad to make other arrangements for you. There are several condominium apartments available in the neighborhood."

Chiun floated through the gate and up a short flight of steps to the double doors. Oval windows decorated each door. Like a small child, he pressed his button nose to the glass and peered within.

The Master of Sinanju turned, his face rapturous.

"It is everything I have ever wanted," Chiun cried.

Remo mounted the steps two at a time and started throwing cold water on Chiun's enthusiasm.

"I don't know, Little Father."

"What do you mean, Remo?"

"I don't think this is worthy of a Master of Sinanju."

"Remo, please," Smith pleaded.

"Where's the moat?" Remo said quickly.

Chiun looked around, as if seeing the grounds for the first time. The building was set back from the sidewalk. It was landscaped with sculpted shubbery, and mock-gaslight electric lamps studded the grounds. Tasteful flowers were in bloom. There were paved walkways and a small blacktop parking lot.

But no moat.

"We can't live in a castle without a moat," Remo said. "What will the Queen Mother say if she comes to visit?"

"A moat can be built," Chiun said.

"A dry moat *is* feasible," Smith said hastily.

"And it's next to a school," Remo added.

"What is wrong with that?" Chiun asked.

"The noise is going to be murder."

The Master of Sinanju looked west, where the sandstone school loomed over his domain.

"The play of happy children will bring joy to our days," he said. "And it will be good for the child who is about to be born. He will have many to play with."

"Chiun, it's a high school."

"This is fitting. The one who is about to be born deserves only the best, highest schools in the land. Emperor Smith, you have chosen well."

Remo groaned.

"Why don't we go in?" Smith said, unlocking the door.

Inside, there were many doors off a central corridor and stairs leading upward.

"It has many rooms," Chiun noted with approval.

"Sixteen in all."

"Not enough," Remo said.

"More than our last abode had by far," Chiun sniffed, eyeing Remo disdainfully.

"For maximum privacy, not all connect," Smith added, throwing one open.

Chiun peered in. He saw a cluster of rooms with open, spacious closets and an immaculate tiled bathroom. Stroking his beard, he nodded sagely and allowed, "Privacy will be important to the mother."

"Cheeta Ching is not living under the same roof as me, and that's final!" Remo snapped.

"You may sleep in the moat," Chiun returned. "After you dig it."

"Thanks a lot."

Remo went to another door and opening it, found an identical cell of rooms, like a mirror image. It also had a spic-and-span bathroom. He frowned.

"I must see the upper reaches," Chiun told Smith.

"This way," said Smith, leading them upstairs.

Upstairs was a group of cell-like rooms. When Remo tried to imagine them with furniture, all that came to mind was a cluster of cramped studio apartments. Every room boasted an identical bathroom.

Then it hit him.

"Hey, this is a freaking condo!"

"Remo!" Smith said tightly.

"Admit it."

Chiun's facial web quivered as if troubled by a sudden ill wind. "Emperor Smith," he said, his sparse eyebrows rising, "tell me of the history of this magnificent structure."

"Yes, Emperor Smith," Remo added archly, "we're all ears."

Smith cleared his throat. His Adam's apple bobbed like a floater popping into the water and up again.

"This building was once a church," he admitted.

"Ha! I knew it!"

Chiun frowned.

"A few years ago, it was completely remodeled as

you see it here . . ." Smith added. "It has never been tenanted."

"In other words," Remo said flatly. "Some developer bought this place at the height of the condo craze, remodeled it, and went belly-up before he could unload the units."

Chiun's beard stroking grew studied.

"I was very fortunate in securing title at a reasonable cost," Smith said doggedly. "It is a unique place. It features all the rooms you could want, privacy, and for the Master of Sinanju, a special meditation room."

Chiun's face lit up. "Meditation room?"

"Perfect for your needs, Master Chiun," said Smith. "May I show you?"

"No," said Remo.

"Yes," said Chiun.

Harold Smith led them up to the squat tower of the former church. From the outside, it resembled a crenellated battlement. From the inside, it was a spacious area with four great windows, each facing one of the four quarters. It was full of spring sunlight.

"This is the meditation room?" Remo scoffed. "Looks more like an indoor handball court. What a joke. Nice try, Smitty, but no sale. Right, Little Father?"

Saying nothing, the Master of Sinanju padded around the room.

He went to the south window, which looked upon the street. The sun was on his face. His chin came up.

After a moment, he turned and said, "It is perfect for my needs."

"I hate it!" Remo said hotly. "I can't stand being inside."

"You may go outside," Chiun allowed.

Remo started away, growling, "Thanks."

"And return with my trunks, of course."

Fourteen trunks later, Remo took Harold W. Smith aside and said, "Nice con job."

"I beg your pardon?"

"Passing off a renovated church-turned-condo as a castle. You must have saved a bundle. Or did some bank pay you to take this white elephant off their hands?"

"The Master of Sinanju appears pleased," Smith said defensively.

"How long does *that* usually last?"

"I have learned that the Master of Sinanju is normally as good as his word. He appears to like this place. And he has given me his word that our latest contract will be executed as agreed."

"Don't pocket your signatures until they're dry," Remo warned.

Moments later, the squeaky voice of Chiun called them up to the meditation room.

Chiun had already unpacked one trunk. From it had come three tatami mats. Chiun had assumed a lotus position on one. The other two sat empty on the floor, facing him.

Chiun gestured for the pair to be seated.

Remo walked up to the mat, crossed his ankles as he had been taught long ago, and scissored into a lotus position on the mat.

With arthritic difficulty, Harold Smith set down his suitcase and eased his long legs down. He ended up in a half kneeling position because his legs lacked the suppleness for crossing.

Chiun spoke. His voice was tinged with ceremonial gravity.

"This is an historic day in the House of Sinanju," he intoned. "For five thousand years, the House of Sinanju has treated with the outside world. Since the days of the first Master whose name has not come down to us, to the glory that was Wang the Greater, my ancestors have given service to the thrones of China, of Greece, Rome, and Siam. The Nubians showered us with gold. The Egyptians made a place for us in their fine palaces. Even the Japanese showed us respect, never venturing into the village of Sinanju even as they conquered the surrounding towns and cities of Korea."

"Whoop di do," Remo muttered.

Chiun closed his almond eyes as if to erase the remark from memory.

"But never before have we been blessed with a castle, a home of fine stone and—"

"Blueboard walls," inserted Remo.

"Blueboard walls," continued Chiun, "rarer even than walls of beaten gold."

"Oh brother," Remo groaned.

"Emperor Smith, known in the annals of the House of Sinanju as Harold the First, beneficent one, the Master of Sinanju humbly accepts your gift."

Chiun bowed his aged head. Smith nodded in return.

"Since this gift meets with the approval of the Reigning Master, I am now free to sign the most recent agreement between our houses."

"I have it right here," Smith said, plucking a parchment roll from somewhere in his coat. It was edged in gold and tied with a blue silk ribbon. He proffered it to Chiun.

The Master of Sinanju accepted it and undid the ribbon. He read the contract over in silence. At the end, he set the scroll on the floor and weighed down each corner with polished stones.

Then, taking up a quill from an inkstone at his knee, he scratched out his name with a flourish.

He blew on it, and satisfied that the signature was dry, lifted the scroll to show all.

"That is satisfactory," said Smith solemnly.

"How many years are we indentured for this time?" Remo asked nobody in particular.

"One," said Smith.

"Too long," said Remo.

Solemnly, Chiun rolled the parchment up and tied it with a gold ribbon, signifying a sealed contract. He extended this to Smith, who took it and tucked it in his coat.

A silence followed. Chiun looked to Smith with expectant features.

Smith looked back, a growing puzzlement on his

thin face. He tested the knot of his tie. He swallowed. He checked his glasses to see that they were pushed back as far as they could go—the way he liked them.

"He's waiting," Remo hinted.

"For what?" Smith breathed.

"It's only a guess, but I'd say the deed."

Chiun's tight smile quirked.

"Definitely the deed," Remo said.

"Ah," said Smith. From another pocket, he extracted a folded group of papers. He extended these. Chiun accepted them.

The Master of Sinanju fell to studying these at great length while Smith shifted position to encourage circulation in his stiffening legs.

"All is satisfactory," Chiun pronounced at last.

Smith started to rise.

"It will be an honor if you would pass the night in our new abode," said Chiun.

"Really, I must be returning to Folcroft."

"It is customary," said Chiun.

"That means do it or hear about it the rest of your natural life," Remo translated.

"Very well," said Harold W. Smith, trying to sound grateful, but instead coming across as constipated.

Chiun beamed. "A wonderful meal will be prepared in your honor."

"Better make that takeout," said Remo. "No stove. No food."

Chiun clapped delicate hands together, producing a report so sharp it should have shattered his fingerbones. "Remo! Quickly—purchase these things."

"I don't think we can get same-day delivery."

"Tell the merchants that these items are to make a sumptuous meal for Emperor Harold Smith, the secret ruler of this gracious land."

Smith looked horrorstruck. "Please do not say that, Remo!" he croaked.

"Don't sweat it, Smitty. Rubber walls don't appeal to me right now. Although they might suit me fine if Cheeta moves in."

"And a television device," Chiun added. "A large one, for within hours, beauteous Cheeta Ching will dispense wisdom and grace upon this generous land."

"Maybe this is a good time to clear the air," Remo suggested.

"You may clear the air after you have cooked Emperor Smith a feast suitable for his regal belly," Chiun countered.

"Cook! I'm the errand boy. Who says I gotta cook, too?"

"Your conscience."

"Huh?"

"Your conscience so says. Are you not listening to it, Remo?"

"No, I am not. I want to talk about Cheeta Ching, her biscuit in the oven, and our future."

"Remo is correct, Master Chiun," said Smith. "I know this is a delicate matter, but it would not be wise to invite Cheeta Ching to cohabitate with you."

Chiun blew out his cheeks at the rude American word. He held his tongue, however.

"I intend no such thing," he said stiffly.

"Good," said Smith.

"Great," said Remo.

"Cheeta the Graceful is a married woman. I will not cohabitate with her. That is her husband's happy duty."

"Great," said Remo.

"Wonderful," said Smith.

"She will only dwell here, she and her offspring."

"No," groaned Remo.

"Have you asked her?" asked Smith.

"Not as yet," Chiun admitted. "I am awaiting the proper time, which will be soon, for she waxes full in childbirth as a yellow moon of fecundity."

Smith cleared his throat. "There may be difficulties, Master Chiun."

"Such as . . ."

"Cheeta lives and works in New York City."

"So? She may live and work in this city of previous emperors."

Remo blinked. "This place?"

"Quincy was the birthplace of two early presidents," Smith said.

"Nice touch," Remo whispered to Smith. "I can see how you sold him on this rock pile."

"Thank you." To Chiun, Smith said, "Miss Ching is bound by contract to work out of New York City. I doubt that she will break that contract for the privilege of living here."

"That remains to be seen," Chiun sniffed.

"Er, of course."

"Cheeta will have no need of employment once her child comes. It would be unseemly."

Remo laughed. "You don't know Cheeta. The original 'I can have it all' superanchorwoman."

"Silence! Why are you not about your errands, slothful one? The day is growing short."

Remo got up. "I'll leave you two to work out Cheeta's maternity leave."

He went down the stairs with no more sound than a puff of air.

After Remo had departed, the Master of Sinanju leaned forward and confided in his emperor. "Do not fret, Oh wise Smith. Remo's dark mood will pass. It is always thus with the firstborn."

"Master Chiun?"

"They always fear being supplanted by the children who follow."

Smith swallowed. "But Remo does have a point."

"Yes, he does," Chiun admitted.

"I am glad you see it that way."

"Perhaps the next time he undergoes plastic surgery, this can be remedied."

Smith looked blank.

"I think he should have a proper Korean nose, like mine. Not one that is so large and ends in an unsightly point."

And the Master of Sinanju winked mischievously.

7

Miraculously, they reached the railhead at M'nolo Ki-Gor without any further incidents.

It had been another day's trek. They had run out of fresh jungle chocolate and were down to their last two baskets of toadstools.

This slowed them down because the Apatosaur every so often got tired of toadstool. They solved this by spacing them further apart. Hunger drove the beast onward.

Skip King had been in touch with the railhead by walkie-talkie and arrangements had been made.

"It's all set," he said as they watched Old Jack lumber toward the railroad tracks. "The train is waiting. All we have to do is get him onto the flatcar."

"And how do you propose to do that?" Nancy asked flintily.

"I was going to leave that up to you, since you're in charge now," King sneered.

It was a problem, Nancy realized. She huddled with Thorpe and the Bantus.

"Any suggestions?"

"Frankly, Dr. Derringer, I don't think there's any way it can be done. If we trank the big bugger, we're talking about ten tons of dead reptilian weight. And getting him to climb onto a flatcar on his own hook is out of the question."

Nancy chewed her lower lip and made thoughtful faces.

"There must be a way."

She looked over to Skip King, who was fanning his sharp face with his bush hat.

"Wait a minute," she murmured. "King set up this whole thing. Surely, he had some semiworkable plan in mind."

"I'll ask him."

Thorpe walked over and conferred with King. Nancy noticed the grin coming over King's lean face and knew what was coming next.

"King wants *you* to ask *him*."

"There's a price attached, I'm sure," Nancy said, striding over to him. "All right, King, I understand you have a plan."

King tried to keep the smugness out of his face and failed. "We have to do it my way. Under my command."

"Why?"

"So people won't say Skip King didn't pull his own weight."

"Let me guess. You're planning to have every moment recorded for posterity."

"I'm a big home movie fan."

Nancy sighed. "All right, King. It's your show. But it's your failure if you screw up."

"Skip King never screws up when he has his way."

"I hate myself for letting this happen," Nancy told Thorpe a moment later.

"Keep your pecker up, as we Brits say."

King called the Bantus together.

"I'm in charge again. Savvy?"

They stared at him.

"I want the trank rifles distributed and every man ready to bring Old Jack down when I give the signal. Any questions?"

No one spoke.

"Good. And let's get those T-shirts turned around, this is going to be recorded for posterity."

No one moved.

"Now!"

Reluctantly, the Bantus peeled off their sweaty, dirt-smeared T-shirts and put them on right side out. None of them talked among themselves, but every man seemed to have the same idea at the same time because they put them on with the Burger Triumph logos on their backs, leaving the fronts blank.

King glared at them. "I give up."

"Missy Nancy in charge again?" one asked.

"No!"

They stalked the Apatosaur, sowing toadstools in its path. Like some tireless beast of burden, it lumbered along. From time to time it took notice of them, but as long as there were morsels to be found along the path, the creature paid the tiny humans no heed.

When they were within a quarter mile of the railroad, King got the expedition organized.

"You, you, and you, keep Old Jack moving. And be ready to use your weapons when I say." He turned to Nancy and Thorpe. "The rest of you tag along. You're about to see genius at work."

The railhead was nothing more than a half rotted platform, a signal house and one rusty length of track. The old Marxist government of Gondwanaland had thought it could save money by building only one set of tracks. They hadn't thought to install a signal system and after six train wrecks in the first year, they spent the money they had saved—plus thirty percent more—installing a switching-and-signal system.

The waiting train consisted of two locomotives in front and a pusher in back. Between them was a heavily reinforced flatcar and a decrepit passenger car.

"That's it," King said. "The way to Port Chuma is straight as an arrow. Once we get Old Jack up on that car, it should be a cinch."

"That's a big 'if,' " Nancy clucked.

"You watch."

King measured out a length of the approach with his feet, saying, "I paced the monster when it was

asleep, so I'd know exactly how long to mark off."
He scuffed an X at either end of the line he had paced
off.

"Okay," he said, clapping his hands together, "everything we need is on the train."

At the train, King was met by a man in a purple
beret and a Boy Scout blue uniform burdened by
heavy ropes of gold braid. He called others out.

Noticing the outfits, Nancy asked Thorpe, "Recognize the uniforms?"

"Can't say that I do."

As they got close, King dispelled all their questions.
"This is Sergeant Shakes."

"Of what?" Thorpe wondered.

King grinned proudly. "The Burger Berets. Our
special purposes strike team. Created just for this
operation."

Nancy and Thorpe looked at one another.

"I don't know whether to laugh or cry," Nancy
undertoned.

"Let's be polite to the gentlemen," Thorpe said.
"Gents, what's your pleasure?"

Sergeant Shakes began offloading great canvas sacks
tied with drawstring. "Bring these over to the line,"
he said.

They got them over and King ordered the back
opened. They looked like post office mail sacks, but
much heavier.

King brought the first leather-and-cable harness out.
It was over a dozen feet long, and the leather was cut
broad and riveted together in layers.

"The idea is to lay these out every so many feet.
Got that?"

Nancy gave one of the straps a thorough examination.
"A harness?"

"Tested until it can take one thousand foot-pounds
of weight per square inch."

"Impressive," she murmured.

"Glad you think so."

"But how are you going to convince Clark Kent to

gather them all up once you drop Old Jack onto these? That *is* your brilliant plan, isn't it?"

"All except the Clark Kent part," King said.

They got the straps laid. King went back and forth, adjusting the intervals, until he was satisfied.

Then they found places to wait, rifles at the ready and videocams *whirring*.

Soon, the ground was rumbling under their feet and the dayglow saurian face loomed out of the bush like the Serpent of Eden.

"No one shoot until I say so," King warned. "Cameramen, come in tight on me."

The creature lumbered closer, the Bantus coming ahead of it, placing food.

"Thorpe!" King snapped. "Tell them to stop. I want a whole pile of it dumped out right where that flat rock is."

Thorpe came out from behind some nettles and collected the last basket of toadstools. He set the basket down onto the flat rock, and found cover again.

Old Jack paused. Its head swung around as if searching for something familiar.

"He doesn't see the damn toadstools!" King hissed.

"I'll fix that," Nancy said, running out.

She got in the creature's path and waved her arms. "Here! Jack! Follow me!"

The beast looked at her. It made a low sound.

"Just a little closer."

It started forward. Nancy backed away. The reptile shook the dry ground with each step, throwing up dusty puffs that hung low a long time in the still African air.

Nancy walked backward until one heel touched the basket. Then she quickly turned and dumped it out, stomping the fungi into a malodorous morass.

"That should do it," she said, joining Thorpe in the bush.

The creature picked up its pace. The thumping of the earth came at closer intervals.

It stopped, straddling the straps and attacked the food that had been laid out for it.

Skip King popped out of the bush and put his rifle to his shoulder. He gave his cameramen three seconds to frame the shot, then fired three times into the thickest part of the creature's tail.

Only then did he shout, "Now! Open fire!"

Rifles poked out of the brush all around, bucked, and made harsh noises.

Tranquilizer darts feathered different places in the monster's anatomy.

Nothing happened.

"Why doesn't he go down?" King wailed, eyes sick.

"It takes a while," Nancy said. "The Apatosaur circulatory system is huge so the tranquilizers have a lot of bloodstream to run before they reach the sleep receptors of the brain."

It took nearly three minutes, but the great legs began shuddering. Slowly the dinosaur eased itself down into an awkward kneel, lowering its stomach to the dusty earth. The head came up from its meal and craned back as if to see why the body was not being supported by the sequoia-thick legs; finally the eyes surrendered and the head came to rest curled back toward the body, like a sleeping cat.

"Shakes—call in the cavalry!"

"Cavalry?" Nancy muttered.

Sergeant Shakes got on a walkie-talkie. Before long the sky was reverberating with the racket of a massive helicopter skycrane. It was white, its stick-thin wheel assemblies hanging insectlike from the gaping space where a cargo container would normally be carried.

Nancy stood watching it with her mouth hanging open and a look of disbelief on her face.

"This can't possibly work!"

"Might," Thorpe allowed.

It did.

Under King's frantic direction, the Bantus swarmed over the inert carcass. The cable ends were brought together on the back of the creature's spine and affixed to cables lowered from the hovering skycrane.

When it was all rigged, King gave a prearranged signal.

"Lift!"

The skycrane began to lift, its rotors making the tawny savanna grass shiver in sympathy. The cables lifted, grew taut, and everyone held their breath.

The head, being lighter, lifted up first. The meaty part of the tail came off the ground.

The helicopter engine whined and grew shrill from strain. It seemed for a long time the weight of the great saurian would defeat it, but then the hindquarters came off the ground, followed by the breast and the belly.

Slowly, the monster was brought over the string of cars and—with infinite patience—aligned with the reinforced flatcar.

King ran around frantically checking and screaming into the walkie-talkie.

"Okay, begin lowering. And the pilot who screws up will be flying a crop duster in darkest Iowa the rest of his life."

The long flatcar platform received the belly with a groaning of springs and a threatening squeaking. The hanging legs bent up at the knees and assumed unnatural positions that brought to mind a dressed turkey, but meant the legs would not be crushed by the weight of the body.

The head, limp and lifeless, dropped into the dirt and looked dead.

"The poor thing," Nancy said plaintively.

The tip of the tail dropped off the end, but the thick root lay safely on the flatcar bed. There came a final groan of complaining steel, and no more.

The skycrane sank lower and the cables grew lax.

"Looks like it's going to work," King said, voice strung tight. "Looks like . . . Yes! Yes! Yes! It's another triumph for Burger Triumph!"

The cables were unsnapped and stowed along the

sides of the cars, ready for later off-loading. Folding gates were raised to form a low cage, but it was obvious that should the cargo ever shift, nothing could prevent a catastrophe.

"Okay," King called, even though everyone was within whispering distance, "we get the head and tail onto the cars and then we're ready to move."

The Bantus took the tail. They wanted no part of the head.

Nancy stayed close to the Burger Beret team as they muscled the head off the ground and tried to find a place to put it.

"The damn neck's too long," King said in exasperation.

"Why don't you just cut the head off?" Nancy suggested.

King looked up, a gleam in his eyes. Then it died. "What am I thinking? No, we can't do that!"

Nancy smiled. "Just testing your brain. It's working—just a little slow."

"How about a little credit for a job well done?"

"We're a long way from Port Chuma," Nancy shot back. "And if you're open to suggestions, I have one."

King looked around to see if there were any cameras recording the conversation. Finding none, he said, "Go ahead."

"The head might fit into the cab of the second locomotive."

King looked from Nancy to the locomotive. Then he stood up and cupped his hands over his mouth. "Hey, everybody, I had a brainstorm! We can fit the head into locomotive cab!"

Clambering down, he mumbled a grudging, "Thanks."

"Oh, don't mention it."

It took nearly every hand to maneuver the head in, but they did it.

"All right, everyone," King shouted, "space is tight so find a place to ride and we'll be off."

"There isn't room for everybody," Thorpe pointed out.

"Let the natives trot alongside the train."

"Be serious."

"Then leave them behind."

"You can't mean that!"

"No? Maybe next time they'll wear the sponsor's shirts with pride."

"If they stay, I stay," Thorpe said firmly.

"Then you stay. The check will be in the mail."

"If *he* stays, *I* stay," Nancy added.

King considered. What he would have said remained unspoken.

"Dr. Derringer, I can handle this from here," Thorpe said. "You stick with Old Jack. Maybe we'll meet up in the States."

Nancy hesitated. She glared daggers at King and took Thorpe's hand in a firm clasp.

"Good luck, Thorpe."

"Cheerio."

King snapped his fingers so hard they stung. "Wait! I almost forgot! Just in case, we've got to send a package ahead."

"Package?"

"A film package."

They called down the skycrane and passed off three video cassettes. The helicopter lifted into the blue sky and rattled off toward the east.

Then the locomotives were fired up. They were steam models. It took some time. Everyone helped shovel coal. Except Skip King. He found the most comfortable seat in the lone passenger car behind the cargo car and popped a beer he pulled from an ice chest.

All the locomotives started up at once.

Great iron wheels screeched as they attempted to revolve. Couplings clanked.

And bearing its monstrous cargo, the train began moving.

They got up to twenty-five miles an hour and held that speed for the remainder of the day. King was talking nonstop.

"I wonder who should publish the excerpts from my biography?" he wondered aloud as a blur of jungle ran past the windows. "*Vanity Fair* or—"

"*Mad* magazine," Nancy finished.

"Don't mind her, boys," King told the attentive Berets, "she's just post-menstrual. It'll pass."

When no one joined in his braying laughter, King took a cold sip and said. "Well, we've all had a rough day."

Less that thirty miles from Port Chuma, the engineer spotted the logs on the tracks and blew his whistle. He hit the air brakes.

It was a European-style engine. There was no cow catcher. Just a pair of spring-loaded rams mounted in the front of the lead boiler.

The brakes took. Screeching, the train slid that last hundred yards, to stop just shy of the barrier of logs.

"What it is?" King muttered. "Why'd we stop?"

The sound of gunfire gave him his first clue.

Out of the bush poured knots of black men in camouflage fatigues with green berets perched on their heads. They carried Skorpion machine pistols.

"Bandits!" King shouted. "Burger Berets, do your corporate duty!"

Nancy grabbed his shoulder. "Are you crazy, King? If there's a gun fight, we'll be certain to lose Jack!"

King shook off the clutching hand.

"Relax baby," he said. "Skip King knows what he's doing." He took an AR-15 away from a Burger Beret, dashed out the glass in the window, and shouting, "Have it your way!" opened fire.

There was immediate return fire and Nancy dived to the floor.

For a firefight, it went on a long time.

The Burger Berets laid down covering fire. Return fire was sporadic. Nancy hugged the floor, face cradled in her crossed arms to protect it against flying glass and splinters.

The popping of the AR-15s filled the car, and she

was forced to clap her hands over her ears. They were still sensitive from the abuse they had taken after King had fired his trank gun in her ear.

"Okay!" King shouted. "Get ready to jump. I'll cover you."

The Burger Berets piled out, shooting.

"Don't worry, Nancy, I'll protect you!"

"Jackass!" Nancy spat. "Who's going to protect Jack!"

"Don't sweat it. God looks out for fools and dinosaurs."

The firing came in percussive waves. King emptied two clips and was ramming a fresh one home when the car door was thrown open and a deep basso voice said in slightly Oxford-flavored English, "You are all prisoners of the Congress for a Green Africa."

Nancy looked up.

A wide-faced black man with a curly black beard was smiling at them with his teeth and menacing them with the muzzle of his machine pistol.

Nancy decided the weapon canceled out the teeth and lifted her hand at the elbows, saying, "We surrender."

"Speak for yourself," King said defiantly. "I may want to tough this out."

"If you don't shoot that idiot," Nancy said in a bitter voice. "I want the privilege."

King looked from Nancy to the black man to Nancy again and lay down his weapon.

"A seasoned jungle fighter can tell when he's out-flanked," he grumbled, throwing up his hands. "I choose to live to fight another day."

Nancy spoke up. "Somebody please tell me that Old Jack is safe."

"You mean *mokele m'bembe?*" asked the basso voice.

Nancy looked startled. "*Mokele m'bembe* is what they call Jack in Gabon."

"And I am from Gabon, come to claim *mokele m'bembe* for my country."

8

Harold W. Smith was explaining the painstaking selection process that resulted in the acquisition of a castle for the Master of Sinanju while he attempted to get the morsels of steamed rice to his mouth with the silver chopsticks provided.

The rice kept falling back, and he succeeded only in getting three or four grains to his tongue each time, and then only because the stuff had a sticky consistency.

"There were several operational considerations beyond simply satisfying the Master of Sinanju," Smith was saying.

"Where does simple come in?" Remo growled, poking at his duck, which he had already pronounced as too greasy. Chiun had countered that the cook should not complain about his own cooking, but should strive for perfection. "Simple is a nice clapboard house with a white picket fence. Simple is not a castle."

"Remo, eat your duck," Chiun said.

"It's greasy."

"The cook was inferior. Continue, Emperor Smith."

"A city large enough for the two of you to blend in was of paramount importance," Smith said. "Small town people tend to be too sensitive to those who do not fit in, and would be apt to snoop."

"Couldn't have us kill every old lady who came to peer through our venetian blinds," Remo grumbled, taking up his bowl of rice. He began eating with his fingers because it would annoy the Master of Sinanju.

"You are eating like a Chinaman," Chiun said, nose wrinkling.

"So I'm eating like a Chinaman. Sue me."

Smith continued. "Proximity to a major airport is critical, of course. You must be able to move on a moment's notice."

"If the world depends on us getting through Boston traffic in less than a day, I'd say the world has a grim prognosis."

Chiun said, "We will walk to the airport if necessary, Emperor Smith. For our gratitude knows no bounds."

"There is public transportation," Smith said. "Another consideration."

"I can see the headlines now," Remo said through a mouthful of rice, knowing it would make Chiun complain about his manners, " 'SUBWAY PASSENGER REFUSES TO GIVE UP SEAT FOR KOREAN MAN; TRAIN PULLS INTO STATION WITH ALL ABOARD DEAD.' "

"Remo, do not speak with your mouth full."

"So, today I'm a Chinaman."

"Today, you are a Chinaman and a Thai. Thais talk with their mouths full. This is why they do not wear beards which might catch expelled rice grains."

"Maybe I'll grow a beard," Remo muttered.

"You have too much unsightly facial hair to grow a proper beard," said Chiun, stroking the thin tendril of hair clinging to his tiny chin. "Do not pay him any heed, Emperor Smith," he confided in Smith. "Remo is in a cranky mood because he will have to sleep indoors tonight, for his moat is not yet ready."

"Har de har har har," Remo said, swallowing.

"Additionally," Smith said doggedly, "I took the demographic makeup of the local population into consideration."

"I have no objection to dwelling among Demographs," Chiun said loftily. "As long as there are an equal number of Republicrats to keep their spendthrift tendencies in line."

Smith set down his rice, giving up.

"You should have no problem shopping for correct foods and other items," he said.

"The rice Remo was able to purchase locally is of good quality. And the duck would have been superb—if prepared properly."

"I am glad everything is satisfactory," said Smith.

"It is," said Chiun. "All we lack is the sound of a child's happy laughter."

"And the sour reek of unchanged diapers," Remo muttered.

Chiun frowned. "Remo," he said in a steady tone, "Soon Cheeta will once again shower this land with her wisdom and grace. Please serve dessert and turn on the television device."

"I do not think my diet will allow me to eat dessert," Smith said.

"Your diet will definitely allow you to eat these," said Remo, pointing to a linen-covered basket set in the center of the circle in which they sat.

Remo reached over and lifted the basket by the handle, snatching away the linen.

"Enjoy."

Smith frowned. He saw a cluster of small horny brown shapes. Gingerly, he lifted one.

"What are these?" Smith asked in a doubtful tone.

"Lichee nuts," said Remo.

"How does one remove the shell?"

"You do it like so," said Remo, digging a thumbnail into the area of the stem and popping the top off to expose the juicy white grapelike fruit. Then he broke away the remaining shell and popped the fruit into his mouth.

Smith attempted the same operation. He managed to crush the fruit in its shell and, embarrassed, swallowed it with bits of shell still clinging to it.

Chiun stared at him in horror. Smith, seeing this, looked to Remo, who was spitting the biggest pit he had ever seen this side of a peach into a flat, silver dish.

"You're supposed to lose the pit," Remo said.

"I do not think I will have another," Smith said weakly.

"Good. But because one is all Chiun and I are allowed. Right, Little Father?"

The Master of Sinanju took his litchi nut between his extra long fingernails and performed an operation that seemed not to break the shell, but suddenly it lay at his feet, along with the pit. The limp white meat went into his mouth. He chewed it for over a minute, until the pulp was liquid. Then he swallowed the result as if it were a refreshing nectar.

"And now it is time for Cheeta," Chiun said in a satisfied voice.

Remo grabbed the clicker and pointed it at the large screen television he had purchased earlier and carted by hand up the stairs. That had been the easy part. Chiun had made him move it sixteen times until the sun was not reflected on the screen.

"Anybody know which channel she's on locally?" Remo asked as he ran up and down the channels.

"Remo! Hurry! I must not miss a moment of Cheeta's—"

"Screed," Remo muttered, stopping when the familiar BCN News graphic filled the screen.

Chiun's tight features relaxed, and his nails touched delicately as his eyes fell on the face of Cheeta Ching, the Korean anchorwoman with whom he had been infatuated for over a decade now. Her face, under a layer of pancake makeup thick enough to pass as cake frosting, was puffy. She was due in six weeks, and Remo dreaded the approaching day.

"Hello. This is the *BCN Evening News* with Cheeta Ching."

Chiun sighed. "What eloquence."

"What crap," Remo muttered.

Smith sat attentively.

Cheeta fixed her predatory eyes on the camera. "Tonight, a startling video out of Africa—and a mystery. Did the Burger Triumph corporation send a safari into the darkest Gondwanaland to bring 'em back alive only to fall into a snare themselves?"

The camera zoomed in on Cheeta's flat features.

"BCN News has obtained an exclusive video of what may be confirmation of what explorers and natives have been claiming for over a century. That deep in the Gondwanaland's imperiled Kanda Tract, an actual dinosaur survives."

Remo brightened. "No kidding!"

"Here is a clip reportedly shot last night by a Burger Triumph-sponsored exploration team," Cheeta announced.

Remo sat up straighter. Chiun's eyes narrowed.

The clip ran nearly three minutes—long for network TV.

It showed an orange-and-black long-necked dinosaur lumber out of a swatch of jungle growth and fall before a withering fusillade of rifle fire.

"A spokesman for Burger Triumph assures us that only nonlethal tranquilizer bullets were employed to stun the creature, which appears to be some sort of dinosaur."

"Brontosaur, you dip," Remo said.

"Remo, hush," Chiun admonished.

"How can she call herself a reporter when she doesn't even recognize a Brontosaur when she sees one?"

"Actually," Smith started to say, "it is a—"

"Silence!" Chiun thundered, and both men fell silent.

Cheeta Ching was still doing a voice-over as scenes of the dinosaur falling onto its stomach were played and replayed.

"After this footage was shot," she said, "the monster was loaded on a train and set out for the capital, Port Chuma. Mysteriously, no trace of the train has been seen in over twenty-four hours. Authorities in Port Chuma express confidence that the train, with its strange cargo, will eventually be found. But as of this hour, there are no new developments to report."

"Which is anchorspeak for 'We don't know nothing,' " Remo said sourly.

"A Burger Triumph spokesman who asked not to be named said the company is considering launching a second expedition to locate the first. Next up, an interview with my personal gynecologist with his third-trimester report. But first, this message."

The screen cut to a different shot of Cheeta Ching extolling the virtues of a home pregnancy testing kit, and Remo and Smith looked to Chiun to see if it was acceptable to talk or not.

Chiun's eyes were narrow. Almost slits. He was very still.

He turned to meet Smith's gaze with his own.

"Emperor Smith, I crave a boon, as ungrateful as it may sound."

"Yes?"

"Dispatch Remo and me to Africa to seek those who are lost."

"Oh no!" Remo said harshly. "I'd rather stay here than go to Africa. I've been there. It's hot and it stinks."

"I will go alone, then," Chiun said coldly.

"Why?" asked Smith.

Chiun made a face. "I cannot tell you, but granting this boon may mean that the House of Sinanju will continue to serve America far into the next century."

Smith looked to Remo. Remo shrugged. Smith cleared his throat. "Well, since these people are American citizens, I suppose you could go. So long as you are discreet."

Like smoke rising, the Master of Sinanju came to his feet. He bowed once. Then, padding over to the TV, he did something that made Remo's mouth hang open in surprise.

He switched off the set just as Cheeta Ching was starting to speak.

"Remo, you and I will look into the Shortsleeve question while Master Chiun is away," Smith offered.

"Nothing doing," said Remo, finding his voice. "I

don't know what's got into Chiun, but if it is big enough to make him turn off Cheeta Ching in midyap, I want to be along for the ride."

They ran the rental van back to the airport, dropped Smith off at the departure terminal, and drove on to international departures.

Remo bought two round-trip tickets to Port Chuma, using a credit card that identified him as Remo Burton, with the Department of Health and Human Services. He had a matching passport.

"Proof of shots?" asked the ticket agent.

"Would someone from the Department of Health and Human Services be going to Africa if he didn't have his shots?" Remo asked in a firm voice.

The agent thought not, and the tickets were surrendered.

Over the Atlantic, they sat in a silence that was not broken until they reached London, where they had to change planes.

At Heathrow, Remo decided to break the ice.

"Care to tell a fellow traveler why he's traveling?"

"No."

"Toss a hint in my direction, then?"

"Reflect upon the lesson of Master Yong."

Remo reflected. In the early days of his training in Sinanju, Chiun used to drum into his head the exploits of past Masters. Each Master, it seemed, was remembered for one special reason. Wang because he discovered the sun source. Yeng because he was too greedy. Yokang because he consorted with Japanese women and caught certain diseases from them. Remo had learned about every Master—or so he thought. In recent years, there had been fewer legends. Remo had assumed it was because Chiun had run out of Masters, but was forced to conclude that the true reason was that in Chiun's eyes, Remo had grown to full Masterhood, the penultimate step toward Reigning Master status, which Remo could only achieve upon Chiun's death or retirement.

Master Yong, Remo could not remember.

He wracked his brain as the British 747 winged its way to Africa.

"Yong, Yong, Yong," he muttered aloud. "Not Bong. He discovered India. Can't be Nonga. He was deaf and dumb."

"Render it in English," Chiun said thinly.

Over his twenty-year association with the Master of Sinanju, Remo had picked up a little Korean here and there until one day he found himself, to his infinite surprise, considering that he had flunked French I three years running in school, fluent in the language.

"Dragon!" he said snapping his fingers. "Yong means dragon."

"Some Masters are remembered for their true names, others—those held in contempt—are remembered by false names so as not to shame their ancestors. It is so with Yong."

"Yeah? What'd he do?"

The Master of Sinanju made a face. He touched his thin beard as if debating the wisdom of answering the question.

"I will tell you if you promise not to reveal what I am about to divulge to Emperor Smith."

"Family secret, huh?"

"A deep shame is attached to Yong the Gluttonous."

"Gluttonous? Are we off to Africa to make the world safe for hamburger companies?"

"Silence! If your ears would hear, your mouth must be still. Preferably closed."

Remo folded his bare arms. It was cool in the big jet and his arm hairs were lifting in response. He willed them to lay flat and they did. It was a minor example of the nearly total control he exercised over every cell in his superbly trained body.

Chiun began speaking.

"The story I am about to tell you transpired in the Year of the Peacock."

"Give me a number."

"I do not know the American year and I do not care," Chiun retorted. "In these days we served the Middle Kingdom, Cathay, a land of barbarians who ate their rice with their fingers."

"Don't rub it in."

"Master Yong—not his real name of course—was summoned to the throne of Cathay. For a great dragon was devouring rice farmers and other subjects of the Chinese emperor. This being how dragons typically passed their days.

"Now the days of which I speak are the old days of Sinanju, before Wang, who discovered the sun source. This was when Masters performed many functions, and not merely practicing the assassin's art. Masters in those days would perform executions for the proper price. For this task, a previous Master had had forged a tremendous sword, known as the Sword of Sinanju. Later, as you know, Remo, the thieving Chinese stole this great trophy, and kept it."

"Until we got it back," said Remo.

"Until Chiun the Great recovered it, aided by a white lackey who may or may not be recorded in the Book of Sinanju under his true name," Chiun said frostily.

"I want to be remembered as Remo the Long-Suffering."

Face impassive, the Master of Sinanju resumed speaking, "When Yong appeared before the Chinese emperor, he had with him the great Sword of Sinanju because in those days one never knew what service Chinese emperors would demand. A courtesan might require beheading. Or the garbage might have to be taken out. To Yong's surprise, it was none of these things. He was asked to slay a dragon."

"Really?"

Chiun nodded. "In those days, dragons were more plentiful than they are now, but still rare. Yong had never before beheld a dragon, although he had heard tales of their fierceness and fury. This particular dragon was known as Wing Wang Wo."

Remo lifted a skeptical eyebrow. "The dragon had a name?"

"This dragon did. Yong agreed to slay the dragon, but not for the usual sum of gold. He asked the Chinese emperor for only one thing in return. The dragon's carcass.

"The Chinese emperor agreed to this. For like all of his line, he was penurious. That means cheap, Remo."

"I figured it out from the context," Remo grumbled.

"It does no harm to explain the difficult words when dealing with willful children," Chiun said. "Now Yong ventured out into the Chinese countryside. And soon he came upon a magnificent if cranky dragon, storming about, its iridescent green-and-gold scales ablaze in the harsh Chinese sun."

"Yong thought he saw a dragon?"

"Yong *did* see a dragon. And knowing that only the foolhardy attacks a foe without first studying him, Yong watched this dragon go about his business of devouring simple peasants."

"Yong didn't stop the dragon?"

Chiun shrugged. "Interrupting Wing Wang Wo's meals was not in Yong's contract. Now be silent, One-Whose-Tongue-Is-Never-Still.

"Soon, Yong devised a plan. First he caught the dragon's attention by bestowing upon him an insulting Chinese hand gesture."

"Flipped him the bird, huh?"

Chiun glared.

"Sorry." Remo fell silent.

"Naturally," Chiun resumed, "this enraged Wing Wang Wo, who blazed ineffectual flames at the ever-nimble Yong. Hurling cutting taunts, Yong lured the dragon to a cave he had explored earlier.

"Seeking to avenge his sullied honor, the dragon naturally followed. For—and you must always remember this, Remo—a dragon's breath is the only thing about them that can truly be called bright."

Remo winced.

"Once in the great cave, Yong hid behind a great stone. The dragon padded past him unsuspecting, the sulphur of its breath blocking its own nostrils. The great arrowlike tail dragged past, and Yong slipped back out of the cave to climb onto a ledge just above the cave mouth, where he had placed the Sword of Sinanju, which was seven feet in length and a mighty weapon."

Chiun lifted an imaginary sword in both thin-fingered hands. His voice shook in the telling.

"Sword held high, Yong waited patiently."

Up and down the aisles, the passengers within hearing paused to listen attentively.

"In time, the dull-witted Wing Wang Wo stuck his thick head out of the cave mouth, whereupon Yong relieved him of this trophy with one swift blow. Chuk!"

Chiun brought the imaginary sword down.

"Ouch," said Remo.

"The dragon whelmed, Yong had its meat stripped away and—"

"He *ate* the dragon?"

Shaking his head, Chiun lifted a long finger. "No. Yong wanted only the bones. For he knew what the Chinese emperor did not. That dragon bones are a potent medicine. Mixed in an elixir and drunk, they prolonged life. Yong drank dragon elixir every month for the remainder of his days, even though twice a year would have sufficed. And that is why Yong lived to a venerable age."

"Yeah? How long do Sinanju Masters normally live?"

"Only one hundred to one hundred twenty years. It is because we work so hard and are unappreciated."

"I feel for you," suddenly remembering that Chiun had turned 100 a couple of years ago. The thought made him feel cold inside.

"Master Yong lived to be an undeserved one hundred forty-eight years in age," Chiun sniffed. "For

he squandered every dragon bone brought back from
Cathay in prolonging his own selfish life. And it is for
this reason, Remo, that Yong is known in the annals
of Sinanju as Yong the Gluttonous."

Mild applause rippled along the aisles. The passengers returned to their magazines and their meals.

"All right," Remo said slowly, trying to figure out
what this had to do with a possible dinosaur in Africa.
"Yong was a pig. But what—" Then it hit him.

"Hold the phone, Little Father."

"What phone?"

"You know what I mean. Are we by chance off on
a wild dragon hunt?"

"I am not aware of any dragons that are not wild."

"Chiun, if you're thinking of grinding up dinosaur
bones just so you can live to be as old as Methuselah,
I think Smith is going to have something to say about
that."

Chiun's hazel eyes grew veiled. "Of course. He is
going to say how pleased he is that he will have a
proper Master to serve him for many years to come.
Perhaps, Remo, when I am one hundred forty, you
will be wise enough in years so I can properly retire
to my humble village."

"By that time, I'll be retirement age myself."

"Americans retire in their prime," Chiun said dis-
missively. "It is a foolish thing."

"Besides, a dinosaur is not a dragon. There is no
such animal. Dragons are mythological."

"Since when are you an expert on dragons?"

"Since never. But when I was a kid, I was a major
dinosaur fan. I still know all the names by heart, Igua-
nodon, Stegosaur, Triceratops, Allosaurus, and the
overwhelming favorite of St. Theresa's Orphanage,
Tyrannosaurus Rex. And what we saw on TV was a
Brontosaurus—assuming the footage wasn't faked."

"It is a dragon."

"Dragons have big bat wings and breathe fire."

"Ha!" Chiun crowed. "A moment ago you refused
to believe in dragons. Now you know all about them."

"I know a dragon from a dinosaur. You're chasing after a freaking dinosaur."

"Merely another word for an African dragon. Perhaps it is a Zulu word. I am sure his bones are as efficacious as a Chinese dragon. If not more so."

"No chance."

"You are obviously prejudiced against African dragons. It's a terrible thing, racism. I will have to drum this white failing out of you once this assignment is over with."

"I give up."

Chiun smiled. "I knew you would."

9

Nancy Derringer sat in the dirt around the makeshift campfire listening to the man who claimed to lead the Congress for a Green Africa. He had identified himself as Commander Malu.

The commander made a long, windy speech about African pride and the rape of the Continent by colonial powers, imperialist thieves, and business interests that put the squandering of natural resources before the land itself.

"What does any of that have to do with hijacking us?" Nancy asked pointedly.

King whispered, "Nancy, don't antagonize him!"

"I asked a question," Nancy repeated. "And I would like an answer."

Colonel Malu scratched his bushy beard. "Very well. Just as the elephant no longer runs in herds and must be protected in preserves, so too must this fine animal be protected from harm."

"Harm! You idiots threw enough lead around to kill us all twenty times over, and you talk about harm?"

"No one was hurt."

"Which is a miracle."

And it was. Nancy still couldn't believe it. After the shooting had died down and they had been taken at gunpoint from the train and made to sit in a circle with the captured Burger Beret team, it was discovered that there had been no fatalities. In fact, no one had so much as been wounded. Unless one counted

Skip King catching his ankle in a clump of nettles and drawing blood.

"I would like to examine the reptile for injuries, if you don't mind," Nancy said in a voice she had no trouble keeping steady.

"And why should I allow this?" Commander Malu asked.

"Because I am a trained herpetologist and responsible for keeping Jack—"

"*Mokele m'bembe,* please."

"*Mokele m'bembe* healthy," Nancy said tartly.

Commander Malu's eyes shifted away. His gaze fell on Skip King, who glared back. "I will allow this," he said slowly.

"Thank you," said Nancy. Two men came up and took her by the elbows. She was lifted to her feet and her bonds removed. Then they escorted her to the train.

King's stern voice floated after them.

"If anything should happen to Nancy, you bastards, there isn't a place on earth you can hide from Skip King."

"Oh please," Nancy said.

"He is very brave, for a white man," Commander Malu allowed.

"His jock strap must be cutting off circulation to his brain."

Malu's laugh shook his great body as if he were pudding. "Ha! You have spirit. A white woman with spirit is a rare thing, I think."

"You obviously don't know any white women," Nancy retorted.

Nancy was given a flashlight, and she walked around the flatcar. The Apatosaur lay torpid, his tiny head tucked into the locomotive cab. His orange lids were closed, and the black-ringed nostrils pulsed and quivered in time to the bellows rhythm of its great dappled body.

Nancy plucked out a few trank darts earlier sweeps had missed and touched the pulsing vein on the long neck. It was steady, like a surging garden hose. The skin was cool to the touch and rather dry.

She turned to the commander.

"Jack is used to having his skin moist. It could crack if he isn't watered down."

Malu beamed. He looked to the heavens. "Perhaps it will rain this night," he said.

"Look, can we cut a deal?"

Concern flicked across his face. "Deal? What sort of a deal?"

"You say you're interested in a green Africa."

"We are."

"There isn't a greener continent on the face of the earth, but I won't argue the point. The company that sponsored this expedition is Burger Triumph. Surely, you have heard of them."

Commander Malu made a face. "Yes. They lace their hamburgers with sawdust."

"I heard that, too. And they made a fortune selling that junk. I'm sure they'd pay a wonderful ransom for the dinosaur."

"And how will we get word of our demands to these people?"

"Send King."

Malu shook his head ponderously. "I cannot do that."

"Why not?"

"A man who is named King is obviously a leader of men," Malu explained. "He may be the most valuable white man we have ever captured. The hamburger people would pay more for him than they would for this fine animal who we would never give up anyway. For *mokole m'bembe* belongs to Africa. And how do I know that this hamburger company has not captured great *mokole m'bembe* just to grind him up to take the place of sawdust in their terrible hamburgers?"

"Oh, don't be—" Nancy frowned. She bit her tongue in frustration. There was no point in arguing. It was typically African logic, as logical as the importance of King's name, and therefore impossible to counter with reason, or even proof.

"So what's going to happen to us?" she asked in a voice she made calm.

"Perhaps there will be a ransom for all of you. I do not know. I must sleep on it."

"Look, you can't expect us to pass the night out here."

"Why not? It is a nice night. Perhaps it will not rain."

"And what are you going to do if Old Jack wakes up?"

Commander Malu grunted. "You will put him back to sleep."

"He's been tranked twice in one day. A third time could be dangerous."

"When one fights for a green Africa, one assumes he will walk in the footsteps of danger."

"You sound like King."

"I will take this as a compliment, coming from a white woman."

"Don't," Nancy snapped.

The commander lost his genial expression. He snapped out a curt order in some language other than Swahili and Nancy was brusquely returned to the campfire, rebound, and set back in her place at the campfire's edge.

"You are all very, very lucky," King growled. "Another minute and I would have torn these bonds free and come looking for you." He leaned over and asked, "You all right, Nancy? They didn't hurt you, did they?"

"If they do, it will be all your fault."

King demanded, "How do you figure that?"

"This was *supposed* to be a research mission. If you hadn't tranked Jack prematurely, none of this would have been necessary."

"You have a funny way of expressing gratitude, you know that? Without my vision, you wouldn't be here in the first place."

Nancy shut her eyes, as if in pain. "I should have gone to McDonald's."

"Their fries aren't as crispy as ours. Everybody knows that."

10

As they stepped off the plane, Remo was saying, "Better let me handle customs, Little Father. It's going to be hard enough to get any cooperation out of the local authorities without getting hung up in customs."

"I will allow you to try," said the Master of Sinanju.

At customs, their lack of baggage prompted concern.

"Why do you not carry bags?" the customs inspector asked in an accusing voice.

"They got lost in London," Remo explained.

"You did not wait for your bags?"

"We were in a rush."

The customs man cocked an eyebrow that pushed his sweaty forehead into thick gullies. "A rush to come to Gondwanaland?"

"Right."

"That means you are spies and are hereby under arrest," he snapped, motioning toward two white-uniformed security police.

"Hold the fort," Remo said. "What makes you say we're spies?"

"Because the only rush is to get out of Gondwanaland. Therefore, you are spies out to uproot our popular president, Oburu Sese Kuku Ngbendu wa za Banga, which means 'The Always-Victorious Warrior Who Is To Be Feared.' "

"Actually, it means 'Rooster Who Mounts Anything Female'," Chiun whispered.

Then the Master of Sinanju stepped in front of Remo.

He spoke a short phrase.

The customs officer looked incredulous. Chiun added another pungent sentence and the man's eyes grew round. He took a step backward, as if confronting his own ghost.

"Now you did it, Chiun," Remo groaned. "What did Smitty say about not getting the locals all riled up?"

Then, shaking his head, the customs officer cried, "Fellows! Come see! Come see! The Master of Sinanju has come to Gondwanaland!"

There was a general rush from the other customs stations. Tourists who had been tied up in hour-long inspections of their luggage—in which fewer items went back into them than were taken out—were waved through as the entire customs force crowded around the Master of Sinanju, begging for autographs.

To Remo's growing surprise, Chiun signed them dutifully and answered excited questions put to him in Swahili.

A customs man came up to Remo, grinning and waving the signature.

"I have the Master of Sinanju's own signature! It is not a great thing?"

Remo glance at the sheet. "He didn't dot the i in 'Chiun.' "

The man looked, his face sagging. He grabbed the next man to walk by and compared signatures. The other man had one with the i dotted. A third man also had one with the i dotted. And a fourth.

An argument broke out over rights to the signature with the undotted i. Remo couldn't follow it because it was in Swahili, but it seemed that all four men decided that the flawed autograph was the rarest one and therefore the most valuable.

They fell into a busy four-cornered fistfight. That, Remo understood.

While they were fighting, Remo picked the coveted autograph off the floor and dotted the *i*.

Meanwhile, the Master of Sinanju was putting the arm on the other customs officers, who each clutched autographs.

Remo had trouble following what Chiun was saying until, suddenly, the customs men were pulling key rings out of pockets and fighting one another for the privilege of throwing their keys at the Master of Sinanju's feet.

Remo stepped in then.

"We only drive automatic shifts," he said. "Everybody else can take their keys back."

Two-thirds of the keys were recovered.

"And we insist upon a car with a good spare."

More keys were taken back. The struggling died down.

"Lastly, the car's gotta be blue."

"What if it is not a car?" one man asked.

"What is it, if it's not a car?" Remo wanted to know.

"It is a Land Rover."

"Then you're in luck. Land Rovers are our favorite."

The owner of the Land Rover began hopping about in happy circles. "I win! I win! I win! The Master of Sinanju is going to drive my machine!"

"Actually, I'm going to do the driving," Remo said, putting out his hand to accept the key. The metal barely touched his fingertips before it was swiftly withdrawn.

"I will have no lowly white drive my car," the owner said huffily.

"You lose your golden opportunity, then."

"He does not," said Chiun, putting out a long-nailed hand. "For *I* will drive."

Remo gulped. "You?"

"I might perhaps be rusty," Chiun allowed. "But the skill will return. It is probably just like falling off a bicycle."

"If it is," Remo said sourly, "try to fall off your side, not mine."

Ten minutes later, they were careening through the crumbling streets of downtown Port Chuma, sending chickens and other livestock out of their path while Remo held on to the Land Rover seat for dear life.

"You drive worse than I remember," Remo was shouting.

The Master of Sinanju scooted up an alley to avoid two East German-built Trabants trying to beat one another through the same intersection.

"But I drive better than the inhabitants of this backward place," he countered.

Remo started to express his doubts when the trash compactor sound of the two Trabants colliding drowned out his words.

"Yes?" Chiun prompted.

"Never mind," Remo grumbled. He looked around. The city still had much the colonial look of Gondwanaland when it was known as Bamba del Oro. The stucco buildings were peeling and had not been kept up. A traffic cop in tropical ducks blew a whistle at them.

Chiun sailed past him without concern.

The whistle turned shrill and angry.

Remo looked back. "Now you did it."

"Do not concern yourself, Remo. He can do nothing. For the policemen in this land are too poor to own automobiles."

"I hope you're right." Remo looked ahead. "Aren't those railroad tracks up ahead?"

"Yes."

"Shouldn't you be slowing down?"

"No." And the Master of Sinanju pressed the accelerator flat to the floorboards, simultaneously turning the wheel hard to the left.

Remo Williams had reflexes and nerves far superior to ordinary people. But even he blinked his eyes at sudden sounds. The Land Rover ran over a stone, and the wheels left the ground. It hurtled toward the hard steel rails. That was when Remo blinked.

When his eyes flew open, somehow the Land Rover was rattling along the crossties between the rusty rails, its tires a hair from scraping the rails on either side.

Despite the bumpiness of the ride, the tires held a true course.

"Mind telling me what you think you are doing?" Remo chattered.

"I think I am seeking a dragon," replied Chiun blandly.

"What makes you think the train the dinosaur is on runs on this track?"

"Because there is only one track. This land is too poor to have more than one. Therefore it is too poor to have more than one railroad line."

"I'll buy that," said Remo, trying to keep his teeth from chipping. "So how do we know we're going in the right direction?"

"*We* do not."

"Huh?"

Chiun lifted a bony finger. The other held the wheel rock-steady. "But *I* do. For the track runs in only two directions. And the other goes into the sea. Therefore we are going in the proper direction."

Remo couldn't argue with that logic, so he said, "I see plenty of road on either side of the railbed."

"Which is true now, but may not be true when the tracks enter jungle," Chiun pointed out, unperturbed.

It was dark. The headlights were bobbing and bucking like flashlights attached to a milkshake machine.

Soon, the city was left behind and all was darkness except for the two funnels of light bouncing ahead of them.

Abruptly, the Master of Sinanju stopped the Land Rover.

"It is your turn," he told Remo.

"It is?"

"I have done the hard part. No thinking will be

needed until we reach the dragon." He stepped from the vehicle.

"Thanks a lot," said Remo, sliding behind the wheel. He waited for the Master of Sinanju to step around and settle into the passenger seat.

Remo got the Land Rover going. It bumped along clumsily until he shook off inertia; then it was like running a stick along a picket fence, only a hundred times worse.

After a while, he had the rhythm and decided he had better start letting Chiun down gently, or this was going to be a very long night.

"Little Father, I hate to be a wet blanket, but this thing we're after, if it's real, is no dragon."

"You have said that."

"It's a dinosaur."

"Which is a Greek word, greatly corrupted by whites."

"Right. Right. It means . . . uh. It'll come back to me."

"Awful lizard," supplied Chiun.

"Close enough. It means terrible lizard. Dinosaurs were terrible lizards."

"And dragon is a corrupt Greek word, *drakon*. Which also means a great lizard."

"I didn't know that."

"That is why I am the Reigning Master and you are driving an automobile along a railroad track. Heh heh heh."

Remo let Chiun's self-satisfied cackling roll over him without a comeback.

"Chiun," he said, his voice quiet, "I just don't want you to be disappointed."

The Master of Sinanju arranged his kimono skirts into a more pleasing fall. "Never fear," he said. "I will not be. For I know that the dragon that will prolong my life lies waiting for me in the night before us."

Remo fell silent. Suddenly, he didn't want to reach the end of the tracks. What if Chiun insisted upon slaughtering the Brontosaur? How could Remo stop him? *Would* he stop him? For if there was one wish Remo could have granted, it was to prolong the life of the person in all the world who mattered most to him—a person who had already lived a full century and could not go on forever. . . .

11

Nancy Derringer couldn't sleep.

Under the circumstances, sleep would have been difficult at best. She was lying on the hard ground and there were fire ants crawling in and out of her clothing. It was night. Pitch dark. But it was not cool. The night air clung to her skin like clammy cotton, heavy and warm, and leeching perspiration from her open pores.

Then there was Skip King.

"I want everybody to know that I haven't given up," he was saying. The other members of the Burger Triumph team, the camera crew and the dispirited Berets, breathed back hushed support.

"We're with you, Mr. King."

"Just say the word."

"Yeah. We can take these third world clowns."

"The first person to try some fool stunt that could only get us or Jack slaughtered," Nancy warned, "I'll kick in the head with both feet and all my might."

King recoiled. "Nancy, what's got into you? We have a chance to escape here."

"We have a chance to bleed all over the ground, too. I vote we wait until morning, and then try to use our brains." She gave King a withering look. "Those of us so blessed."

King squinted at her in the darkness. "This isn't penis envy, is it?"

"How would you know?" Nancy said and rolled

over so she wouldn't have to look at him. The man was impossible. And he had an ego bigger than Old Jack himself. Not to mention a whole lot uglier.

Over by the campfire, Commander Malu of the Congress for a Green Africa was singeing the hair off a dead monkey.

It was a white-nosed monkey. Malu had caught it in a liana snare and strangled it with his bare hands. Nancy had shut her eyes to drown out the pitiful creature's cries of distress, and she jammed one ear against the dirt. But the other ear heard every shriek clearly.

Now the dead monkey was suspended, humanlike hands and feet hanging grotesquely over the fire. Malu had tied its tail around its own neck so it was like an anthropomorphic purse. He swung the dead thing in and out of the flames until the skin was singed crisp and brown and as hairless as a human baby.

"Tonight," Commander Malu said exuberantly, "we will feast on white-nosed monkey stew. M-m-m-m-m."

Nancy looked away.

And she saw the white man.

He was a shadow, a manlike moth in the darkness.

He wore black. Nancy would have missed him entirely, except that below the short sleeves of his black T-shirt, his arms were bare. They showed faintly, like long disembodied moth wings.

She noticed that he had incredibly thick wrists connecting his lean forearms to his strong-looking hands.

As Nancy watched, he slipped into a bush and it didn't even rustle.

"No one should lose heart," Skip King was whispering to the others. "We are representatives of one of the greatest multinational corporations in the entire world. If we don't let the board down, I guarantee they won't let us down. Count on it."

It had been like this half the night. King couldn't stop talking. Some people, Nancy knew, became motormouths under nervous strain. King was obviously that way. But did he really believe that B.S. about

being corporately untouchable? Nancy decided he was
just whistling in the dark.

Then there was a hand at her mouth.

The hand was cool and dry, despite the evening
heat.

A calm male voice whispered in her ear. "I'm a
friend."

Nancy tried to struggle against the hand, but it held
too tight. She felt fingers pluck at her bonds and she
almost laughed into the man's fingers. She had been
tied with wire and pliers. There was no way the man
could undo her fetters without a bolt cutter.

She heard a series of pinging sounds, but no accom-
panying click of bolt cutters.

Then the blood flowed into her hands and the pain
of returning circulation came.

Nancy was lifted bodily and deposited into a prickly
clump of nettles. "Just keep your head down and everything will be all right," the voice told her.

"Who—"

The man faded into the hot darkness. She got a
glimpse of a strong, masculine face dominated by high
cheekbones and deep-set eyes that became skull holes
in a bone-hard face as it withdrew from sight.

He made absolutely no sound among the thorn
bushes.

Nancy struggled to her knees and crawled to the
thicket, parting branches so she could see.

There were two of them out there. The other one
was shorter, frail, and very, very old. His face in the
half-light was Asian. He wore a skirted black garment
that resembled a Japanese kimono, but cut somewhat
looser.

For all his advanced age, the old Oriental moved
like a butterfly. They both did. They fluttered from
man to man, seeming only to touch their bonds, and
they fell loose. Nancy squinted and saw the older one
did not untie the wire—but sliced it with long, curved
fingernails that should have broken under contact with
the bonds.

Skip King noticed the pair suddenly. "Hey!" he yelled. "Who are you two!"

"That idiot!" Nancy muttered. "That colossal fool."

From the campfire, the action unit of the Congress for a Green Africa leapt to their feet and stared through the sparks and fragrant monkey smoke with incredulous faces.

"What is this!" Malu demanded.

"This," cried the old Oriental in a high, squeaky voice, "is the House of Sinanju come to scatter you to the winds."

"I don't know what he's talking about," King wailed. "Don't shoot us!"

The blacks scrambled for their weapons. They brought them up, and unleashed an incredible amount of noise, fire, smoke, and fury toward the crouching prisoners.

Horrified, Nancy was forced to look away. The Skorpions chattered percussively. She heard screams, and visions of a blood massacre transpired before her mind's eye.

Then came a scream so loud and anguished she was forced to look.

It was Skip King. He was trying to get to his feet but his legs were asleep. He was hitting his knees with both fists as if to wake them up.

King was looking toward the campfire.

Commander Malu and his adherents were walking backward as they fired. Incredibly, their weapons were having no effect.

The pair—the thick-wristed Caucasian and the flitting Asian—had separated and were running at right angles to one another, trying to draw the fire.

Behind them, Old Jack slumbered like a great slow-beating orange heart. Nancy's eyes fixed on his mottled hide, fearing to see eruptions. Again, it was a miracle. There were none. Yet.

Then the tiny Oriental disappeared. The terrorists turned their fire on the thick-wristed man. He bobbed, seemingly in two directions at once, and was suddenly gone.

There was a short interval of silence. Then a high scream. It sounded like a lion or a monkey.

Sailing down from the high branches of a tree like black bats pouncing on prey, they came. The white man who reminded Nancy of a black moth and the delicate butterflylike Asian.

They landed in the middle of the paralyzed Congress for a Green Africa.

Stiff fingers lashed out. The crack of breaking vertebrae was distinct and unmistakable in the night.

Two green-bereted men fell like dominos, and the rest ran, spraying their backtrail with automatic weapons fire.

"Don't chase them!" Nancy screamed. "Let them go! They could hurt the dinosaur."

The thick-wristed man froze, as if hesitating. The expression on his high-cheekboned face said that he wanted to chase the others down more than anything else in the world.

The butterfly of an Asian spoke up then.

"Remo, she speaks wisdom," he said, his voice a grim squeak. "Let those worthless ones flee like the dogs that they are."

"If you say so," the other said in a reluctant tone.

And as they turned back, Skip King pounced on a dropped machine pistol and pointed it in the direction of the fleeing hijackers.

Before anyone could stop him, he emptied the clip, saying, "And don't come back, you disenfranchised rabble!"

Everyone looked toward the departing Congress for a Green Africa, expecting to see some fall wounded. They ran until the bush swallowed them.

"You," the man named Remo told King, "have got to be the world's worst shot."

"What do you want? It's dark out."

"You're welcome," Remo said.

Nancy stumbled out of the thorn brush and said,

"You'll have to excuse him. He watched too many Tarzan pictures as a boy."

"Big talk from someone who hid in the bushes while the men were doing all the fighting," King sneered, plucking out a clip and trying to jam in a second.

"I put her there," Remo said. "I should have stashed *you* and kept *her*."

King struggled with the stubborn clip. Not realizing he had been attempting to insert it backward, he threw it into the dirt. "Who asked you to butt in, anyway?" he snapped.

"Uncle Sam."

"The United States?"

"You're American citizens, aren't you? Who did you expect? The Royal Canadian Mounted Police?"

"Actually, I was hoping the Burger Berets would have shown up by now," said King, looking up into the fabulous starfield of the Gondwanaland night sky.

"The who?"

The sound of helicopters in the distance was like the rubbing together of horny wings, busy and insectlike. It grew to a clatter then swelled to a louder, fuller locust sound.

And suddenly the night sky above them was full of helicopters which sent down roving beams of lights.

In the moving patterns of light, snaky lines were dropped and men in midnight blue uniforms began rappeling down.

"Everyone stand clear!" an authoritative voice bellowed. "We're the Burger Berets!"

The man named Remo undertoned to Nancy, "The *what* Berets?"

"Burger."

"As in hamburger?"

Nancy sighed. "I'm afraid so."

She watched as men in midnight blue nylon jumpsuits hit the ground on ivory white boots. Disengaging themselves from the lines, they brought up AR-15 assault rifles.

King was storming about. "What took you so long!"

A man in a purple beret with a gold crown stitched in the front stepped up and executed a crisp salute. He was a colonel. The gold eagles that constituted his uniform insignia told that—although eagles didn't normally clutch a cheeseburger and a bag of french fries in each talon, Nancy realized.

The man in the purple beret executed a brisk salute. "Mr. King, sir. Colonel Mustard reporting."

"Mustard?" Remo said blankly.

"Code name. We're operating on foreign soil, as you know."

"That's no excuse for blowing the mission," King said bitterly.

The colonel looked at a wrist chronometer whose hands resembled french fries. "It's exactly 0400 hours. According to the timetable, we're mission positive."

"Well, you're too late anyway. They got away."

"Is the animal safe?"

"Yeah. No thanks to you." King looked up. The helicopters held their overhead positions. "Are they filming this?"

"Of course, sir."

"Tell them to stop. It's a debacle. The bastards got away. We were rescued by damn civilians."

"The Gondwanaland president gave us personal assurances that he'd keep his people on stand down, Mr. King," Colonel Mustard said stiffly.

Skip King stabbed an accusatory finger at Remo and Chiun. "Look, tell that to *them*. I'm just an ex-hostage." He took hold of his black hair as if to tear it out in chunks, but it was too short and greasy. It slipped through his fingers. "This is a mess. A total mess."

"What's he complaining about?" Remo wondered. "He's free, isn't he?"

"A major PR extravaganza went south when you two showed up," Nancy explained.

Remo shrugged. "That's the biz."

"Believe me, I couldn't be happier. If those corporate clowns had gotten here first, none of us would have survived." Nancy noticed the old Oriental. He was examining the Apatosaur, his head going from side to side like a curious cat's.

King also noticed. He stopped trying to uproot his scalp, and screamed, "Hey! You get away from there. That dinosaur is corporate property!"

The old Oriental ignored King's heated words.

"Didn't you hear me?" King howled.

"I see trouble coming," Nancy warned. "You better tell your friend to step away from old Old Jack."

"He has a name?" Remo said.

"You sound surprised."

The man named Remo shrugged. "It beats Wing Wang Wo."

"I beg your pardon?"

"Skip it."

King was shouting now, "Colonel Mustard. You remove that man right now."

"Yes, sir."

Nancy looked to Remo, who with a bored expression watched his friend about to be surrounded by four bulky mercenaries.

"Don't you think you should step in?" she asked.

"I don't care what happens to a bunch of guys in funny berets."

Nancy blinked. Her attention went back to the old Oriental. He was walking toward the small serpentine head now, his hands tucked in his voluminous sleeves.

Colonel Mustard of the Burger Berets attempted to restrain him with a firm hand on his frail shoulder. The hand descended. The colonel must have had an incredibly tenacious grip, because although he failed to arrest the old Oriental one whit, he was dragged along with him.

King shrieked, "What's the matter with you? He's got to be as old as Methuselah!"

"I—I can't seem to get him to stop," Colonel Mustard said in a voice that seemed to doubt reality.

"Try asking nicely," Remo called.

"Bull. Trip him," spat King.

The suggestion was executed with breathtaking speed. King had barely got the words out when the old Oriental paused, pivoted, and one sandaled foot caught Colonel Mustard across his unprotected kneecaps.

The colonel went down clutching them both, curled in a fetal position and rocking on his spine.

"Not you!" King screamed. "I meant for him to trip you!"

The old Oriental's voice floated back thinly. "Then you should have chosen your words with greater care."

"I want that man stopped now!" King caught himself and began pointing. "I mean, I want you—the Burger Berets—to stop him, whatever his name his."

"His name is Chiun," Remo offered.

"Stop Chiun," King cried.

The Burger Berets started forward.

"He's the Master of Sinanju," Remo added, apparently to see what would happen.

The train engineer was a Gondwanalandian national. He had been crouching off to one side, poking at the abandoned white-nosed monkey stew. He perked up.

"The Master of Sinanju!"

"Yup," said Remo.

The engineer ran and threw himself in front of the old Oriental named Chiun.

"I cannot let you do this," he told the advancing Berets.

"Stand aside. We're not going to kill him."

"No, but he might kill you."

"What are they talking about?" Nancy asked Remo.

"Search me," Remo said in a bored tone.

Nancy watched with frowning wonder creeping into her expression.

Chiun stepped out from behind the sheltering engineer and said, "I cannot let you sacrifice yourself for me, child of Gondwanaland." He threw up his hands, his long wide sleeves slipping from his pipestem arms. "I surrender."

The Burger Berets stepped up to seize him by the wrists—and became airborne. There were four of them. And they flew in four different directions. One human missile rammed Skip King in the stomach with his head and they both went down. The others became human paperweights that flattened assorted brush.

The rest of the Burger Berets withdrew to a safe distance, bearing the still-curled Colonel Mustard like a piece of driftwood that moaned to itself.

Then the old man padded up to Nancy. She swallowed. His face was stiff, his hazel eyes cold as agates.

"You are obviously in charge here," he said.

"Thank you. How did you know?"

"You are the only one not yelling. Yelling is a sign of weakness."

"My name is Nancy Derringer and I'm responsible for the animal you helped save."

"Are you then responsible for this display of ingratitude?"

"No."

"Then you are the one from whom all gratitude flows?"

"Excuse me?"

"He wants to know if you're grateful," Remo offered. "He's very sensitive about these things."

"Yes, of course," Nancy told the little man named Chiun.

The stern face softened, wrinkled in pleasure. A twinkle came into the steely eyes. His voice became a curious purr.

"How grateful?"

"How . . . ?"

"Careful," Remo warned. "It's a trick question."

"I don't think I understand," Nancy said slowly.

The little man, who looked frail but was anything but, pointed toward the Apatosaur stretched on the flatcar and said, "You possess a great treasure in that slumbering dragon."

"Dragon?"

"He thinks it's a dragon," Remo explained.

"Should I humor him?"

"Normally, yes. In this case, no."

Nancy addressed the little old man in a firm voice. "It's not a dragon. It's a dinosaur."

The old Oriental looked to Remo and his face hardened. "You have been whispering lies in this naive woman's ear. Shame on you, Remo."

Remo threw up his hands defensively. "Hey, the word *dinosaur* hasn't passed my lips since we got here. Honest."

"I am sure the company that financed this expedition will offer you a suitable reward," Nancy said quickly.

"I will settle for ten percent."

"Sounds reasonable," said Nancy. Then a thought struck her. "Ten percent of what?"

The old Oriental beamed. His eyes lit up in the darkness, like cat's eyes. "Of the dragon, naturally. A hind leg might be acceptable, provided the thigh bone is intact."

Nancy's eyes went wide.

"He means it," said Remo.

"Not on your life!" Nancy exploded.

"Ingrate!" And the old Oriental flounced about and returned to examining the Apatosaur, which pulsed slowly like a dying organ.

12

It took until dawn was creeping over the bush before they could get the train under way.

There were the unconscious Burger Berets to revive, and the logs to remove from the tracks. Skip King declined to help clear the railbed. He lay on the ground, moaning and holding his stomach and complaining of a hernia instead.

"Grow up," Nancy told him.

"Grow up? I can't even *get* up."

"Then I'll help you."

King scuttled off. "Don't! Do you want to kill me?"

"Right now, I'd be willing to stand aside and watch a herd of bull elephants pound you into pudding," said Nancy yanking him to his feet. King walked about in wavering circles on wobbly legs.

"What's his problem?" Remo asked Nancy.

"No one's quite sure, but my dollar is on undescended testicles."

Remo grunted, and Nancy took it for a laugh.

The engineer was leaning out of the cab, and he shouted, "I am ready when you are, Missy Nancy."

Skip King stopped walking in circles. "Hey! You're supposed to say that native boy stuff to me."

He was ignored.

"You and your friend are free to ride with us," Nancy told Remo.

"We have a Land Rover parked down the trail,"

Remo said. "And if you want a bit of free advice,
you'd better ride with us."

"Why?"

Remo indicated the old Asian with a surreptitious
finger. "I want to take another shot at explaining dinosaurs to him, and I need backup."

"Will it persuade him away from his hankering for
a drumstick?"

"That's the idea."

"Deal," said Nancy. And they shook on it. Remo's
grip felt like something cut from fossilized bone,
Nancy thought. And as she looked up into his deep-
set eyes, she felt her heart leap into her throat for no
reason that she could think of.

Remo turned. The Master of Sinanju was hovering
about the dinosaur like a fussy little hen. "Come on,
Little Father. We're driving escort."

Stepping away from flatcar, the old Korean followed them, padding silently a few paces behind.

"That is the ugliest dragon I have ever beheld," he
said in an unhappy voice.

"And exactly how many dragons have you seen?"
Nancy wanted to know.

"That is my first."

"It isn't even that. It's a dinosaur."

"Pah! It is a dragon. An African dragon. And it
has been cruelly abused."

"No, we just tranquilized it for the trip back to
America."

"How are you getting it back?" Remo asked, interest detectable in his voice for the first time.

"You got me there. B'wana King has worked out
all the details. I'm just the glorified babysitter."

Chiun caught up with them and asked, "Where are
its wings?"

"Wings?"

"I did not see wings. Or stumps where they would
be attached."

"It doesn't have wings."

"But it *does* breathe fire?"

"Not that anyone ever noticed," Nancy said patiently.

"Maybe his pilot light went out," Remo said dryly.

Chiun made a face. Nancy frowned at Remo. But inside she smiled. He was funny in a flat sort of way.

They came to the Land Rover. It was parked down the line, sitting between the rails as if that were a perfectly natural place for it to be.

"You didn't drive it up like that?" Nancy blurted out.

"The shocks are pretty good," Remo said. "Or were."

"So how are you going to get it turned around?"

"Little Father."

The two didn't speak a word. They just deployed on either end of the Land Rover. Remo took the front, and the little man named Chiun the back. They grabbed the bumpers, bent, and Remo said, "One."

They straightened their spines. The Land Rover came up with them, its tires hanging low on loose shocks.

"Two," said Remo in a voice devoid of strain.

They walked in a half-circle until the Land Rover was turned around. They stopped. "Three," said Remo. And they bent down, setting the vehicle back on its wheels.

"How did you do that?" Nancy asked in a shocked-thin voice.

Remo grinned good-naturedly. "Practice. We can actually bench press three Land Rovers each, but we don't like to show off."

"What I just saw was impossible," murmured Nancy, circling the vehicle.

"Then you didn't see it," Remo told her, waving her into the Land Rover. She got in back. Remo took the wheel, the old Oriental beside him.

Remo got the motor started and they began bumping along.

Every bone in Nancy's slim body rattled. She began wishing she'd packed a jogging bra and folded her arms under her chest. That helped. By the time they got up to a reasonable speed, Nancy found it tolerable. If she kept her teeth clenched tightly.

Keeping her mouth closed proved impossible. The Old Asian was talking in a high squeaky voice. Not talking so much as complaining.

"Perhaps we should speak to the King of Gondwanaland," he was saying.

"About what?" Nancy asked, puzzled.

"Proper respect."

"He means gratitude, as in reward," Remo called over his shoulder.

"Excuse me," Nancy said. "But why on earth do you want a leg off an Apatosaur?"

"A what?" Remo and Chiun said simultaneously.

"Apatosaur. That is the scientific name for the species."

"Lady, I had every plastic dinosaur toy ever made. That's a Brontosaurus back there."

"You should get current. Modern paleontologists call it a Apatosaurus."

"What's that mean?"

"Deceptive reptile."

Remo made a face. "I like Thunder Lizard better. Sounds more dinosaurian. Like Pterodactyl. That was another neat dinosaur I used to collect."

"Pterodactyls were not dinosaurs, I'm sorry to inform you."

"The hell they weren't."

"Listen, I don't know where you went to school—"

"St. Theresa's Orphanage. Never mind where it is. Or was."

"Fine. But knowledge about dinosaurs has changed dramatically over the last decade or so. You see, what you used to know as the Brontosaur never really existed. That is, its bones were confused with another sauropod. We now call it Apatosaur."

"It's still the biggest dinosaur that ever was, right?"

"No, there are bigger. Supersaurus. And Ultrasaurus. All sauropods like Apatosaurus. And let's not overlook Seismosaurus, the biggest known sauropod.

You'd have liked him, Remo. He was known as Earthshaker Reptile."

"Your Greek is abominable," Chiun said disdainfully. "I cannot understand half of what you say."

"Dinosaurs are classified into orders, such as saurischia, which are lizardlike, suborders like sauropoda, the four-footed herbivores like our own Old Jack—"

"Can I explain this to him?" Remo asked plaintively.

Nancy leaned back in her seat. "If you can."

"Chiun, try to follow this. Back before there were humans, dinosaurs ruled the world. They were giant reptiles."

"Not all of them." Nancy said quickly. "Some were birds."

"Like Pterodactyls, right?"

"Wrong. Like Triceratops."

Remo hit the brakes. Nancy almost landed in the front seat with them.

"Triceratops!" Remo exploded.

"Yes."

"Triceratops with the three horns? Built kinda like a rhino?"

"Yes."

"A *bird*?"

"Yes!"

"Since when?"

"Since they came on the evolutionary scene during the Late Cretaceous period. We now know they were Ornithischia, bird-hipped."

"They're birds because of their freaking *hips*?"

"Simplified for the twelve-year-old mind, yes."

"Bulldookey," said Remo. "Birds don't grow horns and run around goring other animals."

"The modern ostrich does."

"That's the bird that hides its head in the sand at the first sign of trouble? Right?"

"True," Nancy admitted.

"Then I rest my case. No way a Triceratops would hide its head if a Stegosaur trotted by. He'd bite the other guy's head off, and hide *that*."

"For your information, a modern ostrich can kill a full-grown lion."

"With what? His fluffy tailfeathers?"

"No, by pecking the lion into submission with his beak. Ostriches are fierce and mean-tempered, and if you place an ostrich skeleton beside an Iguanadon skeleton, you'd see what I'm talking about."

"I'd see squat, because one's a reptile and the other is a goofy bird. End of story. Where did you get this crap, anyway?"

"You can look this up in any modern encyclopedia."

"Wanna bet?"

"Certainly. Let's say ten thousand dollars, shall we?"

Nancy offered her hand to shake on it. Remo hesitated.

"Too rich for your blood?" Nancy asked sweetly.

"I have to think this through," Remo muttered.

"I thought so."

"Thought what?"

"All talk and balk, that's you."

Remo frowned. "Little Father, what do you think?"

"Only a fool would wager against a woman who owns a dragon," the Master of Sinanju said thinly.

Behind them, the train was rattling along, getting closer. The steam whistle blew one long blast when it rounded a shallow turn and the engineer sighted them.

"Unless you're looking forward to abandoning ship," Nancy suggested, "I suggest you start us rattling along again."

Fuming, Remo got the Land Rover going. He was silent a while, then he asked, "Triceratops didn't have feathers, did they?"

"No."

"Good."

Nancy couldn't resist. "But you know, Pterodactyls had hair," she said in a bright voice.

"They did not!"

"Sorry to pop your bubble, but you should really read up on these things."

"You are both talking nonsense," snapped Chiun.

"Why would we do that?" Nancy wanted to know.

"To dissuade me from living to the fullest span of my years."

Nancy frowned. "Say again?"

"I'll tell it," Remo said. "One of his ancestors had a close encounter of the dragon kind a few centuries ago, and made off with a whole skeleton."

Nancy perked up. "Do you still have it, Mr. Chiun?"

"The proper form of address is Master, and no, Yong consumed it to the last finger bone and wing rib," Chiun said flatly.

"Your ancestor *ate* a fossil skeleton?"

"No, he drank it."

"Chiun's ancestor supposedly slew a dragon," Remo explained.

"A true Chinese dragon," Chiun sniffed. "Not like your ugly thing."

"Thank you," said Nancy.

"And he ground up the bones to make some kind of medicine, so he could live forever, or something," Remo added.

"In the East, dinosaur bones are sometimes ground up and mixed in philters," Nancy said thoughtfully. "They are believed to be very beneficial. How far along did your ancestor get, Master Chiun?"

"He squandered one hundred forty-eight winters," said Chiun.

"Squandered?"

"Chiun thinks he should have saved a few bones for his descendants," Remo added.

"Oh."

They drove along in silence. The sun was climbing the sky, turning it the color of brass. The jungle birds were screeching and calling. Somewhere a hippo bellowed. And Nancy began to sweat profusely.

She noticed that Remo and the old Oriental named Chiun were not sweating and wondered why.

"We don't sweat," Remo said unconcernedly.

"Nonsense. All mammals sweat. Or pant."

"We don't pant either."

"What is a mammal?" asked Chiun.

"A dinosaur is a reptile and we're mammals," Remo explained.

"Does that mean monkey?"

"A monkey is a mammal, just like us," Nancy said.

"Just like *you*. I am Korean."

"What does that mean?" Nancy asked Remo.

"I am not like whites," Chiun said stiffly, "who believe they are the offspring of monkeys."

"That's a fallacy," said Nancy.

Chiun indicated Remo with a long-nailed finger. "Tell this baboon."

"Hey! I resent that."

"Humans are descended from a monkeylike primate ancestor, not a monkey per se."

"Some have not descended very far," Chiun sniffed.

"Chiun's people think they're descended from the Great Bear that came down from the sky, or something," Remo explained.

"Bears are mammals, too," Nancy said. "But that still doesn't explain why neither of you are sweating in this heat."

"Chiun can explain it better than me."

"We do not sweat because we understand that we do not have to sweat," Chiun said flatly.

"You *have* to sweat."

"Enemies can smell sweat. To sweat is to die."

"That's a very mammalian sentiment," Nancy said dryly, "but that doesn't change the basic fact that you have to sweat in order to cool your body."

"We sweat when we wish to," Chiun allowed. "In private."

"Sweating is optional," Remo added.

"Are you saying you can stay cool without having to sweat?"

"That's about the size of it," Remo said.

"What you are describing is supermammalian physiology," Nancy said slowly.

In the front seat, Remo and Chiun looked at one another, lifted doubtful eyebrows, and said nothing.

"That would be an amazing adaptive response," Nancy went on.

Remo shrugged. "Hey, what do you expect? We mammals outlived the dinosaurs, didn't we?"

"An accident."

"My foot. Dinosaurs died out for two reasons. They were too slow and too stupid."

"Wrong."

Remo snapped his fingers. "Oh yeah, right. Three reasons. It got too cold. They were cold-blooded. So they couldn't stay warm when the ice age came."

"Wrong again."

"Okay," Remo said sourly, "let's hear *your* theory."

"It's not my theory. But never mind that. It boils down to an asteriod or comet strike. It threw up dust particles that blocked out the sunlight, killing off the plants that the herbivores subsisted on, and when the carnivores that ate the herbivores had no food source, they died out, too."

"Prove it."

"Geologists have discovered a worldwide layer of iridium deposited in the earth's soil about sixty-five million years ago, coinciding with the end of the Cretaceous, when the dinosaurs began dying off. Iridium is rare on earth, and could only have gotten into the soil from an extraterrestrial object striking the planet and dispersing the particles in the atmosphere. There's a 110-mile crater down in the Yucatan Penninsula called Chicxulub, which is the probable impact point. If you don't believe me, you can look it all up."

"Anything else I should know while my childhood memories are burning to the ground?" Remo said glumly.

Nancy smiled. "Let me see. We now think dinosaurs were smarter than previously believed. And faster. Much faster."

"That thing back there obviously excepted."

"Well, we haven't seen it gallop, but it *is* possible."

Remo snorted. "Give me a break. It's too fat to gallop."

"You *are* out of date, aren't you? Apatosaurus is much more agile than the old Brontosaur was thought to be. According to tendon scars found on their fossil skeletons, they could rear up on their hind legs to reach food in the tall conifers and ginkgo trees of the Upper Jurassic."

"Crap. Crap and double crap. That thing would have trouble getting out of bed. It's the original 'I've fallen down and I can't get up' dinosaur. That's why there are no more dinosaurs. They were slow and dumb. Mammals beat them at the evolution game."

"Wrong again. Dinosaurs may have been superior to mammals. At their height, they occupied every ecological niche above the size of a chicken. If not for a cosmic accident, they would still be dominant."

"I don't believe it."

"I don't believe *you,*" Nancy shot back. "You're a grown man and you have the belief system of an eleven-year-old boy."

"I do not believe either of you two," Chiun sniffed. "You are both carrying on like two children, and making less sense. And I do not understand half the words you are speaking."

"Well," Remo said defensively, "any way you slice it, it's not a dragon."

"In that," Nancy said, "you and I are in rare agreement."

"It is an African dragon," said Chiun. "There are Chinese dragons, and English dragons, and African dragons. The meat that sheathes its mighty bones is not important. Only the bones themselves."

"And you may not have one," Nancy said quickly. "Get that through your sweet little skull, please."

"Ingrate."

"What about the one whose name I can never remember," Remo said suddenly. "The lizard with the sail on his back.'"

"Dimetrodon?"

"That's him. He was a lizard, right?"

"Oh, I wish you hadn't brought Dimetrodon up."

"Why not?'"

"He's not even considered a dinosaur anymore."

"What was he—blackballed for biting?"

"No, he was an early mammal-like reptile."

"Next, you're going to tell me Tyrannosaurus Rex was a kangaroo," Remo said sourly.

"A woman who would deny a dragon its proud heritage is capable of anything," Chiun said in a bitter tone.

13

Word travels fast in the bush.

By the time the train rattled toward the shantytowns that lay scattered outside of Port Chuma, the rails were lined with curious Gondwanalanders.

They cheered the locomotive's chugging approach. Cheers of delight, awe, and surprise attended the sighting of the great flatcar and its saurian cargo.

At each point, the Master of Sinanju waved to the admiring crowds. They waved back with enthusiasm.

"It is good to find a land that appreciates us," Chiun told Remo. They were seated in the passenger car now. Nancy sat in a facing seat.

"I think they're excited about the dinosaur," Remo told him.

"Pah!"

"Of course, I could be wrong," Remo admitted.

"We will know when we reach the capital. Where no doubt the king waits to greet me."

"Gondwanaland is ruled by a president, not a king," Nancy pointed out.

"When he is seen in my company," Chiun sniffed, "his subjects will demand that he be crowned, for it is well known in these lands that he who befriends the Master of Sinanju sleeps serene in his castle."

Nancy leaned forward and whispered to Remo. "Have you given thought to committing him?"

"Only if I want to watch men in white coats being dismembered before my eyes."

Nancy, remembering how Chiun had made short work of Colonel Mustard, said, "I assume he knows some kind of exotic martial art."

Remo nodded. "Bruce Lee taught him everything he knows."

Chiun spat noisily out the open window.

"What brought that on?" Nancy asked Remo.

"Ritual purging. I'll explain later."

"Don't bother."

Skip King came back from consulting with his Burger Berets, who had decided to ride on the roof when Chiun came on board at a water stop. He clutched his walkie-talkie, and his face was worried.

"I've been in touch with Port Chuma. Word's already reached the capital."

"Is that good or bad?" Nancy asked.

"Not good. The rabble are demanding that Old Jack stay in Africa. We're going to have to run the train straight to the docks and load him aboard the ship."

"What kind of a ship hauls dinosaurs?" Remo asked.

"A fabulous one. If there's time, we might let you see it."

"Gee, can we?"

"Ingrate," sniffed Chiun.

"What's his problem?" King asked Remo. "We let the two of you hitch a ride with us after your shocks died—even though you screwed things up."

"He likes grateful people," Remo said of Chiun.

"Who doesn't?"

"Especially grateful people who are free with their gold."

"No chance. The board would have paid him to stay away. Do you realize the archival footage we lost?"

"I keep thinking of the blood that wasn't spilled." Nancy said dryly.

"Women don't understand these things."

"King, there are problems taking Old Jack to America," Nancy said.

King grinned. "And I solved every one of them."

"I doubt it. What about the long ocean crossing?"

"It won't be long. Less than twelve hours. He'll probably sleep through the whole thing."

"What kind of a ship can cross the Atlantic in twelve hours?" Remo asked.

"A fabulous one," King said.

"Like the one that brought King Kong to New York?" Remo asked.

King made a disdainful face. "This is the nineties. We don't do boats in the nineties. But we have to be ready to move fast. There are cranes waiting to make the transfer. We'll do the press conference with that as a backdrop."

"Press conference?" Remo asked. "What happened to moving as fast as possible?"

King looked injured. "I said fast, not panicked. This is a great opportunity for the Gondwanaland people. We're going to open up Burger Triumph franchises all over this backwater as a gesture of the corporation's eternal gratitude for the president's help."

"Selling what?" Nancy asked dryly. "White-nosed monkey burgers?"

King started to frame a comeback. His fox face froze, and his beady eyes took on an inward look.

"You okay?" Remo asked suddenly.

"Not if what I think is happening is," Nancy said.

"Huh?"

"B'wana King is wondering if the board will go for the monkey burger idea."

By the time they clicked into the dock turnaround area, the cranes were swinging into place.

A reviewing stand was set up, covered in purple-and-orange bunting—the Gondwanaland national colors, chosen by throwing darts at a paper rainbow. And attired in a purple-and-orange general's uniform and cocked leopard-skin hat was president of the twentieth century, Oburu Sese Kuku Nebendu wa za Banga.

The train nudged the rotting kapok-wood bumper

that marked the terminus of Gondwanaland's only national rail line, and stopped. The engineer blew a long last whistle blast.

And Skip King leaped from his seat and said, "Okay, let's go! Camera crew—do your stuff. Half of you record the transfer. The other half have ceremony duty."

"I'd better check the ship," Nancy said. "It has to be a suitable environment, or I must veto the transfer."

King scowled. "I need you at the ceremony."

"And Old Jack needs me to look out for his welfare."

Skip King drew himself up to his full five-foot-six-inch height. "We're in civilization, now," he said levelly. "Where there is a natural pecking order and men run things. I let you get a little out of bounds back in the bush, but all that's over with now. I won't speak of it if you don't."

"I intend to submit a fully detailed report of your pompous behavior to the board once we're in the States. And if you don't want to have to explain a dead Apatosaurus, I suggest you keep your pecking order—not to mention your pecker—out of my project responsibilities."

King's neck turned red. The color crept up to his face. He bared his teeth in something that was not a smile.

Then Remo said, "Or you can go a few rounds with Chiun and me."

The red went out of Skip King's face so fast someone might have turned on a spigot.

"Okay," he said grudgingly. "Do your check. But I want you up on that podium when the president gives his speech."

"Thank you," Nancy said frostily.

A Captain Relish escorted them down to the docks. He was very polite and kept a respectful distance.

Nancy had expected a large freighter, possibly a container ship or even a small oil tanker.

There were ships tied up along the wharfs. But nothing large enough to float a forty-foot dinosaur.

Sitting just off the beach in the calm tidal water was a gleaming white shape that looked like a crashed 747. It resembled an airliner, but the wings were snubbed off close to the wing roots. There were no engine nacelles. But mounted high in front of the swept-back tail were two large propellers set on a single shaft.

The spine of the craft lay open to the blazing sun in two sections, and lines from great cranes dangled into them.

Remo asked. "What is *that*?"

"It is obvious," sniffed Chiun. "A crashed plane."

"No," said Captain Relish. "It's an ekranoplane."

They looked at him.

"It's a wingship, a wing-in-ground craft, or ekranoplane as the Russians call it."

"What do the Russians have to do with this?" Remo asked.

"They devised this baby for landing troops on foreign soil. It flies like a hovercraft, but much faster and with a bigger payload. The way it works is the tail props start her moving along the water like a boat, then those two Kuznetsov turbofans mounted on the nose ahead of the wing there blast air under the wingroots, creating lift. She skims along the deck slick as you please. Isn't that great?"

They all stared at him some more. And Remo asked, "Wouldn't it be simpler to fly like a plane?"

"Not because of the ground effect," said Captain Relish. "You see, when a plane flies high, wingtip vortices are created, producing drag. Slows the craft down. Remove the ends of the wings and fly close to the ground, and the problem is solved. When the Soviet Union went belly up, they decided to rent the monster out. This model is called *Orlyonok*, or *Little Eagle*."

"Let me see if I have this straight," Remo said. "You cut the wings off so it will fly better?"

"You got it," said Captain Relish, grinning proudly.

Remo turned to Nancy. "You should get together with him."

"Why?"

"Because you two obviously have a lot in common. What he said makes about as much sense as feathers on a Triceratops."

Nancy made her voice firm. "I am not—repeat *not*—authorizing that we fly Old Jack to America," she told Captain Relish. "And that's final."

"Dr. Derringer, you don't understand—"

"I understand plenty. You tell that jerk King that's my decision. And it's final."

"Uh-oh. Too late."

Nancy looked where Remo was pointing.

Two cranes were at work, carefully hoisting the dinosaur off the flatcar. The body lifted quivering, the head and tail hanging limp as if dead. The forked tongue protruded.

"Those idiots! They haven't secured the head and tail."

"I guess they're in a rush," said Captain Relish. "I hear the natives are restless."

Working in unison, the crane bore the great Halloween bulk closer and closer.

Nancy turned to Remo and Chiun.

"I need your help."

"Name it," said Remo.

"Yes," added Chiun. "Name it and a price will be determined later."

Remo winked as if to say, "Don't worry about it."

"Deal. I need you two to guide the head down safely. I know you can do amazing things, can you handle that?"

"Sure," said Remo.

"For a price to be determined later," Chiun said blandly.

"We'll worry about that then," said Nancy.

Captain Relish escorted them to an inflatable pontoon bridge that carried them over the shallow water to an open passenger door in the side of the anchored craft.

"The cargo bay is aft," he said, leading them through an interior that very much resembled a truncated passenger jet. A door in the rear gave into the cargo area. It lay open to the dazzling African sun.

Nancy gave the area a quick once-over. She turned to Captain Relish. "I think you'd better leave. Captain. That's ten tons of reptile meat about to come down in a relatively confined space."

The captain ducked out.

The cranes' operators brought the beast over to the waiting cargo hold of the ekranoplane. They were good. They got it into exact position without unnecessary jockeying. It blocked the sun.

Slowly, the cables began paying out.

"Okay," Nancy said nervously, as the creature's shadow grew. "We shouldn't have to worry about the tail. But if the head folds under the body, it could be crushed. At the very least, the windpipe could be constricted."

"Just grab the head and keep it from the body, right?" asked Remo.

"Right. You can do that?"

"Sure."

Nancy withdrew to a safe distance, where she made white-knuckled fists on and off during the remaining part of the fifteen-minute operation.

She saw it all, and questioned none of it.

The whiplike tip of the tail touched first and began coiling like a serpent dropping into a box. It was the other end she was worried about.

The undersized head, mouth slightly open and eyes closed, inched closer and closer to the stainless steel of the bulkhead floor.

Remo and Chiun took up positions under it. Small as it was in comparison to the thick neck, the head dwarfed them both. Like construction workers guiding a girder into position, they took hold of the snout and chin and with a nod to each other, walked it away as the body continued down.

The head was heavy enough, Nancy knew. But the greater weight lay in the tremendous pumpkin-striped neck.

Somehow, the pair knew exactly what to do. They moved left when the neck began to kink right and vice versa. They seemed to have an instinct for the way the reptile's weight was redistributing itself. It was as if, Nancy thought, they used the creature's own inert muscles against itself. That, more than their eerily effortless strength, impressed her most.

When the great padded feet touched the floor, they had the neck almost fully elongated. This was the crucial part.

Then it was over. Suddenly, effortlessly. The legs folded up on either side of the great bulk of the body and the wrinkled underside touched the floor. The ship hardly jarred.

And the neck, fully elongated now, lay flat, with the head resting on its chin.

Nancy came up and looked the beast over without saying a word.

The Master of Sinanju watched her and said to his pupil, "She is not very effusive in her gratitude."

"Give her a minute," Remo said. "She has to check everything out. Like you, when we fly."

"I am not flying in this maimed air vehicle. It has no wings."

"I don't get it, either."

Nancy let out a yelp of annoyance.

They ran to meet her.

"Damn Damn Damn Damn!" she was saying.

"What?" asked Remo.

"I forgot to sex the beast."

"Oh," said Remo.

Chiun took Remo aside and whispered, "What manner of female wishes to mate with a dragon?"

"She doesn't mean it that way."

"What way does she mean it?"

"She's trying to figure out what sex it is."

"It is a female," Chiun called.

Nancy looked up. "How can you tell?"

"Male dragons have larger heads. Females but tiny ones, because they have smaller brains. Just as with human females."

"Thank you for that illuminating bit of information," Nancy said thinly.

Chiun wrinkled up his tiny nose. "She does not sound grateful."

"Give her time," said Remo.

"I am willing to be patient as long as I receive my dragon bone," Chiun allowed.

"Nobody said anything about her being *that* grateful."

"A toe bone then. Until the beast dies a proper death. Then I may claim the leg bone of my choice."

"Do they even have toes?" Remo asked.

"True dragons do."

"But this is an African dragon. You never know about them. Maybe you should check."

His whole face wrinkling now, the Master of Sinanju floated up to the animal's rear right leg. He bent to examine the fleshy pad. Nancy noticed this and asked, "Looking for thorns, by chance?"

"I am seeking a toe."

"Why?"

"To see if this monstrosity has one."

"Well, it does. Several of them. Happy now?"

The Master of Sinanju straightened. He looked into Nancy's faintly humorous eyes.

"I will be as soon as the largest toe is removed and given to me."

"Are we back to that?"

"I have never left," snapped Chiun.

Outside the craft, a great roar went up. At first, it sounded like a cheer. But the sound went on and on and grew angry. Nancy didn't understand a word of it. But anger, she understood.

"I'd better see what that is," she said.

"It is the king, appearing before his subjects," said Chiun.

"You understand what they're saying?"

"No, I understand the sound that is made by subjects of a strong king."

"Sounds more like a lynching in progress, if you ask me," Remo said.

"That's why I'm looking into this," said Nancy. "Will you two watch Old Jack?"

"Fear not," said Chiun in a loud voice. "No harm will befall this noble animal while the Master of Sinanju is his protector."

"And I'll stick around in case Chiun gets carried away playing 'this little piggy,' " said Remo.

"Pah!" said Chiun.

Nancy rushed for the forward exit hatch.

14

Skip King sat in the VIP row behind the podium at which the president of the Republic of Gondwanaland was shaking his thick-fingered fist at the growing crowd.

The crowd was shaking its fists back. Both sides looked angry, but who could tell? This was the Third World, where shaking fists might be the local equivalent of a Hitler salute, or merely wild applause. King had taken dozens of corporate seminars, where he was taught that in Great Britain tabling a proposal meant the opposite of what it did in the U.S., that the deeper you bowed to a Japanese counterpart the more respect you showed—and lost—and that when an Arab sheikh took your hand while walking, it didn't mean he had fallen in love with you. Necessarily.

King had taken a crash course in Gondwanalandian customs, but his mind had been so overloaded with the visions of what this project would do to his career he could hardly pay attention, never mind take actual notes. He knew he'd spend most of his time in the jungle, anyway. Who cared which side of the road people drove on?

So he sat listening to the back-and-forth shouting in an incomprehensible language and hoped against hope this was an example of enthusiastic support and not the first stages of rioting.

Placards and signs were going up now. King sat up in his wooden folding chair, between the sweating war minister and the sweltering cultural minister, both of whom looked like they had been submerged in a fry-o-lator until brown, and craned to see them.

Some of the placards were in Swahili, but most were in crude, semiliterate English.

King saw one that read, KEEP AFRICAN BRONTO-SAUR IN AFRICA.

Another proclaimed, ENDANGERED AFRICAN SPE-CIES ARE AFRICAN—NOT AMERICAN!

"Oh-oh, this could get real ugly real fast," said King, looking around. "Where the hell is that bossy blonde? Maybe a good look at her knockers will settle these clowns down."

At that point, President Oburu switched to English for the benefit of the Burger Triumph archival camera crew.

"In recognition of the hospitality of our poor nation to the people from the Burger Triumph company," the president was saying, "the Americans have agreed to set up Burger Triumph franchises in both our major cities. These wonderful franchises will be available through my first cousin, the minister of commerce."

King smiled. Maybe that would do it. People who ate monkey meat should be damn grateful for a taste of good old Americana microwaved and slapped between halves of a bleached-flour bun.

Instead, the crowd turned uglier.

"We do not want the white man's cheap meats!" they shouted.

"We want our Brontosaurus! It will bring Gondwanaland many tourist dollars!"

"Yes. We want our Brontosaur!"

The crowd took up the chant. The placards began to lift and dip in time with the angry refrain.

"We want our Brontosaur! We want our Brontosaur! Keep Brontosaurus in Gondwanaland!"

President Oburu turned away from the microphone and looked to King with the expression of a bulldog faced with an unclimbable fence.

"You wish to try?" he mouthed.

King got up. Straightening his tie, he strode purposefully up to the President of Gondwanaland and, keeping his distance from the microphone, made a show of shaking the president's big fat-with-gold-rings hand in both of his.

"I got it covered," King said confidently.

The president turned away, palming a sweaty well-folded envelope crammed with U.S. dollars, and took his seat.

King addressed the microphone. He had taken endless Burger Triumph seminars in public speaking. He knew all the tricks. He raised both arms and waited for the shouting to die down. His arms got very tired and his face hurt from smiling.

But he wore them down. The dull roar soon settled into an angry muttering. And King lowered his arms and began speaking.

"People, don't think of this as a dead loss. Think of it as a net gain."

The angry mutter swelled.

"I mean, you're not losing a lumbering slow-witted dinosaur. You're gaining a fast-growing slice of the American dream. Burger Triumph fries are the best on the planet. Our nondairy shakes come in six different flavors. And we only use the finest Hungarian steer beef in our Bongo Burgers. Shipped directly to Port Chuma from Warsaw—or whatever the capital of Hungary is these days."

He was booed. A thousand fists shook at him.

Through it all, Skip King kept his corporate smile fixed as the bars on a prison door. He raised his arms for silence. This time, the crowd won.

"Keep Brontosaur in Africa! Keep Brontosaur African!"

Then Nancy Derringer slipped to the empty chair at the end of the VIP row.

"Wait a minute," King shouted. "Here's somebody you have to hear." The roar continued unabated. King found the volume control, set it to max, and said,

"May I present the foremost authority on dinosaurs in the universe, the lovely Nancy Derringer!"

While the crowd was covering its ears, he waved Nancy over.

"Come on, baby," he hissed. "Save the corporation's bacon here."

Nancy stepped up to the microphone as if walking on glass.

"What do I say?" she asked, eyes uncertain.

King kept his hand on the mike. "Anything. Quiet them down. We gotta get out of here before they stampede." He took his hand off the mike and said, "And here she is, as talented as she is built: Nancy Derringer!" Then King beat a hasty retreat to his seat.

Blushing, Nancy addressed the mob.

"I know how you must feel . . ." she began.

The crowd booed.

"But in the interest of science, this is the best way."

They hissed.

"We have facilities in America to humanely house the animal."

They hooted.

"And it's my hope that the Apatosaur will be returned to the wild after a suitable interval of study."

At that, the crowd laughed in derision.

Someone took off their sneaker and threw it. It bounced off the podium. Nancy kept it from toppling with both hands.

"Really, you must try to understand. This is for the animal's welfare."

"Boo!" someone shouted. "You are going to slaughter it and feed rich Americans the meat."

"Oh, be serious. Who told you that?"

"I have read this in the *International Enquirer*."

"Oh, come on."

A rock sailed up and landed on the tiny bald spot at the top of Skip King's head.

"Oww!" he cried, jumping up with both hands covering his head.

The skies rained hard objects.

King turned to President Oburu. "Do something!"

The president turned to his nephew, the minister of the interior, and spoke rapidly. The minister of the interior leaned over to his son, the deputy minister, who then consulted briefly with his half brother, the chief of the secret police, who stood up and lifted a silver whistle hanging from a gold chain about his thick neck and blew into it.

The Gondwanaland authorities had obviously prepared for this eventuality. On signal, pepper gas grenades popped and fell into the crowd. Military vehicles rumbled into view and water cannon began knocking down the audience closest to the stage. People began running, but the ground was a river. They slipped and slid and all was bedlam.

In the confusion, King shouted to his camera crew, "Cut film! Don't record this! Everybody understand that?"

Then he was at Nancy Derringer's side saying, "Don't sweat it, Nance. I'll protect you."

"You! This is all your fault!" She raised her hand to slap him in the face, but King covered his face in time.

"Now, now, you're just hysterical with fear. Come on!"

The sound of tear gas shells brought Remo to the side door of the ekranoplane. He threw it open and immediately the sting of pepper gas drove him back.

"Remo, what is it?" Chiun asked.

Remo coughed his lungs clear. "Trouble."

"I am charged with guarding this fine animal," Chiun said imperiously. "You may quell the troubles if you wish."

"I counted every toe," Remo warned. "Twenty. There better be twenty when I get back, too."

"Tattletale!"

Remo charged his lungs and plunged out of the *Orlyonok*. A wave of Gondwanalanders pounded toward him, holding handkerchiefs or sleeves and other bits of clothing in front of their mouths and noses. Their eyes were red and teary. And they were in no mood to give way.

Remo, blowing a slow but steady stream of carbon dioxide through both nostrils to keep the pepper gas from entering his lungs, ran directly at them.

He veered, looking for an opening. He found one, zipped through, and immediately changed direction. It was like running against a tide that was also running. Remo sensed the flow of bodies around him, drew their motion into his own, and avoided every stumbling form and groping, outstretched hand.

But there came a point where there was no more space in the crush of bodies. He changed tactics in midrun, leaping suddenly into the air. One foot came down on the head of a man. The man felt only a slight scuff that disturbed his springy peppercorn hair, and the foot was gone. Remo's other foot touched another head and impelled him along.

He ran over the ground, so fast that people brushed at their hair and looked over their shoulders in time to see a white man seemingly running on air.

Technically, Remo was running on *hair,* but no one understood that. They were too busy fleeing to imagined safety.

He reached the stage, where the speakers were crouched down, trying not to breathe the noxious onion-flavored fumes.

Remo found Nancy struggling with Skip King to get off the podium.

"Time to go," Remo called.

"How?" Nancy coughed back. "Everything is blocked. We're trapped."

"Leave that to me. Let's go."

Remo offered Nancy his hand. Immediately, King pulled her away.

"Butt out! This is *my* rescue. Stick with me, Nancy."

"Remo, I would appreciate any help that separates me from this toady," Nancy said tightly.

"You got it," Remo said. He reached out and took King by the throat, squeezed, and King came to his feet with his teeth clenched and an obedient expression in his sharp face. Even his eyes looked clenched.

"Whatever you want me to do," he croaked. "I'll do it."

"That's a smart attitude, because your spine feels unusually brittle today."

"I thought so, too," King said unhappily.

"Just stay with me," Remo said, guiding them along.

"My camera crew!" King said, stopping. "We can't leave them!"

"Since when did he become a humanitarian?" Remo asked Nancy.

"Since he entrusted the videotapes of the expedition to the camera people."

"Oh," said Remo.

"This way! This way!" King yelled, waving his arms to get the crew's attention.

The video team was dispersed about the stage and below. They pushed their way to King's side.

"Everybody all right?" Nancy asked.

"Never mind that!" King snapped. "Are the packages safe?"

"Yes, Skip," said the chief of PR.

"Call me Mr. King when the cameras are off! Got that?"

Remo led them to the side of the stage, through a loosely packed part of the crowd. The tear gas was beginning to thin, but the water cannon were hosing everything in sight. The ground was wet and muddy. The security police were laughing and knocking down anyone still on their feet, the high-pressure streams pushing them into shacks and other immovable objects.

Remo brought them to one of the giant cranes. He climbed it and took the edge of his hand to the base of the framework. Metal snapped and parted. Slowly, the crane began to lean drunkenly.

As if looking through a surveyor's transit, Remo

sighted through the skeletal framework. He gauged
where the derrick might fall, pounded in the lattice at
one side, and took another sighting.

Satisfied, he gave a hard, two-handed push.

With a squeaking screech, the derrick began to fall.
Remo yelled, "Timber!"

But it was the sound of the derrick's tortured framework that made everyone in its shadow look up and
break in all directions like ants in an earthquake.

The derrick crushed two water trucks that happened
to be in the way, forming a bridge to the waiting
wingship.

Remo helped Nancy up onto girderwork. King
scrambled up, on his own. The video crew took up
the rear.

They worked their way along and dropped off at
the end. That put them within sprinting distance of the
pontoon bridge to the wingship. The crowd, chased by
security police, were busy fleeing in both directions
along the waterfront, leaving the area clear.

"How's that for service!" Remo asked.

"Wonderful," Nancy said. She turned. King had
managed to ingest a mouthful of pepper gas. He was
coughing uncontrollably and squinting blindly through
his pain.

"Here, let me help you," she said sympathetically.

"Are you crazy! What if there are government cameras running! How will it look—Skip King being
helped by a girl?"

"Stumble along on your own, then," Nancy snapped,
stepping onto the pontoon bridge.

They reached the side hatch and King ducked into
the rest room. The strenuous sound of his retching
and heaving came for several noisy minutes.

Captain Relish took command.

"Everyone to their assigned seats," he announced.
"The pilot is getting ready to launch this bird."

"I'm staying with Old Jack," Nancy said.

"Not a good idea," Captain Relish said.

"Maybe not, but it's my idea." She started aft.

"I'll help you count toes," Remo said.

Captain Relish got in Remo's way. "Sorry, sir. You're not part of the team. I can't let you aboard without authorization."

"Think again. I just saved everyone's butt."

"Mr. King will have to authorize this." The sound of running water abruptly stopped in the rest room. "Throw him off the plane!" King shouted. Then heaved some more.

"Try and make me," Remo told Captain Relish.

At that moment, the Master of Sinanju appeared in the doorway through which Nancy was heading.

"Remo, I am not staying on this vehicle, which cannot possibly fly," he said coldly.

"Damn."

"Nor will I continue to consort with these ingrates."

"You win this round," Remo told Captain Relish.

Nancy looked to Remo. "Look me up in the States?"

"Maybe," said Remo.

The engines started to whine. The Master of Sinanju slipped from the wingship. Remo ducked out after him, his face a storm cloud. The pontoon bridge was cast off and the hatch was slammed unceremoniously shut.

Remo and Chiun stood on the beach to watch.

The great dorsal cargo doors were settling into place. At the tail, the two props began turning, each in the opposite direction. They built up speed and the craft inched forward.

Remo turned to Chiun.

"What's the idea? We could have hitched a ride home."

"Hush. I must watch. It is possible the craft will sink and an entire thigh bone will be mine for the taking."

Remo folded his arms. The prop backwash was beating the remaining pepper gas away from the patch of sand where they stood.

The *Orlyonok* was moving now. The two props pulled it into the harbor. Fishing boats got out of the way.

There were two giant turbofan exhausts set on either side of the nose. They began roaring and blowing, angling forced air under the wingroots.

The wingship leaped ahead and was suddenly floating above the waves. It skimmed out to sea at a steady speed.

"Guess it works after all," Remo muttered, watching it. "And you can kiss that thigh bone *sayonara*."

Chiun narrowed his hazel eyes at the departing tail.

"Come, Remo." And the Master of Sinanju leapt toward the water.

He lifted his skirts and soon was splashing into the surf. Then, as if finding submerged steps, he was racing across the waves, employing the same technique Remo had used to run atop human heads without breaking human necks.

Remo plunged after him. His feet found the water's natural buoyancy and he used this to propel himself forward.

The ekranoplane was still building up air speed. They overhauled it after a five-minute run, and first Chiun, then Remo caught up with the starboard wingroot and leapt onto its shiny surface.

There they lay flat, adhering like stubborn starfish as the slipstream buffeted them.

The *Orlyonok* skimmed out into the Atlantic.

No one noticed that it carried two extra passengers. Until Skip King happened to look out a starboard window hours later and imagined he saw the aged Korean calmly sitting on the trailing edge of the wing, his back to the slipstream, which pressed his clothing so flat king could almost count the bumps along his spine.

King blinked. Imagination. It had to be. Without telling anyone, he took a seat on the opposite side of the wingship.

There, he thought he saw the other one—Remo—

stretched out on the wing, sunning himself as if on a huge aluminum lawn chair.

Some sixth sense caused Remo to become aware of King's eyes on him. Abruptly, Remo sat up and gave a little wave. King lifted his hand to wave back, then had a sudden change in priority.

The sound of his heaving and wretching floated out of the washroom for the next hour. Intermittently.

15

The ekranoplane *Orlyonok* thundered across the Atlantic Ocean in exactly eleven hours, twenty-eight minutes, and sixteen seconds.

Her nose engines began to throttle down, and Remo, who had passed the trip stretched out on the port wing, sat up. The reduced slipstream threw his dark hair around, and he kept his face turned away from the blasting air.

Shore breezes brought a conglomeration of smells to his sensitive nostrils—smog, food odors, car exhaust. Civilization. The ekranoplane was nearing land. It was night. The moon outlined a shelf of pale sand. A beach.

Then the nose engines cut out and the wingship settled into the water, her tail propellers pulling her toward shore.

Remo stood up. It was possible to stand up now. Over the prop roar, he called, "Hey, Little Father. Ready to make landfall?"

"The tardy cook dinner," Chiun squeaked back.

And Remo jumped off the leading edge of the blunt wing. His feet carried him in front of the wingship. Once past the gleaming white nose, he spotted the Master of Sinanju, pipestem arms pumping, legs flying under his broad kimono skirts, keeping pace.

Remo pushed himself harder. The wavelets under his feet felt like slippery elusive pebbles that tried to repel footing. But Remo's flashing feet moved on so quickly that they found purchase enough to keep him moving ahead, but not enough to break the surface tension of the water.

Then there was a *chunking* of hard-packed beach sand under his shoe leather.

"I win!" said Remo, turning toward the water.

Chiun was nowhere to be seen. Remo saw the big wingship coming in, but out on the water there was no Master of Sinanju.

"Oh man," said Remo, starting back. He had just set both shoes into the cold water when behind him, Chiun's squeaky voice said, "You were slower than usual."

Remo whirled. There was Chiun, standing there, pointing to Remo's sopping shoes.

"And you have wet your feet."

"They're wet because I thought you'd fallen in."

"Anyone who would think that deserves to walk about with his shoes full of seawater."

Remo walked back, his shoes simultaneously squishing and making gritty sounds.

"I didn't see you overtake me," he said.

"And if you do not learn to see with both eyes, you will never see the hand that strikes you dead," retorted Chiun, a faint light of triumph in his hazel eyes. "We will have fish tonight," he added blandly.

"Maybe there's a good restaurant around here, wherever here is."

They looked around. The beach and docks looked unfamiliar. The wingship continued gliding toward the empty beach. Tugboats were chugging to meet it. The *Orlyonok* settled into a slow glide and the tugs bumped at its wings, stopped it, then backed off as other tugs began nudging the wings from behind.

Slowly, they guided it toward the beach. The craft nosed onto the gritty sand, crushing sea shells and driftwood, and its hull made an extended grating sound before it came to a dead stop.

"Let's pretend we're a welcoming party," Remo suggested.

"I will welcome a toe bone and nothing less."

They circled around to wait patiently by the hatch while it was unlocked and thrown open.

Colonel Mustard poked his head out.

"Greetings," said Chiun.

"Miss us?" asked Remo.

Colonel Mustard grew round of eye and mouth and pulled the hatch back with both hands.

Remo caught the door edge. Mustard pulled harder. Remo gave a casual yank and the colonel landed in the sand, face first.

Skip King barged up to the door, demanding, "What is going on here?"

"Welcome wagon," Remo sang out.

King let out a shriek and stumbled back into the craft.

Nancy Derringer showed up next. "How on earth did you two—" She saw the purple-bereted figure sprawled on the beach and changed her question. "What is he supposed to be?"

"Colonel Mustard, in the sand, with egg on his face," Remo said.

"Funny."

"How's the Bronto?"

"Apatosaur. And he's sleeping like a little lamb."

"Some lamb."

Nancy looked around. "That's odd."

"What is?"

"I don't see any press."

"I wouldn't complain," Remo said.

"I'm not. It's just that I've come to expect the glare of hot lights every time I turn around."

"No press," King shouted from within the craft. His voice held a nervous tremble. "We're in a press blackout."

"Why?" Remo called back.

"We don't want the public to see Old Jack until we're ready to unveil him."

"Where are we anyway?" Remo asked Nancy.

"Dover, Delaware, home of the globe-girdling Burger

Triumph Corporation." She looked to the beached ekranoplane. "This is the part that worries me most.
Offloading Old Jack and transporting him through the
city. We've already subjected him to enough strain as
it is."

Remo noticed two barge-mounted cranes standing
off in the harbor.

"Here we go again."

"Yes, and I'm worried those cranes aren't up to the
job."

"Excuse us a minute," Remo said, motioning Chiun
away. The two consulted for some moments and
returned.

"We have an idea," announced Remo.

"Yes?"

"But it's not likely to make too many people
happy."

"Will it insure Old Jack's survival?"

"Guaranteed."

"Then I don't care. Just tell me what I have to do."

"Take a short nap," said Remo.

"Excuse me?"

But before Nancy could hear the reply, steely fingers had her by the neck and squeezed down on her
spine. She heard a faint click, and when she woke up
an unknown period of time later, she was sitting in
one of the comfortable ekranoplane passenger seats,
surrounded by other expedition members, who snored
and grunted in their chairs.

Except Skip King, who for some reason was on his
knees with his face jammed under his seat flotation
cushion.

Nancy felt very sleepy and her memory was hazy.

Then the howl of metal under stress caused her to
jump bolt upright. It seemed to be coming from the
cargo bay. Nancy leapt to the door. It was closed,
dogged shut. She tried to undog it. The wheel seemed
to have been welded immobile.

Rushing back, she jumped to the main exit door.

The locking lever refused to budge, and from the rear of the plane came more howls of metallic complaint.

The wingship had a double deck, like a jumbo jet. She raced up the spiral steps to the observation deck. The pilot and copilot were asleep in the cockpit, but aft of it was an observation bubble. Nancy mounted the short carpeted steps and stared out.

"Oh God!"

The tail of the plane was off. It had fallen backward and was canted to one side. Between the dismembered tail and the passenger and wing area, there was no plane. Just hull plates and the exposed ribs of the mainframe, which had fallen away from the naked keel.

The Apatosaur was slumbering on the open air platform that had been the enclosed cargo bay floor, its black-and-orange skin shining in the moonlight. It seemed undamaged by the incredible explosion—for what else could it be?—that had blown open the cargo hold.

Then an airframe rib moved and fell into the sand. Nancy shifted position to see what had brought it down.

And there was Remo, casually placing a foot on the next rib. He set his weight on it. Nancy judged he couldn't weigh much more that one hundred fifty-five pounds, but the rib snapped off like a dry branch.

Remo looked up, happened to see her, and gave her a thumbs-up sign.

Nancy waggled fingers back. Weakly.

Then she sat down and had herself a good shake.

"This isn't happening," she told herself.

Not long after, the main hatch was ripped free and Nancy pounded down the steps and out.

"Check it out," Remo said, face calm.

She ran past him and to the rear. The Apatosaur was still in a drug-induced stupor. She found no marks on his leathery orange hide and breathed a long sign of relief.

Chiun appeared, seemingly out of nowhere. "Do not worry, it has all its toes."

"I don't know how you did it, but—"

Something rumbled up on the high ground. A horn honked. It sounded like a diesel truck, and they all looked toward the high end of the beach.

Monster headlights appeared first, shooting rays into the night sky. Then as the great forward tires eased down into the soft sand, they dipped, blinding them.

"What on earth is that?" Nancy breathed.

"At a guess, the official Brontomobile," Remo said.

With a hiss of air brakes, the lumbering multi-wheeled vehicle came to a stop. The headlights were doused, and they we able to see again.

"Looks like a missile carrier," Remo ventured.

"Leave it to King to buy the biggest toys," Nancy sighed.

"And we'll leave it to you to get the Bronto onto that thing safely, okay?"

"Where are you going?"

"Our work is done. So this is where we cut out."

Nancy grinned. "Didn't the Lone Ranger say that once?"

Chiun lifted his chin. "I am not leaving without proper compensation."

"You have your castle," Remo said. "So what's the beef?"

"Castle?" Nancy asked.

"Long story. Catch you around sometime."

Remo started away. On impulse, Nancy reached out and snagged his lean arm. It felt as strong as it should—given the fact that he had just disassembled a giant aircraft without resorting to tools.

"I owe you a lot," Nancy said simply. "Care to swap phone numbers?"

Remo hesitated. Reluctantly, Nancy let go of his arm, her brow furrowing. "I know I crushed your childhood fantasies, but—"

"We do not have a telephone," Chiun said.

"We don't even have furniture yet," Remo added.
"Tell you what, give me your number."

Nancy handed him a business card.

Remo looked at it. "Cryptozoology?"

Nancy smiled. "Call me sometime. I'll explain it to
you. Deal?"

"Deal."

And then they were gone.

Nancy's eyes went to the crew scampering down
from the dinosaur hauler, back to the Apatosaur
sleeping peacefully in the exploded hull of the ekranoplane, and she mumbled to herself, "I don't know
how I'm going to explain all this." Then she shrugged
mentally and added, "Then again, why should I? This
is B'wana King's responsibility. Let *him* explain it."

She smiled as she ran to meet the carrier crew.

16

Remo and Chiun had to walk two miles before they found a roadside payphone.

"Well, I feel good," Remo was saying. "I did my good deed for the week."

"May you feel so elated at my funeral," Chiun said bitterly.

Remo frowned, "Look. One, I don't believe that crap about dragon bones being the fountain of youth. And two, it wasn't a dragon. And saving it was our mission. Smith will be happy."

"Not when he learns that he is doomed to a too-short life due to your inflexibility."

"Got news for you," Remo said, fishing into his pockets for a quarter, "I don't think Smith will buy into that fable, either."

The Master of Sinanju turned his back on his pupil. Remo thumbed the one button down until the automated dialing system brought him Harold Smith's lemony voice.

"Remo. Where are you?"

"The wilds of Delaware. Mission accomplished. The Bronto is on the beach. They should be loading him onto the carrier about now. And best of all, we have the eternal gratitude of a Dr. Nancy Derringer, who gave me her card. It says she's a cryptozoologist, whatever that is."

"It is one who searches for creatures who may or may not exist," said Smith, showing no surprise at learning the dinosaur was real. "I am pleased all went well. And I have interesting news for you."

"Yeah?"

"You will remember Roy Shortsleeve, the death row inmate you believe is innocent?"

"Yeah?"

"I have looked into his background. Shortsleeve and two other men went on a camping trip in August 1977. The murdered man was found shot with Shortsleeve's rifle. Shortsleeve has steadfastly maintained his innocence from the trial to now. He claimed the third man on the trip, a coworker named Doyce Deek actually committed the murder. But Deek insisted it was Shortsleeve."

"One man's word against the other, huh?"

"The evidence against Shortsleeve was otherwise circumstantial," Smith admitted. "If Deek did it, he might be persuaded to confess."

"Got a line on Deek?"

"He is now living in Gillette, Wyoming. No visible means of support."

"Wyoming. I'm on my way."

"I am not going with you," Chiun called out. "My days are growing short and I wish to savor every precious hour."

"What is Master Chiun saying?" Smith asked.

Remo sighed. "He took a fancy to the Bronto."

"I am not surprised. It is a remarkable find. I would like to see it myself."

"Chiun is disappointed he didn't come away with a souvenir. Like a big toe."

"A big *toe*?"

"Seems dinosaur bones are the main ingredient to some witch's brew that makes Masters of Sinanju live to ripe old ages."

"Great longevity can be yours, too, Emperor Smith," Chiun called out. "Just speak the words that will speed me on my way."

"Tell Master Chiun I have no wish to live beyond my alloted span," Smith told Remo.

"Not only great longevity, but virility belongs to he who partakes of the bones of the dragon," Chiun proclaimed.

"Er, I am virile enough, thank you," said Smith.

"Don't tell me, tell him," Remo said sourly. He put his hand over his mouthpiece. "Nice try Chiun, but Mrs. Smith is built like an overstuffed sofa. I think Smith could care less about his virility."

"He does not know what he is missing."

Remo took his hand off the mouthpiece. "Okay, Smitty. I'll bundle Chiun on the next magic carpet to Castle Sinanju and get on my way to deal with this Deek character."

When Remo had replaced the receiver, he found the Master of Sinanju looking up to the night sky, his face forlorn.

"I am unappreciated."

"You are not. You own a brand spanking new castle."

"I am unappreciated in a foreign land and a castle will no longer console me, for I do not know how long I will have to enjoy it." He shut his eyes.

"I knew this wouldn't last," Remo said. "Come on. Let's find some transportation. Smith has an assignment for me."

Chiun eyed Remo suspiciously. "You are trying to get out of cooking dinner."

"I'll buy you dinner at the airport, okay?"

"I am being abandoned at an airport. I never thought you would stoop this low, Remo."

"Stoop to what?"

"Parent dumping. I have seen this terrible practice on television. Cheeta Ching decries it often. Now it is my turn. I am being dumped."

"You are not being dumped!"

Chiun bowed his aged head. "I am being fed a farewell meal and left to fend for myself."

"Oh, cut it out."

*   *   *

At the airport, the Master of Sinanju announced that he was not hungry.

"You sure?" asked Remo, suspiciously.

"I am sure that I am being abandoned."

"Bulldookey."

"But do not think simply because I am being abandoned by you," Chiun said in the loud, attention-getting voice. "that you no longer owe me a final meal."

"Keep it down, will you?"

A passing stewardess stopped, set down her folding baggage cart, and asked, "Is there a problem here?"

She directed her question at Chiun not Remo.

"No, no problem," Remo said quickly.

"I am being abandoned by my adopted son," Chiun said plaintively, lifting a corner of his kimono sleeve to one eye.

The stewardess glared at Remo, "You should be ashamed of yourself. This poor old man."

"Look, I have to get him on the next flight to Boston."

"Do you live in Boston, sir?" This to Chiun.

"No." Chiun gave Remo a cold stare.

The stewardess glared at Remo again.

"He lives outside Boston," Remo said. "And I just want to get him home. Look, I brought him his ticket and everything. All I have to do is get him on the freaking plane."

"I am forced to travel on an empty stomach," Chiun complained, snatching the ticket from Remo's hand.

The stewardess patted Chiun's frail-looking hand, saying, "There, there. Don't fret. Let me take you to travelers' aid. Are you hungry?"

"My appetite seems to be returning now that I am in your caring hands," Chiun said.

"I'll be happy to treat you to a nice meal. You look as if you haven't eaten in weeks."

"I am in the mood for fish."

They started off together.

"Fine," Remo called after the stewardess. "Feed

him. But whatever you do, don't let him con you into loaning him any money. He's as rich as King Midas."

"My ancestors were rich," Chiun told the stewardess. "For they were secure in their families. But I am in my twilight years and have no sons to call my own. Therefore, I am poor."

"You know," the stewardess said. "Cheeta Ching did a special report on this only last month. It's called granny dumping."

"A gross name for a gross practice. Did I mention that I am a personal friend of Cheeta Ching?"

"Really? She's my hero. Especially for having a baby at forty. She's so . . . so Murphy Brown!"

"She could not have done it without me. Did you know that?"

"I think her husband had a little something to do with it. He's a gynecologist, you know. Talk about having it all!"

Remo went to his gate, and talked his way into an earlier flight to Wyoming. He was looking forward to having a conversation with Doyce Deek, who had let a man rot on death row for a crime he never committed.

Remo knew exactly how that felt. He planned on explaining how it was to Deek—in excruciating detail.

17

As the converted missile carrier lumbered through the night, Nancy Derringer was amazed at how smoothly the transfer had gone.

There had been some rough spots before the big cranes had hoisted Old Jack from the remnants of the wingship, true. But those had been confined to Skip King's tantrums and carrying on when he found the *Orlyonok,* for which he was directly responsible, a broken derelict.

"How am I going to explain this to the board?" he moaned as the wingship crew compared notes. They had all remembered waking up in their seats to find the ship destroyed. No one remembered falling asleep. No one remembered anything.

"Simple," Nancy had suggested. "We beached, there was an accident, and the ship broke apart. We were all knocked unconscious."

"That's it! Pilot error. Why not? It works for the F.A.A."

"It was no pilot error. It was an accident."

"You don't understand. This is corporate politics we're talking about. There has to be a scapegoat. It's the way the game is played, and you're my backup."

"I am not your backup. Get clear on that point."

"Forget about me ever mentoring you."

They had to beach the barge, but it worked out better that way. A beached barge could not capsize. The cranes toiled briefly, under the watchful eyes of the Burger Berets, swinging the limp creature onto the padded carrier.

Everyone pitched in at that point, guiding the dinosaur's head to a safe landing. One of the cranes was needed to drape the thick tail onto the carrier. The beast was secured with heavy cable.

"Perfect." King said. "We're ready to roll."

The moon had become lost in a storm front. The darkness was absolute. Even so, transporting a ten-ton reptile up the lonely Delaware coast was not about to come off smoothly.

Yet, it did. The roads were virtually deserted.

"I can't believe our luck," Nancy said, riding in a company car with King. They were directly behind the brontohauler, as King called it. Three cars loaded with crack Burger Berets rode point.

"Don't," King said flatly. "The board had the roads blocked off."

"The board has that kind of clout?"

"The board has that much money to throw around," King retorted.

"Somehow I don't much care for the way the board throws money at problems instead of reasoning them through."

"In our league, baby, things move so smoothly that thinking is optional."

"That, I believe."

King frowned in the darkness. "That didn't come out right."

"Oh, yes it did."

They were barreling along a stretch of wooded road. The carrier, on twelve fat tires, each the size of their own car, dragged them along in the steady suction of its passing.

"I'll be glad when we get where we're going," Nancy breathed. "I feel like I personally carried Old Jack all the way from Africa on my shoulders."

"Me, I feel great. I'm Skip King, the man who brought the last living Brontosaur back from Africa alive. I wonder if I'll make the cover of *Time*?"

"Probably not," Nancy said in a cool voice.

"Why not?"

"I think they'll put Jack's picture on the cover, if anyone's."

"Damn, that's right. Those bastards probably will. Damn. Maybe I can get into the picture, somehow."

"Maybe if you put your head into his mouth."

King blinked. "Brontos don't eat people, do they?"

"Of course not."

"Maybe it's worth a shot then." King reached over and chucked Nancy under the chin. "Thanks, kid. You're all right."

Nancy rolled her eyes.

The walkie-talkie on the dash crackled.

"Mustard to Mogul. Mustard to Mogul. Acknowledge."

"Mogul is my code name," King said proudly. Into the walkie-talkie, he said, "Go ahead, Mustard."

"We have some vehicles blocking the road up ahead."

"Roadblock?"

"Looks like."

"Must be state troopers securing the road," King muttered. "Go on ahead and get them to clear the way for us. Fast. We don't want the carrier to have to brake unless we have to. That thing is a juggernaut."

"Roger. Out."

Through the steady rhythm of the carrier they heard the lead cars accelerate. Several moments passed. Then, unmistakably, there came the rattle and *pop pop pop* of small arms fire.

"That can't be gunfire!" Nancy said.

Abruptly, the red brake lights—all sixteen of them—flared along the carrier's rear end. Massive brakes engaged and the giant wheels kicked up acrid rubber smoke as momentum pushed the locked tires along.

The brontohauler began slewing.

Nancy moaned, "Oh no. It's going to jacknife!"

The carrier didn't jacknife. But it was a near thing. Knuckles white, King swerved to avoid a collision.

He ended up on the soft shoulder of the road. He popped the door and lifted his head up to see.

The carrier was sliding on locked tires to a sloppy halt. There was another silence. Then the gunfire broke the stillness, louder and more spiteful this time.

King grabbed up his walkie-talkie. "Mogul to Mustard. What's happening?"

"You won't believe this, Mr. King," Colonel Mustard panted, pausing to snap off a shot. *"We're under attack!"*

"Not again!" Nancy said.

"Can you make out who it is?" King asked in a heated voice.

"No, sir, they're wearing camos and ski masks. But there is something you should know."

"What?"

"They're wearing green berets."

"It can't be! We left those third world do-gooders back in Africa."

"I can't say it's them, but they have the same haberdasher. We're returning fire."

"Return fire, hell! Wipe 'em out!"

Nancy hissed at him in the dark. "Are you crazy, King? A firefight is insane."

King looked at her incredulously. "What do you want—to let them just steal the animal?"

"If I have a choice between a dead dinosaur and a kidnapped one," Nancy bit back. "I'll take the latter. Gladly."

"The board didn't spend millions just to lose out on the product tie-in of the century."

Nancy jumped out of the car. "Use your head. Where could they possibly take Jack? Back to Africa? Order your goons to retreat."

"I'm giving the orders around here." King hissed into the walkie-talkie, "Burger Berets! Do your duty! Sing out!"

And from the near distance, repeated in the walkie-talkie, came a crackling battlecry.

"Have it your way!"

Then the percussive chatter of automatic weapons fire cannonading through the night like a crackling intermittent rain.

Listening to it, King pounded on the car roof. "Damn, I wish I had a gun!"

"So do I," Nancy said bitterly. "And you in my sights."

"You're just overwrought."

Then, the most blood-chilling sound Nancy Derringer had ever heard in her life lifted over the unremitting small arms fire.

Harruuunkk?

King grinned fiercely. "They must have nailed one of the bastards!"

"That was Jack!" Nancy cried.

"*Old* Jack?"

But Nancy was rushing to the brontohauler. Skip King froze. If he pulled her back, she might be eternally grateful. On the other hand, she'd been threatening to write him up to the board.

"Maybe I should leave this to Kismet," he said, ducking back into the car to wait out the mortal storm.

Nancy Derringer heard the sound a second time. The black tip of the Apatosaur's whiplike tail was twitching.

"Oh God, the tranks are wearing off! Now now! Not now! Please not now!"

The pumpkin bulk still lay flat on the hauler body. Nancy circled around to the front. The head lay flat like that of a stunned serpent. The eyes were half open, the square, goaty pupils hooded. The orbs were filmed and cloudy. It was not aware of its surroundings. And obviously too weak to stand. A minor blessing.

Nancy gave the rough leathery hide a reassuring pat. "Don't you worry, Punkin. Mama's going to get you out of this. Somehow . . ."

She stopped under the oversized cab. Both doors were open. The drivers had joined the firefight, which seemed to be all around her now. Tracers zipped through the dark woods just ahead.

Nancy had started climbing the aluminum ladder to the driver's compartment when out of the shadows a masked man emerged.

Nancy saw him and yelled, "Put that weapon down! Do you want to kill the poor creature?"

"Get down from that thing," warned a gruff voice. A stocking mask covered all but the mouth and a thin circle around the eyes. The man's skin was black. No question. And he wore the signature forest green beret of a member of the Congress for a Green Africa.

"All right," Nancy said tightly, "but watch where you point that thing, please."

She clambered down.

The masked man approached. "Hands up."

Nancy obeyed. She tried to keep her face blank. Inside, she was boiling.

The masked man in the green beret approached. He carried his Skorpion machine pistol carelessly, waving it about.

Nancy tried to reason with him. "You don't expect to just steal a ten-ton dinosaur, do you?"

"If we can't," the man said casually, "then we'll just kill it."

It was the wrong thing to say. Nancy felt her mind go as blank as her face. She hadn't planned it. She hadn't planned anything. But her toe was in the man's groin before she knew she had kicked up and out.

Her opponent went, "Ooof!"

And his Skorpion hit the ground. Nancy leapt for it. Her hand touched the still-hot barrel. "Ouch!" She fumbled for the stock and brought the weapon around. She pointed it at her attacker.

The terrorist was holding himself and walking bent-legged.

"Settle down," Nancy warned, getting the feel of the unfamiliar weapon.

"Bitch! You kicked me!" His voice was very high.

"I'm as surprised as you are about it. Now stand still."

The man stopped. He stood in a bowlegged stance, holding his crotch, his teeth bared in pain.

"You gonna pay for that, bitch."

"Fine. Just so long as you stay exactly where you are, and don't let go of your organs of thought."

"Got no choice," the man grunted.

Nancy noticed his voice then. His accent was not what she had expected. There was none of the Euro-African gumbo flavor of the previous attackers. It sounded more American somehow.

"Who are you, anyway? You couldn't have beat us back to the States."

"That for you to figure out, bitch."

"You *are* an American."

"Congress for a Green Africa be international."

"Hmmm."

Clicking footsteps behind her caused Nancy to whirl. She pointed the Skorpion at the approaching figure.

"Halt!"

"Nancy—what are you doing?"

Nancy almost shot the familiar voice in her surprise. "King?"

Then she was jumped from behind. They struggled for the weapon. The terrorist was stronger. Inexorably, he was using the extended weapon as a lever to force her to her knees. He was winning.

And in her ears, Skip King was saying, "For God's sake, Nancy! That man is a professional killer. Don't fight him. You can't win."

Maybe it was her anger at King. Maybe it was a sudden and terrifying awareness that the muzzle was pointing directly at the slumbering Apatosaur. But something gave Nancy Derringer the strength to resist as she tried to bring her heel down on his instep.

His feet kept shifting. It was no good. Her breath came in hot sobs.

"King—" she grunted. "Help—me."

Then her opponent's thumb found the trigger guard
and the gun started erupting fire and stuttering noise.

Nancy forced the muzzle down, praying she wasn't
too late. The weapon was spitting at a cluster of oversized tires and then at the ground. Abruptly, it was
emptied.

Nancy let go and stepped back, her face white and
shocked. And a fist connected with the point of her
chin. She kept her feet, her eyes blinking furiously.

Dark shadows were moving all around her, but she
barely comprehended what they meant. She was out
on her feet.

When her head cleared, Nancy was sitting up
against the big hauler tires and Skip King was bending
over her, shining a flashlight on her modest cleavage.

"What happened?" she asked in a thick voice.

"I saved you," King said smugly. "You owe me
your life."

"You did?"

"Absolutely. Ahem, I hope you'll keep that in mind
when it comes time to write your expedition report."

Nancy pulled herself to her feet. She looked
around. It was still dark. The air was heavy with the
smell of gunsmoke.

There were clots of Burger Berets moving around
sweeping through the roadside trees.

"What happened?" Nancy repeated.

"The Berets beat off the bad guys. What else?"

Eyes clearing suddenly, Nancy whirled. "Punkin!"

"Who?"

"Old Jack! Is he hurt?"

"Not that I can see," King said, sweeping the dappled brute's bulk with his flashlight.

Nancy took it away from him. "Give me that!" She
climbed onto the cab, using the light to illuminate
every square inch of wrinkled hide. There were no
visible cuts or wounds.

"A miracle," she breathed, coming down off the
cab.

"You *could* throw a little gratitude around," King said sourly.

"I could. But I won't."

"That's cold."

Nancy speared the light in his eyes. "Yes, cold. Exactly how you'd feel if you woke up and found your top blouse buttons unbuttoned. And don't try to deny it, either!"

King's lean lips grew pouty. "I was checking for wounds. In case you needed a medic."

"How many dead?" Nancy demanded.

"None."

Nancy blinked. "None! After all that shooting?"

"You sound disappointed."

"Confused is more like it. What happened to the one I nailed?"

"You mean the one who conked you over the head?"

"Whatever. Answer the question, please."

"He got away. I would have nailed him myself, but I was too busy—"

"Sexually assaulting me."

Skip King lifted placating hands. "Don't say that. Please don't say that. The board is very down on sexual harassment this quarter. I don't know what got into them. But please don't call it that."

Colonel Mustard came up at that point. "Mr. King, we've finished our sweep. It's all clear. We can move out now."

A serpentlike head lifted in the darkness and from it came a low *harrooo* of a sound. Nancy held her breath. The head settled back into place and the eyes fell closed.

"We'd better get a move on, or baby is going to make our other troubles seem tame," King said uneasily.

"We'll settle this later," Nancy spat. "This time I'm riding on the carrier."

"Suit yourself," said King, stomping away.

As the Berets got into the cars and the transport

team clambered into the cab, Nancy gave the hauler a quick once-over.

The tires were whole, she found. The body hadn't a single bullet pock. Nor the ground.

"Strange," she muttered.

Then she noticed a long black streak on the fender above the tire she had shot. She ran her hand along it. The fingertip came away black. Smudged.

"Gunpowder burn," she said. "But where are the bullet holes?"

Her flash picked out a sprinkling of spent cartridges. She picked up one. It was still warm.

Then the hauler's diesel engine was rumbling and she doused the light and climbed aboard, a worried notch appearing between her eyes that stayed there the rest of the trip.

She was looking at the ragged, powder-burned tip of the cartridge.

18

Doyce Deek liked nothing more than to kill.

The kick of a Marlin .444 lever-action rifle against his shoulder was sweet music to his ears. The eruption of blood from a fresh wound was a too-brief painting, the smell of gore wafting on the breeze, metallic and tangy, were more pleasing than the scent of flowers after a spring rain.

Right now, in the sagebrush hills north of Gillette, Wyoming, with the Devil's Tower national monument thrusting up against the endless sky, Doyce Deek laid the crosshairs of his Tasco scope on the bronze flank of a pronghorned antelope.

The antelope was poised on a rise. It look around, white tail switching, as if scenting danger. Deek took his time. He ran the crosshairs down from the flank to the big tawny hindquarters. He could shatter that hip and still split the narrow skull before the animal could hit the dust.

Then again, head shots were pretty spectacular. He shifted his sight to the head. He got the left eye, big and black as the heart of a bull's eye, centered in the crosshairs. There was a lot to say for a clean head shot. The crack of the skull, the splash of hot brains. True, you didn't get as much of a pump of gore from the head as from the flank. But the satisfaction of looking into the kill's eyes in the instant before death all but gave him hard-on.

So, with the morning sun climbing the brass bowl

of the clear Wyoming sky, Doyce Deek lingered over his kill.

The trouble was, Doyce Deek really, really preferred other game. Human game. Antelope were fine. Their eyes had that hunted look that people got when they found themselves staring into the end of a hunting rifle. But antelope never understood what hit them. The crack of the bullet might stir their eardrums in the final moments of life, but they wouldn't hear it. The brain was usually dead by the time the sound got to the target.

It was different with human prey. But Doyce Deek couldn't afford to hunt human prey anymore. Not after that time in Utah when he stalked two men through the desert for two days. He killed one. The other had gotten away. Deek might have hunted him down, but since everyone at work knew that the three of them had gone camping together, it would look suspicious if only Doyce Deek came out of the desert alive.

Deek had started back to civilization after planting his rifle where the third man, Roy Shortsleeve, had left his abandoned belongings. Then he fingered Shortsleeve for the murder. It had been that simple.

The Utah State Police never did a background check, never learned that in other states where he had lived Doyce Deek had a habit of inviting friends and coworkers on camping trips and coming back alone. And never figured out that Roy Shortsleeve had been condemned to die for something he didn't do.

Doyce had testified against Roy those many years ago. He had kept in touch with the prison, as each postponement came. And when the time came, he planned to be a witness when they injected Roy Shortsleeve with liquid death.

He was looking forward to it, in fact. In a way, Deek liked to think, it was going to be his thumb on the plunger. He only wished it could be. Doyce really, really liked to kill people. No special reason. He just liked it.

In the meantime, he had to settle for antelope.

But this specimen in particular seemed skittish. Its head swept away and back. It had a scent. Not Deek's. He was upwind. Cayote, maybe.

Doyce Deek had decided to go for the head shot when, abruptly, the antelope bolted.

"Damn." Deek laid his rifle down.

It sprinted a good fifty yards and came to a nervous stop, its white tail bristling. He brought the scope up. Its nostrils pulsed with agitation.

Deek let it calm down, then drew a bead on the wary left eye.

He began squeezing down on the trigger and held his breath.

"Damn!"

Savagely, Doyce Deek stood up. The antelope was leaping along now, cutting through the sage.

"What is with you!" he snarled. Could it be psychic? Deek had never heard of a psychic antelope before. This one seemed to know exactly when to hightail it.

Deek started down off the rise. What the hell? Stalking was half the fun, anyway. And the day was just starting. Maybe he'd get lucky and a light plane would fly too low. Now that would be a kick. Bodies raining from the sky like milkweeds.

From a crook in a tree, Remo Williams watched the man with the hunter's rifle come down into the valley.

Once, he could have identified the make of the rifle. Now it was just a carved stick with a pipe shoved through it, as far as Remo was concerned. That was how far the Master of Sinanju had elevated him from the world of guns and mechanical things.

Way back in his Vietnam days, when he was a Marine sharpshooter, Remo appreciated firearms, their grace and raw power. His ability with an M-1 had earned him a nickname. "The Rifleman." Long ago. Now he saw them in a different light. Crude machines.

All noise and smoke and as subtle as a baseball bat with a railroad spike driven through the thick end.

His weapons were his hands, his feet, and most of all, his mind. He was a Master of Sinanju. He was the human animal raised to the pinnacle of perfection. In his way, he was the most ferocious killing machine since Tyrannosaurus Rex.

It made a grim smile come to his thin lips to think that. Remo Williams, Human Tyrannosaur. He hoped they were still lizards.

Remo had killed many men in his life as America's secret assassin. In the beginning, in those long-ago days, he enjoyed it, enjoyed the awesome power he wielded. Later, after that cruel joy had been pummeled out of him by the Master of Sinanju, it cooled to pure professional pride.

Today, he was not going to kill a man. He was going to right a wrong. But that didn't mean he couldn't get a kick out of it.

The man with the unimportant rifle found a clump of sagebrush and carefully lay down in it. He slipped the barrel through the clump until the muzzle was pointed at the skittish antelope.

Remo had a fistful of small round pellets. He thumbed one into his free hand, set it so that it perched on his hard thumbnail, held in place by his crooked forefinger.

He watched the man. He wasn't moving now. But his coarse woolen shirt expanded with each breath. The cloth would fall still in the instant before he pulled the trigger on his prey, Remo knew.

Remo used to daydream about hunting big game. He never had. And in the years that separated his old life from the being he was now, that idle daydream had faded into insignificance.

He had come to understand killing in a new way. He no longer ate meat, and since there could be no joy in the work of the assassin, hunting animals for sport seemed beyond cruel to him. It was senseless.

People feeding their egos at the expense of innocent animals.

The shirt stopped moving. And Remo flicked the pellet.

This time, he waited until the last possible second. Whistling, the pellet struck the antelope on its hindquarters and it sprang away.

The rifle bullet sliced through the air exactly where the antelope's head had been, to kick up an eddy of dust yards beyond.

The man with the insignificant rifle cursed and jumped to his feet.

Remo slid off the tree branch to commiserate with the poor hunter who was having a bad day.

"That bastard of a buck did that on purpose!" Doyce Deek was raging. He wanted to break his rifle over his own knees. He wanted to kick a cactus. There were no cactus in this part of Wyoming. It was cattle country. Always had been.

The antelope was running in a ragged, bullet-eluding zigzag. It would be in the next county before long.

"Hell, there's other pronghorns," he said.

"Not for you," a confident voice said.

"Huh?" Doyce Deek brought his rifle down and around until he found the source of the voice.

It was a man. Coming from the south. He was not dressed for hunting. He wore tan chinos and a black T-shirt.

"Who in blazes are you?" Deek demanded, not lowering his weapon.

"The spirit of the hunt."

"Ha. You look more like the spirit of the pool hall."

"That's my night job," said the man. His eyes were set so deep in his head that the climbing sun threw them into skull-like shadow. He walked with an easy, confident lope. His wrists were freakish, like cartoon water mains about to burst under pressure.

"Did you see that buck! Consarned thing up and lit out on me!"

"Thunderation," said the man, coming on despite the threat of the Marlin rifle. His voice was thin, his accent eastern. His "thunderation" might have been an understated taunt.

On reflection, Doyce Deek decided it *was* a taunt. He decided that the moment he realized he was all alone out here with the man. The obviously unarmed man.

He grinned wolfishly. He brought his rifle up a hair.

"I don't cotton much to easterners," he said.

And he fired.

The shot was clean, sweet. The bullet should have gone exactly where the man's smile was. Maybe it did. Because the man didn't move, other than to keep approaching real casual-like.

Levering another shell into the chamber, Deek fired again.

He blinked. The powdersmoke was in his eyes. And the man was still coming on, like he had all the time in the world.

"You ain't really the spirit of the woods, are you?" he muttered in a weak, reedy voice.

"Nah," said the man who seemed impervious to bullets.

"Them I'm gonna keep shootin' you 'til you lay down and die!" snapped Doyce Deek, bringing his weapon up once more. This time, he saw something he hadn't before. He forced his scope eye to stay wide and not blink like before. He held his breath and fired. The bullet moved too fast for him to see where it did go, but the skinny easterner seemed to see it coming. He shifted his shoulders as if to let the bullet blow on past; it straightened again with such eye-defying speed that the action was a kind of after-image blur.

He was fast. Not magic. Just fast.

So Doyce Deek tried for a sucking chest wound. That always put the fear of God in a man.

He laid the scope to his cheek, sighted along the barrel—and nothing!

He switched the rifle's field of fire. The man was gone!

Doyce Deek never felt the rifle leave his hands. He didn't feel the bore jamming up his rectum, either, the gunsight ripping his dormant hemorrhoids til they bled.

But suddenly he was squatting on the ground, with the stock dangling between his legs and the skinny easterner was taking Doyce's own hands, helpless as a child, and making him take a good strong grip on the rifle. He forced Deek's own thumb into the trigger guard and held it there.

"I'm going to give you a choice, pardner."

"What kind of a consarn choice involves having a Marlin .444 jammed up my own ass?"

"A hard one."

"Uh-oh."

"Option one," said the confident voice of the easterner. "You pull the trigger and kiss your butt *hasta la vista*."

"I'm kinda leaning toward option two."

"Confess to the murder that Roy Shortsleeve is doing time for."

"That ain't exactly a healthy option, either."

"Think you can handle the trigger by yourself—or do you want help?"

"I got a car phone in the pickup. Think you could fetch it here? I'd like to call Utah about a little misunderstanding."

"That's the option I was hoping for."

"Yeah, but it could have gone the other way."

"Never happened yet."

Doyce Deek made his eyes round. He squinted with the left one.

"You done this before?"

"This? I do this stuff all the time."

"I mighta guessed, on account of you done it all slicklike from the git-go."

Remo carried the man under his arm two solid miles through the open sagebrush wilderness to the waiting pickup. The dangling rifle bounced with every step, and with each bounce Doyce Deek made a funny little noise deep in his throat.

At the pickup, Remo set him carefully on the ground so the rifle wouldn't accidentally discharge. He dialed, waited for the ring, and held the phone receiver to Doyce Deek's unhappy face while he confessed in excruciating detail.

After he had hung up, Doyce Deek had a simple request.

"Separate me from this rifle, won't you?"

"Nope."

"I done what you said."

"So? Everybody does. I don't give points for cooperation."

"Oh."

And a hand—not a fist, but a hand—came up in Doyce Deek's long face and took consciousness away from him.

Remo left him in the pickup and walked back to Gillette, whistling. Satisfaction. There was no substitute for it.

Harold Smith received the report without comment.

"Chalk up one for the good guys," Remo said. "Now how about Dr. Gregorian?"

"Perhaps later. I am still compiling information on him."

"How much information do you need to understand the guy is on a quasilegal killing spree?"

"Enough to be certain."

"*I'm* certain."

"I may need you for something else," said Smith.

"Yeah?"

"Last night, there was an incident involving the Apatosaur."

"Bronto," snapped Remo. "Get it right."

"My understanding is—"

"Look, which sounds more like a dinosaur? Apato or Bronto?"

"I will admit that I prefer the latter, but—"

"But nothing. Go with tradition. It's Brontosaur. So what happened?"

"I gained access to the Burger Triumph electronic mail system, which is buzzing about the creature's arrival," Smith said. "Information is sketchy. The corporation has evidently clamped a lid of secrecy on the entire incident, but it appears some terrorist organization attempted to hijack the animal en route to their corporate headquarters."

"It can't be the Congress for a Green Africa," Remo muttered.

"Why would it be or not be them?" Smith asked in a puzzled voice.

"Chiun and I chased them off back in Gondwanaland. They were upset about endangered species or something."

"Please hold, Remo." And through the earpiece the hollow, plasticky click of Harold Smith's long fingers working his computer keyboard came like castanets in spastic hands.

"The Congress for a Green Africa," Smith murmured. "A little-known African ecoterrorist group. Formerly known as the Congress for a Brown Africa in its nationalistic phase, and the Congress for a Black Africa in an earlier black power incarnation. It was founded in the late 1960s as the Congress for a Red Africa."

"Red?"

"Their funding originated in Havana."

Remo grunted. "From the way they cut and ran from Chiun and me, they should call themselves the Congress for a Yellow Africa. But I don't see them following the Bronto all the way to the U.S. Unless they have branches all over the world."

"Unknown. Perhaps you might reestablish contact with Dr. Derringer, inasmuch as you have her confidence."

"Is this an official assignment all of a sudden?"

Remo asked. "I thought the idea was to appease Chiun, and rescue the expedition."

"Remo," said Smith, "a sovereign African government has allowed an American corporation to take possession of a native animal of incalculable value to the world scientific community. When the dinosaur's existence is confirmed, the eyes of the entire world will be focused on how the animal is treated. U.S. prestige could be at stake here."

"Gotcha," said Remo. "Does Chiun know about this?"

"I have not been in touch with Master Chiun."

"Maybe we should leave him out of this."

"Do what you think is best, Remo."

"Always," said Remo, hanging up.

19

Nancy Derringer had to admit it. She was impressed.

The sauropod habitat was perfect. A sunken bowl covered with hard-packed dirt and jungled with fronds, trees, and tough, edible lianas. There were even hard rocks scattered about as potential gizzard stones. True, there was no jungle chocolate or orange toadstools, but they could be flown in. Why not? A company that could build a dinosaur habitat in the basement of its world headquarters could afford to run fresh food between Port Chuma and Dover, Delaware as often as necessary.

Old Jack, Nancy was pleased to see, had woken up. He had not yet levered his great body up from the dirt, but his head was up and swinging about. To look at the head alone, the creature brought to mind a massive python, sleepy and even a little stupid.

The goat-pupiled eyes regarded her with no trace of comprehension.

"How's the boy? If you are a boy, that is."

The creature seemed to recognize her voice. It made a low noise—a curious sound, not threatening at all.

Nancy took a fragment of toadstool she had pocketed in Gondwanaland and speared it on a thin branch she had broken off in an examination of the habitat before Old Jack had come around.

Leaning over the stainless steel rail, she offered the morsel.

The curious sound came again. The head lifted, the heavy lids lifted, too. The eyes cleared, grew interested.

"Come on, Punkin. Come on."

The creature moved its massive legs, pushing its wrinkled knees downward. But muscular strength was not there. The body trembled and surrendered to weakness. It eased its great belly to the dirt floor in defeat.

Swaying, Old Jack brought his small head as high as he could. His neck was not long enough to close the gap between his snout and the aromatic food.

Nancy knelt and shoved the stick downward through the lowest rail.

The creature hesitated, the morsel was only inches away.

"Go ahead, Punkin. You can do it. Come on."

The mouth yawned, exposing peglike teeth and the head crept forward, serpentlike.

Nancy steeled herself. If necessary, she would drop the stick. Those teeth, though blunted by chewing hardwood branches, could take her hand off at the wrist with a casual snap.

But the movements of the Apatosaur were so languid they disarmed her. Nancy relaxed. The forked tongue licked out heavily to caress the toadstool. Liking what it found, the mouth crossed the last inch and Nancy let go as the stick was taken in the firm grip of many teeth.

She stood up and watched it gulp the toadstool, branch and all, into its long gullet.

"Good boy. Or girl."

The click of footsteps on parquet flooring brought Nancy around. Her face, soft with pleasure, abruptly fell into tight lines.

"King."

Skip King saw the hovering orange head and brightened. "He's awake?"

"Obviously."

King gripped the rail, grinning. "Great! The board is on the way down."

"They are?"

"Are you kidding? They couldn't wait."

"I wish they would. I don't want to disturb Punkin."

"Old Jack. Unless the board decides different. Which I think they will."

"Why should they?"

"Because they'll want maximum name appeal when the thing goes on tour."

"Tour!"

"Hey! Settle down. That's why I came ahead. I don't want you to go all hormonal in front of the big guys. The board wants to set up a twelve-city tour, to tie in with our new monster burger promotion."

"Promotion, my butt! Our agreement expressly stipulates that there would be no such circus. This is the last surviving dinosaur, as far as anyone knows. We can't subject it to lines of gaping primates poking it with sticks and throwing french fries at it."

"Please. No french fry slurs in front of the board. They're sensitive about the fry perception thing ever since it came out that our fries are cooked in lard."

"I object in the strongest terms to a tour," Nancy said firmly.

"Hey, don't get upset with me. Take it up with upper management. I'm merely a corporate servant, just like you. And try not to forget it. Without Burger Triumph, this big brute would be languishing in Darkest Africa, unloved and unexploited."

"Which is where I'm beginning to wish I'd left him."

"Sour grapes make sorry wine," King sniffed, leaning over the rail. "Hey, big Jack. Remember me!"

Harrooo!

The head came up with unexpected speed. King leaped back, startled. Saurian eyes regarded him coldly.

"What's with him?"

"Maybe he remembers you shooting him," Nancy suggested.

"Dinosaurs aren't that smart. That's why they're extinct."

"A common misapprehension," Nancy said. "Let me suggest you keep your distance."

"Doesn't matter. I don't need a pet. Not when this bag of meat is my ticket up the corporate ladder."

The *ping* of an arriving elevator floated across the wide, well-lit basement area.

King straightened his coat and said, "That's the big guys. Remember. Play it cool, and everything will work out for the best."

Nancy made her face placid as she watched the board of directors of the Burger Triumph Corporation cross the polished floor. There were six of them, all well fed and prosperous. And probably none of them so much as sniffed their own product, never mind ate it. They looked like stuffed-lobster types.

King made formal introductions. "Gentlemen, I don't believe you've met Miss Derringer. Better known as Nancy, the greatest dinosaur-minder in the world."

"It's *Dr.* Derringer," Nancy said, mustering her composure.

"She prefers to be called Nancy," King said.

Nancy bit her tongue and shook a half-dozen cool hands. A minute after she had repeated their names aloud to commit them to memory, she had forgotten them. They were that faceless.

And beside them, King was waving to the floating Apatosaur head, saying proudly, "Now meet the most colossal contribution to U.S. culture since the invention of onion rings. Heh heh."

His laugh was a solitary sound in the great basement.

The six members of the board leaned over the rail and stared at the unhuman face regarding them. One puffed on a cigar. The others wore no particular expression. They might have been looking at a stack of freeze-dried hamburger patties and not a living thing.

"What do you think?" King asked anxiously.

"Kind of ugly for a corporate symbol, King."

Skip King's face fell. He swallowed hard. "When I was a kid, there was a gas company that had one as its logo."

"I remember it," another board member said slowly.

King brightened. "See?"

"Didn't they go out of business?" asked another.

King's face fell some more. He was paling by degrees.

"The coloring says Halloween," a fourth board member murmured. "Not appropriate for a summer tour."

"We can paint it to match the season," King said instantly.

"We will not!" Nancy flared.

"Nancy," King hissed. Clearing his throat, he said to no one in particular, "Anything the board wants, it gets. Heh heh."

"That's it!" Nancy said, getting between them and the reptile. "I must object in the strongest terms to the whole concept of a tour. The animal hasn't been stabilized. We have no idea how—or even if—he will acclimate to captivity. And the strain of transport could be catastrophic."

King snorted. "Crap! We brought him from Africa to America. We proved it can be done. A tour is doable."

Nancy looked to the board members. They stared back with noncommittal expressions. The might have been thinking. A moment later, it was clear they had not been.

King said, "Miss Derringer has been under a lot of strain. You'll have to forgive her."

"Strain?"

"It's all covered in my report," King said.

"Report!" Nancy exploded.

"I stayed up all night writing it," King said defensively. "No grass grows under my feet."

"And butter doesn't exactly melt in your mouth, I see."

"We have read Mr. King's report," the man with the cigar said. "You have done an excellent job, Miss Derringer. Why don't you take a month off? With pay, of course."

"A month! And who will tend to the animal?"

"I have that covered," King said hastily.

"I refuse."

"I'll have her removed from the building," King offered.

Nancy blinked furiously. Her eyes went from King's eager-to-please expression to the six faces of the board of directors, whose own expressions were unreadable. When none of them objected to the suggestion, King motioned to a pair of Burger Berets stationed at the elevators.

"Escort *Miss* Derringer to the door," he said.

Nancy froze. Her fingers became fists. Then, all the tension drained out of her.

"I can walk out under my own power, thank you."

And she did. Flanked by two guards.

Echoing in her ears was Skip King's self-satisfied voice, saying, "I have the entire tour itinerary worked out, if you gentlemen care to see it. . . ."

Skip King waited until the two Burger Beret guards had returned. He had set up a pair of easels in front of the dinosaur terrarium.

"Why don't you two take twenty?" he said. "Out of the building."

The pair went away without a word. And King faced the board of directors.

"Now that we're alone," he said, grinning, "would you gentlemen care to see the projections I've worked up for Operation Bronto Burger?"

The man with the cigar nodded.

"We are now entering phase two," King said, extending a telescoping pointer. He tapped red points on a map of the nation. "Phase two envisions a six-month, twelve-city tour of our Brontosaurus. During which time we anticipate moving over six million units on our all-beef monster burger tie-in promotion."

King removed the map placard and exposed one showing graphs and cost projections.

"Once that target volume has been achieved, our subject dinosaur will be returned here and phase three will begin."

He removed the graph placard. The next one showed an Apatosaur, with its body separated into segments, each segment indicating its gross weight.

"After the beast is discreetly but humanely euthanized, the carcass will be rendered and the meat frozen for a one-year period of bereavement. After that, phase four.

"My office will then issue press releases announcing that the meat has been preserved in the interest of science and has been scientifically determined to be edible. Everybody with me so far? Good."

King shifted to the other easel, removing a blank placard. Under it was a mockup of a billboard showing a man sitting on the fender of a Ferrari, a blonde in a silvery evening dress draped over him. Both were trying to take a bite out of the same hamburger.

"We will market our deluxe Bronto Burger as a special one-time-only offer at five thousand dollars and ninety-nine cents per quarter-pound burger," King said. "Soft drinks and fries extra."

The board nodded in unison. King went to the next placard, which showed a family picnic. The adults were wearing Burger Triumph crowns and the children played with plastic dinosaurs. Everyone had a hamburger.

"For the downscale market, bronto-meat-flavored extract will be laced into our regular monster burgers at ten ninety-nine per unit. We will play up the unique taste, the novelty, and the once-in-a-lifetime offer. Only one burger to a customer. And toys for the kiddies, of course. Our estimated gross is seventy million."

"Sounds doable so far, King. But how does the Bronto Burger taste?"

"We don't know. Yet."

"What if the public won't go for it?"

"What if it tastes like snake meat?"

King grinned broadly. "Remember our unofficial motto, 'The public's curiosity is stronger than its stomach.' Just in case, a no-refunds policy will be strictly enforced."

"The animal looks mighty sick. How do you know he'll survive the tour?"

"I've got that covered," King said, collapsing his pointer. "Unless she's quit in a huff, Nancy Derringer will keep him healthy if she has to donate her own blood to do it. Best of all, she doesn't suspect us. In fact, no one will ever suspect us, because of the fake attacks we arranged. After they're through serving as an honor guard, the Burger Berets will be quietly disbanded. And the so-called African environmentalists will catch all the flak. In short, the operation is foolproof."

The man with the cigar exhaled a slow, thoughtful cloud of aromatic smoke. "King my boy, proceed with confidence. The board is behind you."

"You don't know what that means to me, sir. Ever since kindergarten, I've ached for a shot at the big time."

The board filed out. After the elevator had closed on them, Skip King, beaming like an altar boy at his first communion, turned to the Apatosaur and blew it a kiss.

"See you later, you gorgeous seventy-million-dollar rack of reptile!"

As King walked off, a forlorn *harrooo* followed him. And the Apatosaur's head settled to the ground, eyes slowly closing.

20

Nancy Derringer had called everyone she knew. Her lawyer. Her friends at the International Colloquium of Cryptozoologists. Everyone. Her lawyer had been blunt.

"If I sue Burger Triumph, they'll have me for lunch. Sorry."

Her colleagues were more sympathetic.

"We'll picket."

"We'll help you kidnap the dinosaur."

"We'll do anything!"

In other words, long on enthusiasm, but short on practicality. That was typical cryptozoologist thinking. Since the Colloquium was not so much an organization as a loose interdisciplinary alliance, there was no muscle behind their expressions of support.

In her furnished apartment provided by Burger Triumph for the duration of her term of service, Nancy fumed and fought back hot tears.

"How could I have been such a fool?" she said bitterly.

A rapping at the door brought her off the sofa.

"Who is it?" she called through the door.

"Remo."

Nancy threw open the door. And there he was. Lean and casual in a crisp white T-shirt, but somehow as exciting as if he wore Navy dress whites.

"You don't know what it means for me to see a

friendly face right now," she said with relief. "Come in, please."

"Nice place," Remo said, looking around.

"It's bought and paid for—just like me," Nancy said ruefully. She shut the door and clapped her hands once softly. "So—what brings you back into my life so soon?"

"I hear the bronto was attacked after we left you."

"How did you know that? As far as I know, the company was able to keep a tight lid on it."

"Let's just say that somebody told somebody who told me."

"Have it your way. It was the Congress for a Green Africa again. The Berets beat them back. Old Jack must be the luckiest reptile on earth. He came out without a scratch." Nancy folded her arms and dropped onto the sofa, her face clouding over. "I wish I could say the same." Her voice was a hair from cracking.

Remo's face grew concerned. "You okay?"

"I wasn't fired, but let's say I've been put in ice. Now I'm trying to figure out how to worm my way back into the board's good graces before Old Jack goes the way of his ancestors. He needs hour-by-hour monitoring, and there's no one on staff who's qualified."

"Why do I smell gunpowder?" Remo said suddenly.

Nancy looked up. "Do you?"

"Definitely. Burned gunpowder."

Nancy sniffed, frowning. "I don't smell anything."

Remo followed his nose around the room until he came to a small purse lying on a chair cushion. He picked it up.

"Be my guest," Nancy said tartly. "I enjoy having my personal belongings rummaged through by men I dimly know."

Her mouth parted in surprise when Remo's hand came up holding a spent rifle shell.

"What are you doing with this?" Remo asked.

"I forgot all about that," said Nancy, coming out of her chair to join him. "I picked it up during the attack on the hauler. It struck me as strange, but I wasn't sure why."

"It's a blank."

"How can you tell?"

"I used to fire blanks for practice when I was a Marine," Remo explained. "They pour the powder into the cartridge and crimp the open end shut. When the bullet is fired, the crimping is blown open just like this."

"My God! That explains why no one was hurt during all that shooting. They were firing blanks!'"

"Who were?"

Nancy stopped, blinking like a moth fluttering at a lightbulb. "Well, take your pick. Either the Congress for a Green Africa or the Burger Berets. What on earth is going on?"

"Let's check out the place where you were attacked."

Less than a hour later, Remo pulled a rented car over to the side of a piney wooded road south of Dover. They got out.

"I'm sure this is the spot," Nancy was saying. "It was dark, but I recognize that big boulder over there. Yes, here's where the hauler went off the road. See the tire gouges?"

"Look for spent shells," Remo said.

Nancy paced, her eyes on the ground. "I don't see any now, but the ground was littered with them before."

"They must have sent back a cleanup team."

"Who did?"

Remo bent and lifted a dirty brass shell casing from the furrows of tire tracks.

"Bingo!"

Nancy peered at it closely. "It looks just like the other one, except for the color. What does that prove?"

"The Berets were armed with American assault rifles, right?"

"True."

"Remember what the other guys had for weapons?"

"The same vicious little machine pistols they had in Africa."

"Yeah. Firing short rounds. Nine millimeter. Like this one. Let's see your shell."

They compared shells. Nancy's was distinctly longer and made of steel, not brass. But it had the same burned, ragged end as the other.

"That's a .223 cartridge you got there," Remo pointed out. "That means both sides were firing blanks. Might explain why no one got hurt in Africa, too."

"Oh, that can't be!"

"Why not?"

"It just can't." Nancy's frowning face fell into slack lines. "One moment. There *was* something off about one of last night's terrorists."

"Never met a terrorist who was on," Remo said dryly.

"No, this one spoke black English. American style. I had the feeling he wasn't part of the African unit that hijacked the train."

"A terrorist is a terrorist—unless they're shooting blanks."

"What is going on here?" Nancy breathed in an incredulous voice.

"Simple. It's some kind of publicity stunt."

"Staged for whose benefit? There was no press."

"Search me. But we gotta get you back in the saddle."

"How?"

Remo made an unhappy face. "I hate to do this."

"Do what?"

"But I don't think there's any other way."

"I hope this isn't what I think it is," Nancy said, her tone matching Remo's.

Remo nodded grimly. "I gotta call Chiun back into this."

"Wonderful. But what good will he be?"

"Chiun just happens to be a close personal friend of Cheeta Ching."

"The TV anchor?"

"I'll bet a Brontosaur to an Apatosaur she jumps on your story like a Tyrannosaur on a Dimetrodon. Literally."

Nancy smiled grimly. "I'll take that action."

It turned out to be easier than Remo had thought. Back at Nancy's apartment, he picked up the telephone to call the Master of Sinanju. Then his face went slack.

"What is it?" Nancy gasped.

"I just remembered. We don't have a phone."

"Oh, no."

"Maybe the guy who put me on to this can help."

"And who might that be?"

"Don't ask."

"I won't," Nancy said, lifting an arch eyebrow.

As Nancy watched, Remo blocked the phone with his body and touched a key. She didn't see which. But he held it down without dialing further.

A moment later, he was speaking in low tones. Nancy caught only cryptic snatches of the conversation.

"Think you can help?" Remo finished. He listened a few minutes and said, "Great."

He hung up grinning. "The new phone is supposed to be installed today. He's going to put an expedite on it. Could be hooked up within the hour."

"Whoever he is, he must have a lot of clout if he's plugged into Burger Triumph's grapevine and AT&T both."

Remo's grin turned tentative. "So, what do you want to do to kill time?"

"Care to hear some dinosaur stories?"

"Is there a second option?"

"Unfortunately, no."

Remo's face fell. He dropped into a chair and folded his arms defensively. "Okay, but be gentle. I don't want all my illusions shattered."

*   *   *

The phone rang as Remo was trying to grapple with the concept of dinosaurs being neither warm-blooded nor cold-blooded, but capable of shunting between metabolic options.

"I liked the dinosaurs we had when I was a kid better than these new ones," Remo muttered unhappily. "You knew where you stood with them."

Laughing, Nancy put the receiver to her ear and said, "Hello?" then jerked the earpiece away as if it was hot.

"Chiun, right?" said Remo.

"He seems more than a little upset."

Remo accepted the handset and said, "What's up, Little Father?"

Out of the receiver came a horrendous squeak.

"Remo, Remo, a calamity has happened!"

"I know, but with your help, I think we can get Nancy reinstated."

Chiun's voice grew annoyed. "What are you babbling about?"

"Nancy got the old heave-ho. What are *you* talking about?"

"I am speaking of my terrible encounter while exploring the streets near my castle."

"Mugger?"

"Worse," Chiun spat. "I encountered a Vietnamese."

"Uh-oh."

"The neighborhood is rife with Vietnamese. I also saw a woman I took to be Chinese. Or possibly a Filipina."

"But no Japanese, right?"

"I am afraid to find out. Oh, Remo this is impossible. I cannot dwell among lowly Vietnamese. What would my ancestors say?"

"Lock the castle door every night?"

Chiun grew so angry he hissed.

"Okay, okay, you're pissed. Smith got you again. Why don't you take it up with him? He gave you this number, right?"

"I was so beside myself. I did not know what to say. I have accepted his castle and signed his contract. I am bound by these things, Remo."

"So we move. I can live with that. But skip it for now. Listen, Nancy needs your help."

Chiun's voice grew cool. "The woman knows my price."

"Forget dinosaur toes for a minute. We're on Smith's clock now. No perks."

"Pah! I am too distraught to think properly."

"We need to ring Cheeta Ching in on this," Remo said.

Immediately, the Master of Sinanju's voice grew softer.

"Cheeta. Smith wishes me to contact beauteous Cheeta?"

"Right away. Here's what you tell her. . . ."

The first thing Cheeta Ching wanted to know when she heard the familiar voice of the Master of Sinanju was, "Is Ringo with you, Grandfather?"

"Ringo?"

"That hunk with the wrists."

"No," Chiun said shortly.

"Oh. Next time you bump into him, could you tell him for me Cheeta has been thinking of him?"

"Perhaps. But I am calling for another reason. It is about a woman whose plight you should know. . . ."

Skip King was in an upscale singles bar in Dover, trying to hit on two blondes at once when a familiar voice came from the big-screen TV.

"You say you were let go by a vice president of Burger Triumph, who was sexually harassing you?"

King grunted. "Hasn't she dropped that kid yet?"

Then to his horror, the crisp voice of Nancy Derringer answered Cheeta Ching's pointed question.

"I wasn't let go. I was shunted aside by a glory-seeking Neanderthal named Skip King. I brought the dinosaur project to him and the minute he got the animal to this country, he pushed me out the door."

"This is about power, isn't it?" Cheeta asked.

"Isn't it always?" Nancy said.

"Dinosaurs and sexual repression," Cheeta said in a shrill voice. "Is modern man less evolved than modern woman? For a different perspective, here is science correspondent Frank Feldmeyer."

"Oh God." King said, gaping at the screen. "I'm toast."

"They're waiting for you," the head of security told Skip King when he burst breathless and panting into the lobby of the company headquarters.

"Are—they mad?"

"You know the board. It's hard to say."

"Did—did they say anything about me? Anything bad?"

"Not to me. But they're in the boardroom and they've been there a solid hour."

Sweating, Skip King took the elevator to the top floor. "An hour. I've cost the board of directors an hour, and it's after business hours. An hour times six. Oh God! I'm costing the board six hours of their personal time. I'm burnt toast."

The board of directors looked up in unison when Skip King pushed open the glass doors. The CEO was seated at the far end, in a leather chair that had a tall, thronelike back. His cigar smoked in his fattish fist.

Along the sides, the others sat in similar oversized chairs.

"I came as soon as I heard," King croaked, reaching for the chair at his end of the long conference table.

The CEO gestured with his cigar.

"Don't bother. You won't be staying."

King gulped. "You—you're not—firing—me?"

"We think you should take some reflection time, King. Let things sort themselves out."

"But I can't. I'm ramrodding the Bronto project."

"We have that covered."

"Covered? What are you going to do when the press starts pounding on the doors for interviews? That Derringer dame just told Cheeta Ching we've got a full-grown Brontosaurus Rex in our basement. And I'm the guy who captured it. The media will be howling for my story."

"Right now," came a cool voice from the high-backed seat directly in front of him, "the media is howling for your head."

Eyes wide, Skip King peered over the chair. Looking back at him were Nancy Derringer's upside down blue eyes. They were not friendly.

"Dr. Derringer has agreed to come back on board during the transition," explained the CEO.

"I thought it was the least I could do," said Nancy dryly.

"Look, I won't stand for this. I won't be cheated of my moment of glory."

"Skip," a senior VP said. "You wouldn't buck the board, now would you?"

"I—I might. Anything is possible when the corporate ladder breaks under your feet. I might even write a tell-all book. You never know with a corporate comer spurned."

The board regarded him with unblinking, unreadable eyes.

The CEO gestured to the door with his cigar. "Give us a moment, would you King? We need to confer."

King paced the rug outside the boardroom for twenty minutes. His jacket grew heavy with perspiration.

"This isn't happening," he muttered. "This isn't happening. I'm Skip King. I'm headed for the top."

When he was called back in, he found the board sitting placidly. Nancy looked unhappy. That was a good sign. He forced himself to breathe normally.

"We've decided you can stay with the project," the CEO said bluntly.

"Great. You won't regret—"

"Under Dr. Derringer."

King scowled. "A woman. I can't work under a woman."

"I suggest we take Mr. King at his word," Nancy said coolly.

"On second thought," King said hastily, "I can give it a shot. Why not? I'm a people person."

"Excellent. Take a seat, Dr. Derringer is making recommendations."

King sat. He folded his hands on the table until he realized how it looked. Then he hid them under the table so no one could see them tremble.

Nancy cleared her throat and said, "I have just examined the animal. It is clearly depressed."

"That's the most ridic—" King started to say. He shut up.

"And not adapting to the habitat. It's too early to tell what the problem is. I'd like to do a blood workup, toxicology tests, but of immediate concern is to move Punkin—"

"What happened to Old Jack?"

"Punkin is a more customer-friendly name," the CEO murmured.

King shut up again. The woman was smooth. She had them eating out of her hand. His eyes went around the room, wondering which one of them she was sleeping with.

"As I was saying," Nancy resumed, "Punkin must be moved as soon as possible. To a more suitable environment. Also, a more secret one since the press has been flooding the switchboard with inquiries."

"Now whose fault is that?" King snapped.

The CEO stood up abruptly. "King, help Dr. Derringer with all the arrangements."

"Yes, sir," King said unhappily.

On their way out, the board of directors stopped to give Nancy their compliments. King was ignored. That hurt most of all.

After the board had gone home, King stood up stiffly. "I guess I'll have to make the best of this. Where are we moving him?"

"That's classified," Nancy snapped, gathering up her files.

"Not from me."

"*Especially* from you."

"Then how can I help if I don't know where we're taking Old Jack?"

"Because B'wana is going home for the evening."

"You can't order me home."

"Would you rather I ask the board to do that?"

"You play a hard game of ball for a girl without any."

"Try not slam the door on your way out," Nancy said. "It's made of glass. Like your ego."

After King had left, Nancy went to her new office. Skip King's name was still on the door. By morning, that would be changed. At her new desk, she dialed her home number.

"Remo? Nancy. It's all set. We're moving Punkin tonight."

"Need any help? Chiun should be here in an hour or two."

"No. No time. Better wait for him. And stick by the phone. I'll call if I need you."

"Let's hope not. I'm in no mood to stand between Chiun and the wishbone of his choice all freaking night."

21

Burger Triumph World Headquarters was a forty-story office tower surrounded by low satellite buildings. A golden crown surmounted the tower, making the lower buildings seem like kneeling subjects before a monolithic emperor. The park was accessible by a single service road and surrounded by a security fence.

The press was kept outside the fence. The security guard at the gate was under explicit instructions. If questioned about a dinosaur, laugh in their faces.

He did. And as the night wore on and the phone calls to the corporate building went unreturned, the press gave it up.

By three o'clock in the morning, the coast was clear.

Nancy Derringer was giving the Apatosaur's a last once-over. It regarded her with sleepy eyes. It had shifted position since she had last been here. It was a good sign. It should be strong enough for the transfer.

She lifted the walkie-talkie in her hand and said, "Open the gate."

At the opposite end of the sunken habitat a steel door lifted like a guillotine blade being raised into cutting position. A dim tunnel was exposed.

From within, a fan began blowing, carrying a fruity scent to the Apatosaur nostrils. It stirred, craning its long neck around.

"There you go, Punkin. Food."

The reptile sniffed audibly.

"You can do it," Nancy encouraged. "You're hungry, aren't you?"

The creature found its feet with ponderous dignity. It backed up, turned, and sent its long drooping neck into the tunnel.

Nancy had her fingers crossed. "Keep going."

The shoulder disappeared as the creature followed its nose. When the sound of noisy eating came, only the tail was visible.

This went on for twenty some minutes and tailed off. Then it stopped all together.

A voice crackled from the walkie-talkie. "He's gulped down every last avocado, Dr. Derringer."

"I'm on my way," Nancy said. "It shouldn't be long now."

The great basement gave a long shudder and there was silence except for the slow slapping of the reptile's tail against the ground.

Nancy climbed down and slipped into the tunnel.

Captain Relish met her in the narrow square tunnel. The dinosaur hauler had been backed into the sloping tunnel, so that its bed lay flush with the floor.

The Apatosaur had collapsed peacefully in the confined space, ready for transport.

"The sedatives worked perfectly, Dr. Derringer," said Relish. "Care to do the honors?"

Reluctantly, Nancy tranked the creature herself, hating every pull of the rifle trigger. Only a half dozen shots were required to insure an extended sleep.

Nancy handed the rifle back to Relish. "All right, secure him and we'll be going."

Nancy watched the Burger Berets cable the Apatosaur down.

When they were done, they went out a side door and around a concrete tunnel where the cab of the brontohauler lay outside the other end of the basement tunnel.

"I'm driving," Relish said.

"Fine." Nancy took a seat in the middle of the oversized cab. The backup driver took the outside passen-

ger seat. Relish got the diesels started and the hauler
lurched forward.

Nancy was looking out the back window as the rest
of the hauler emerged, bearing its cargo of sleeping
Apatosaur.

"Ingenious, isn't it?" Relish grunted.

"Anything that avoids stressing the animal has my
heartfelt appreciation," Nancy said distantly.

"Is something wrong?"

"No," Nancy said hastily. "We should be fine once
we reach our destination."

"Which is?"

"Classified until you need to know. Just take Highway 13. North."

"You're the boss."

A huge overhead door rolled up and they rumbled
out of Burger Triumph World Headquarters and into
the night. Soon, they were out of the office park and
traveling north.

Nancy settled down for what she hoped would be a
short uneventful ride. She didn't like sitting between
two Burger Berets—not understanding how they fit
into the apparent charade with the Congress for a
Green Africa. But once the creature was in neutral
territory, it should be possible to wrest control of it
from the corporation. If not with lawyers, then with
the help of Remo and Chiun—whoever they really
were.

On a quiet stretch of Route 13, not thirty minutes
later, a small van roared up behind them and tried to
squeeze past the hauler.

Relish eyed them in his side mirror. "Are they
crazy? Trying to pass us? We own the damn road."

"Must be press," the other Beret muttered.

Engine racing, the van strained to pull past the lumbering vehicle. Captain Relish gave the wheel a nudge
to the left. The hauler responded. Forced to swerve,
the van ran up on the soft shoulder of the road, almost

wiped out, and pulled ahead. Its red tail lights dwin-
dled, then flared.

Far ahead, the van screeched to a halt, blocking the
road. Its headlights were in their eyes, blinding them.

"Hit the brakes!" Nancy cried.

The hauler slid to a long, slow stop, its side doors
sliding open with a harsh squeal.

And out came shadowy figures who stepped into
the headlights. A quartet of masked men in camos and
wearing jaunty green berets. Short-barreled weapons
gleamed.

"Not again!" Relish snapped.

"It's a bluff!" Nancy shouted. "Drive through
them!" Then she thought, *Why I am telling them?
They know who's been firing blanks all along.*

At that moment the Skorpion machine pistols came
up, smoking and shaking and chattering.

The windshield spiderwebbed before Nancy Derringer's shocked blue eyes, and on either side, a Burger
Beret was slammed back into his seat with his face a
ruin of blood and brain and bone.

My God! Nancy thought. *The bullets are real!*

Then the masked men were knocking in the glass
of the cab doors.

22

The Master of Sinanju was beside himself. "Oh, Remo, what can I do?" he squeaked plaintively.

Remo was sprawled on Nancy Derringer's couch watching a nighttime talk show hostess attempting to coax a group of adults dressed in disposable diapers to talk about their sex lives. "Simple," he told Chiun. "We move."

"I cannot move. It is the first castle Emperor Smith has bestowed upon me. To move would be an insult."

"So? Smith can stand it. He might not even care."

"And I have bargained dearly for it."

"Ah-hah. The real reason emerges."

The Master of Sinanju ceased his fussy pacing and settled on the center of the rug. "I am a prisoner in my own castle of hostile Vietnamese and I am fated to die soon. No Master of Sinanju has ended his days so bitterly since Hung."

While Remo was trying to remember the lesson of Hung, the phone rang. Remo picked it up, saying, "Sinanju Dragon Rendering Service. You find 'em, we'll grind 'em."

"Remo," a voice croaked.

"Smitty? What's wrong? You sound awful."

"Two Burger Triumph Berets were found on a deserted stretch of Delaware highway within the last twenty minutes."

"Yeah?"

"According to my monitoring of Burger Triumph

interoffice electronic mail, the two dead men were the driver and his relief."

"What about Nancy?"

"There is no word on her fate," Smith said

"Damn. And we've been cooling our heels waiting for her call."

"Remo," Smith said, tight-voiced. "I want that Apatosaur found."

"Just point us in a direction, Smitty. I guarantee results."

"I have been unable to make sense of your report of staged firefights between the Burger Berets and the Congress for a Green Africa. But someone at the company must know something. Find that person and shake the truth from him. Work your way up the corporate ladder if you have to."

"My pleasure." Remo hung up. "Come on, Chiun. Let's go calling."

Skip King was walking the halls of Burger Triumph headquarters aimlessly. The board was in seclusion. No one was talking. Especially, no one was talking to Skip King, the company leper.

And worst of all, he no longer had an office. He had been locked out of his own. So with no desk to call his own, King was reduced to walking the halls, loitering at water coolers, trying to find out what was happening.

"This is fiendish," King confided in a middle-level clerk.

"Actually, this is how the CIA treats field operatives who screw up," the clerk said cheerfully. "They recall them to Langley and make them roam the halls, trying to look busy."

"You're a lot of help," King snarled, crumpling up his paper cup and throwing into a basket. He stormed over to the elevators. Maybe there would be more information on the next floor. If not, at least he still had his key to the executive washroom. Maybe he would set up an impromptu office there.

The elevator doors slid open and King started in. He noticed the lift was occupied. Then he noticed by whom.

King started to retreat but a hand connected to an extraordinarily thick wrist grabbed his power red tie and used it to yank him back. The doors closed on his yelp of surprise.

"Going up?" Remo asked casually.

"Actually, I was going down," King said glumly.

"Looks like you ride with us. Funny, we were looking for you, too. Let's have a private talk in your office."

"I don't have an office. They gave it to Nancy."

"Okay, let's have a talk in Nancy's office."

"I don't have the key."

"You won't need one."

The elevators settled at the top floor and Skip King stepped off, with Remo and Chiun a pace behind him. He knew better than to run.

At the office door, King said sheepishly, "Here it is."

The little Korean stepped up to the pebbled glass and used one long fingernail to score the glass. The sound hurt King's ears. Remo gave the circle a tap. The glass popped in, and he reached inside to turn the doorknob.

"In you go," said Remo.

King stepped in. "You know I'm not impressed."

"No?"

"Anyone can slip a glass cutter under their fingernail."

"Maybe. But not us. Where's Nancy?" Remo asked, without wasting any more time.

"I don't know. I heard she was riding shotgun when the brontohauler was hit."

"Hit by who?"

"Search me."

"He is lying, Remo," said Chiun in a cold voice. "His sweat reeks of falsehoods."

"That's ridiculous," King snapped.

And suddenly Skip King felt a viselike pressure around his ankles. The rest was a blur of sound and noise and motion—and once the blood rushing to his head cleared his vision, he realized he was being dangled out his former office window by his ankles.

"Let me go!"

"You don't want that. You want to be pulled back in safely. Right?"

"Pull me back in to safety—fast," King screamed, his tie slapping his face.

"First some truth. Who hijacked the hauler?"

"It must have been those Africans."

"Try again. We know the Africans were shooting blanks. So were the Berets. What's the story?"

"I don't know what you're talking about!"

"He is lying, Remo," came the squeaky voice of Chiun. "His voice shrieks his perfidy."

"I don't like being lied to," Remo said, an edge in his voice now.

"I don't blame you!"

"Ever heard of the melon drop?"

"No."

"It's an old Korean custom. Someone lies to you and so you dangle him by both ankles and play melon drop. Guess whose head substitutes for the melon?"

King guessed. "No! Please!"

"Ready for the one, two, three, *splat* part of the ritual?"

"Okay! Okay! I'll talk."

"You're already talking. Talk truth."

"The board must be behind this! It's gotta be them."

"Why?" Remo asked.

King let the words come out of him in a spray. "This whole Bronto thing is part of a marketing plan. We're putting Old Jack on tour. When it's done, we're going to euthanize him."

Chiun's wrinkled features grew perplexed. "Euthanize?"

"Dino dumping," said Remo grimly.

"The fiends."

"That's right," King agreed. "They're fiends. The idea is to sell Bronto Burgers at rare-art prices. The board expects to clean up. They must have moved the time-table up without telling me."

"What do you think, Chiun?"

"I think there is no limit to the barbarism of this land, where Vietnamese are allowed to live in the finer provinces and people would eat dragons."

"As opposed to skinning them for the magic bones?"

"One buries a dragon after it has breathed its last. It is the only proper thing to do."

"Why?"

"So a new dragon will grow from the organs, of course."

"I give up," said Remo, hauling King back into the room. King staggered over to the wastepaper basket and, getting down on hands and knees, began heaving into it.

"Let us hie to this board of evil, Remo, and remove their scheming heads."

"Not without checking in first."

The Master of Sinanju indicated Skip King, his head in the steel basket.

"That one has ears."

"I'll fix that," said Remo as he reached into the basket and squeezed a place near King's spine. He went limp and the bubbling sound of him exhaling into his own vomit came.

Remo got Smith on the phone.

"Smith, forget everything you heard about African environmentalists. This is a Burger Triumph scam all the way."

"What?"

"They have it all worked out. A promo tour, an accidental death. Guess what happens next?"

"I cannot imagine."

"Every yuppie in the universe getting in line for a once-in-a-lifetime taste sensation."

Smith's gasp was a dry, shocked sound. "You don't mean—"

"It'll be bigger than cabbage patch dolls, except you can eat Bronto Burgers."

"Have you traced the animal?"

"No. But we scared the truth out of King. He says the board has moved up the timetable."

"Interrogate the board."

"Just wanted you to know before we did it."

"Try to do this delicately. Burger Triumph represents a significant slice of the American economy."

"They don't lie, they don't die. How's that?"

"Satisfactory," said Smith.

Skip King was still bubbling away when Remo hung up. On the way out the door, the Master of Sinanju kicked the basket over. King fell with it and began breathing normally.

The board of directors of the Burger Triumph corporation wasn't sure what to make of the thick-wristed man and his colorful companion.

They tried to bluff their way through the intrusion on their emergency board meeting.

"Are you employed here?" asked the CEO.

"No. We're dissatisfied customers."

"Dissatisfied?"

"We like our Brontosaurs on the hoof and not between slices of stale bun."

"I do not follow."

"They are temporizing, Remo," the old one warned the other.

"Must be expecting help," said the one called Remo.

He walked around the table, running his fingers along the polished cherrywood top. He stopped when he came to the right-hand corner at the CEO's elbow, reached under, and yanked a push button out by its wiring.

He dangled it in the CEO's face. "Who'd you call?"

"Security. And I suggest you two plan to leave quietly or charges will be filed. Federal charges."

"Lordy me," said Remo.

The Burger Berets burst in a moment later. There were four of them and they toted AR-15 assault rifles. Captain Mustard led them. He paled at the sight of Remo and Chiun. He started to back out of the room, but his team was in the way.

"Nice guns," said Remo.

"Please put your hands up," Mustard ordered in a quaking voice.

Remo's confident smile didn't involve his eyes. "Remember to load them this time around?"

Captain Mustard and his Berets hesitated, looked momentarily blank, and various uncomfortable expressions crawled over their faces.

Remo looked to the CEO and said, "You know, I think they forgot their bullets again."

The CEO stood up and shook an angry fist. "Shoot them! They've threatened the board and by implication all your jobs!"

The Burger Berets made a valiant attempt. Their lack of ammunition was a serious handicap, but it probably saved their lives. As the weapons filled the boardroom with noise and flame and gunsmoke and not much else, Remo and Chiun moved among them, using their jaunty purple berets to gag them—after first relieving them of the weapons and all limb volition with hard fingerstrokes to shoulder and hip joints.

They made a pile in one corner, and Remo addressed the board. The Master of Sinanju stood behind him like an emerald-and-gold genie, his hands tucked in his sleeves.

"The scam is out in the open," said Remo, his voice clipped. "So tell us where the bronto is and maybe you won't have to end up like Skip King."

"How—how did Skip King end up?" a man quavered.

"Breathing his own puke."

The board of directors looked queasy and the CEO said, "We have no idea what has happened to the poor animal. We agreed to allow Dr. Nancy Derringer to transport it to a secure place, and the hauler did not arrive. We were just discussing what it could mean when you two barged in."

"You aren't trying to tell me this hasn't anything to do with Bronto Burgers?" Remo said skeptically.

"Obviously Dr. Derringer has tricked us."

Remo started to scoff when the Master of Sinanju said thinly, "He is speaking the truth, Remo."

"I can smell their sweat," said Remo.

"As can I. But it smells of truth."

Remo looked dubious. He lowered his tone. "Their pulses are racing. That means they're lying, right?"

Chiun shook his head coldly. "It means that they are frightened. If they lied, their pulses would jitter."

Remo looked from the Master of Sinanju to the board and back again. "So who hijacked the Bronto? It sure wasn't Nancy."

"There is only one person left," Chiun intoned.

"Can't be Colonel Mustard. He's in a pile with his beret in his mouth." Then it hit him. Remo snapped his fingers. "King?"

Chiun nodded firmly. "King."

"Damn." Remo slipped from the room, calling back, "Anyone who interferes is hamburger. Literally."

Chiun hung back a moment. "I have spared you your miserable lives," he told the trembling board. "I will expect your gratitude to be without measure."

Then he was gone.

"I move we all submit our resignations," the CEO said stonily.

When no one answered right away, he added, "On the condition that the severance packages are commensurate with our contributions."

The motion was seconded, voted on, and passed unanimously. That left only the dicey question of to whom to tender their resignations.

Skip King was gone when Remo and Chiun reached his former office. They followed the trail of partial footprints to the elevator bank. King had stepped in his own vomit and tracked it along the carpet.

The head of security in the lobby confirmed that King had left the building.

"What kind of car does he drive?" asked Remo.

"Why should I answer that question?" the guard wanted to know. "Did you two sign in? I don't remember buzzing you in."

"We do our own buzzing. Watch."

The man had a computer terminal at his station and Remo laid a hand on it. He described a quick circle and reversed it.

The guard noticed that the data on his screen was breaking up. An electronic beeping came from the system. It sounded panicky. "How are you doing that?" he gulped.

"This?" Remo said. "This is nothing. Watch this." And Remo ran his hand back and forth along the side. The glass cracked and the broken screen hissed in the guard's face like an upset alley cat.

The guard spat out information in quick bursts. "Red. Infiniti. License plate says KING 1."

"Let's go, Little Father. It's time to crown the king."

They floated out of the building.

23

Skip King had climbed the corporate ladder the hard way.

He had started working the drive-in window of a Burger Triumph in Timonium, Maryland, was soon catapulted to store manager, then regional supervisor, and by the tender age of twenty-eight he was working out of the corporate headquarters.

There was one and only one reason for his success. He saw himself as a cog in the corporate machinery. On the franchise level, that meant maximizing the profit even if it meant returning to work after hours and salvaging the unsold burger meat and stale fries and bringing them in the next morning before the day crew arrived.

He saved the company twenty thousand dollars in his first six months as manager. As regional supervisor, he saved six figures by shuttling leftovers between stores. The board never questioned his methods. They only saw the bottom line and the bottom line was what they cared about.

And what Burger Triumph, Inc. cared about, Skip King cared about. He had no social life, acquired no friends, and didn't care.

When he had been promoted into the heady, button-down atmosphere of the main office, at first Skip King didn't think he could make it. There was no spoilage to salvage. He wasn't going anywhere as a junior product researcher until he requested what was thought to be the dead end of all dead ends. A transfer to the company cafeteria. As manager.

Within three months, the subsidized cafeteria actually showed an unheard-of profit. The board didn't care that the plastic utensils were being cleaned in Skip King's apartment sink every night for reuse and only the cheapest army surplus food was being served to lower echelon staff. The board ate in their private clubs and fine restaurants, so they didn't hear the complaints of staff. They only saw the bottom line. And they only cared about the bottom line.

One gleaming rung at a time, Skip King scaled the shiny ladder of success. It had not been easy. His lack of business education had caused many doors to slam shut in his glowering face. Middle management looked more and more like Skip King's destiny.

Until the night he slipped an updated resumé into his employee file, listing himself as a graduate of Wharton Business School. Magna cum laude. Because he had never heard of summa cum laude.

It was a potentially dangerous move, but King, noticing the high turnover in Burger Triumph personnel—even at its corporate headquarters—figured he was even money to get away with it.

The next time he put in for a vacant position higher up in the company, he talked up his degree in business administration—and found himself in the marketing division. From that day on, Skip King was a Wharton man. And he made sure everyone—from the secretaries to the janitorial staff—knew it.

His fellow employees found him insufferable about it, but not one called him on it. They preferred to change the subject, or duck into a men's room stall when they saw him coming.

Five years after first entering the building, Skip King was made VP of marketing and found himself sitting with the big boys in marketing meetings.

He adapted well. He learned to read the board. To sense when it was safe to agree or disagree. He was one of them. A comer. The organization man. There was no limit to the heights he might reach.

Until the Bronto Burger project unraveled.

It had been a bitter pill to swallow. Demoted overnight. And on the verge of his greatest fame. It had been Skip King's idea from start to finish. It had been Skip King who had stood before the board and vowed to fall on his sword if anything went wrong. With an agreed-upon golden parachute in place if he was forced to resign to preserve the company's good name.

Demotion wasn't honorable. Demotion was not something Skip King had bargained for. And working for a woman who'd never seen the inside of Wharton was intolerable.

Briefly, Skip King had contemplated suicide. For what was life without the reassuring steel rungs of the corporate ladder under one's climbing feet?

Then he got angry. Angry at the board of directors who would humiliate him, Skip King, who dared go into the heart of deepest Africa to make their bottom line the greatest in fast-food history.

It was in that cauldron of righteous anger that Skip King decided to get even. And as long as he was in the getting-even business, he thought, no sense in not getting rich in the process.

It had been the easiest thing in the world to set up. Everyone was in place. Like chess pieces. It was just a matter of getting them to jump in a new direction, and not just diagonally. Skip King had never been good at chess. There were too many rules, too many invisible barriers to victory.

As he drove through the Delaware night, wiping his own vomit off his lean wolfish face, Skip King knew there would be no more rules for him.

Not after tonight.

Nancy Derringer awoke with a start.

Her eyes were slow to focus. Her head hurt. There was a funny smell in her nose and a bitter taste in her mouth. The taste was from the dry sponge someone had jammed between her teeth before gagging her with a length of cloth.

Then she remembered the Burger Berets' faces turning to raw meat and the men in the ski masks pulling the bodies from the hauler and taking their place.

They took the bloodied seats and one got the hauler moving while the other pushed Nancy's face to the floorboards and pressed a cold, wet cloth to her face, holding it there until she had passed out. Ether. That was the smell clogging her nostrils.

Nancy looked around. It was dark. The air smelled stale. She was lying in dead, musty hay. There was a nimbus of white light ahead of her. She crawled to it. Boards creaked under her weight.

Gradually, a vista came into view.

She was in an old barn. In the hayloft. The white light made the barnboards look like weathered old tombstones.

In the center of the barn, parked in the hot glow of hanging trouble lights, was the hauler. And stretched out on its bed was the Apatosaur, looking like some prized mutant pumpkin awaiting judging. It looked dead. If it was breathing, Nancy couldn't see it.

There were men moving around the hauler. They wore camouflage utilities, but their faces were bare. Black men. She watched their faces carefully. Five minutes of study confirmed what Nancy had suspected. None matched the faces of the African members of the Congress for a Green Africa.

One of them was speaking now.

"This is one big mother, ain't it?"

"I wouldn't get too close. It might wake up and snap off your fool head."

"It eats heads?"

"Relax," a third voice put in. "It's a vegetarian. A few groats and he's happy."

The accents were American. All of them. They were Americans. But what did it mean?

Nancy crept back from the edge of the loft so she

wouldn't be seen. She tried breathing steadily to clear
the ether stink from her nostrils. Maybe it would clear
her head, too. None of this made any sense and she
desperately wanted it to make sense.

Most of all she wanted Old Jack to survive the
night.

The honking of a car horn brought her crawling back
to the edge. She watched the black men go to a side
door, weapons at the ready. They looked nervous.

"Who is it?" one hissed.

A man was looking through a knothole in the
barnboard.

"It's King!"

"King?" Nancy murmured.

"Let him in," a man said.

And Skip King, looking nervous and flustered,
stepped in through the unlocked door.

"Everything okay?" he asked.

"It just be growling in its sleep, is all."

King went the Apatosaur. He walked around the
hauler. "I think it's starting to come around."

"Are we in trouble?"

"You got it cabled down tight?"

"Yeah. But how tight does it need to be? That's
the question."

King said, "That bossy blonde knows the answer to
that question. I'd better ask her. Where is she?"

One of the hijackers used his thumb to indicate the
hayloft. "We stuck her up in the loft."

Nancy wriggled back out of sight before King's gaze
could lift in her direction. He was talking again.

"Get ready to make the call. We may have to put
the arm on the board sooner than I thought."

"This had better work, King," another voice growled.
"If this gets out, we're top of the list of perps."

"Don't sweat it. I know how business works. The
board will pay the ransom just to hush things up. The
last thing they want is for it to get out that they were

planning to sell ground Brontosaurus to the American public."

In the musty gloom, Nancy Derringer blinked her eyes rapidly. She heard the words, but they rang in her ears like some discordant gonging. What did he mean?

Then King was climbing a creaky ladder and his fox face was silhouetted against the back glow of lights.

There was no point in pretending, so Nancy sat up and glared at his approaching figure.

"I see you're awake," King said smugly.

Nancy made an angry noise in her throat. It came out of her nose, buzzing.

"Simmer down," King spat. "Let me get this thing off you." He untied the gag, and reached cold fingers into her mouth for the gag. Nancy spat out the bitter sponge taste then followed it with sharp words.

"You bastard! What are you up to?"

"Call it a sting."

"Sting?"

"The board stung me. I'm stinging them back. If they want Old Jack in one piece, they have to pay me. A cool five million. That's enough to retire on."

"But why?"

"You saw how the board humiliated me. And you're asking why?"

"Yes, I'm asking why. Two men are dead and the last Apatosaur on earth is at risk because your scrotum is as swelled as your head?"

"Since when are you such a big board booster?"

"Since you went off the deep end."

King smiled in the twilight. More than ever, his smile struck Nancy as foxy. "You wouldn't think so much of those stiffs if you knew what I know," he said.

"I'm listening."

"They never intended to find a good home for Old Jack, you know. All along, they were planning to run his carcass through the grinder and make Bronto Burgers."

"I don't believe it."

"Too audacious, huh?"

"Too stupid. Only a cretin like you could imagine such a thing."

"As a matter of fact," King said in an injured voice. "It was my idea from the very beginning."

And Nancy knew he had been speaking the truth. The realization caused a coldness to settle into her marrow. She wanted to throw up, but there was nothing in her stomach to regurgitate. She settled for staring at King as if he were a ghoul that had stumbled out of a fresh grave.

King asked, "Listen, those cables? Will they hold him down if he wakes up?"

"I have no idea. I tranked him for a two-hour ride, with an hour safety margin. He could come around any time now."

"Uh-oh. What do we do?"

"You call the authorities before you get in any deeper," Nancy snapped.

King stood up. "Like you said, two men are dead. It doesn't get any deeper than that."

King walked to the edge of the loft. He cupped his hands before his mouth and shouted down. "Check the hauler. Maybe there's a trank gun on board."

Nancy was considering rolling into the back of King's calves and knocking him off his perch when one of the hijackers came through the side door.

"There's a car coming!" he hissed.

"Douse the damn lights!" King yelled.

The lights were connected to a single portable battery. Someone disconnected it and the barn became a great black space in which there was no sense of orientation.

Then in the blackness, a sound. Low, mournful, but blood-chilling in its implications.

Harrooo.

24

The sound came again, louder, freezing the blood of everyone on the old barn's dark confines.

Harrooo.

Then something snapped with a metallic twang. Great suspension springs groaned as the hauler shifted on its huge tires.

"Is that what I think it is?" a wary voice croaked.

"The lights!" King cried. "Turn the lights back on!"

"Something's moving down here. Something *big*."

Another voice said shrilly, "The groats! Whose got the damn groats?"

Nancy Derringer strained to see through the inky dark. It was impossible to see more than doubtful shadows.

"Don't shoot! Whatever you do, don't shoot!" she pleaded.

"Shoot if you have to!" King howled. "Don't let it get away. It's worth five million, dead or alive."

Harrooo.

Remo popped out of his rented car. A moment before, the decrepit old barn had been leaking light from chinks and knotholes and a corner of the roof like a gray old jack-o'-lantern fallen into ruin.

Every fragment of light went out at once.

"Must have a sentry posted," Remo muttered.

The Master of Sinanju said coldly, "It does not matter. We have the fiends where they cannot escape our wrath."

"Yeah, well they're probably not firing blanks now. We gotta do this so Nancy and the Bronto aren't hurt."

Then they heard the sound.

Harrooo.

"Damn," said Remo. "Now we really have problems." He turned to Chiun. "Listen, I gotta have your word that no matter how this goes, the Bronto comes out of it in one piece."

"That is our assignment," Chiun said in a thin voice.

"Keep that in mind. No accidents, no taking advantage of opportunities. Got me?"

The Master of Sinanju screwed up his tiny face into an amber knot of wrinkles. "I know my emperor's wishes."

"Okay. Now let's take them."

They split up, attacking the barn from opposite approaches.

And the foghorn sound of the Apatosaurus came again—and with it the unmistakable complaints of heavy cables straining and snapping.

The *blat* of automatic weapons fire was followed by barnboards being knocked off their frame supports.

Abandoning stealth, Remo moved in for the side door, his face angry.

Below the hayloft. Skorpion machine pistols were spitting long tongues of yellow fire, throwing intermittent shadows about the huge barn interior.

The freakish light illuminated the Apatosaur throwing off its chains. Its goat eyes were coursing about the room, searching, frightened. A rear leg unbent itself and found momentary purchase on the right rear set of oversized tires. The rubber burst under the weight and the Apatosaur's leg slid off. The barn shuddered and shook when the padded leg touched the floor.

The hauler suspension wasn't equal to the stress. It snapped. The opposite tires broke like thick-skinned balloons. The entire rear end fell and the great pumpkinlike rump of the Apatosaur slowly slid to the hay-strewn floor.

It was screaming now, its mouth open and set like a frightened snake.

"Don't shoot!" Nancy screeched. "It won't hurt you if you leave it alone."

"Do what you gotta," King yelled.

Bound hand and foot, Nancy rolled toward King's standing form. *That does it. You're going over the edge if I have to go with you*, she thought fiercely.

Then the side door came off its hinges, jumped six feet, and brought down a man who was trying to draw a bead on the Apatosaur's small, questing head.

Simultaneously, a cluster of boards at the back splintered and fell and a high, squeaky voice filled the shot-with-gunfire darkness.

"Surrender, minions of the hamburger king. For your doom is surely upon you."

Recognizing the voice, Nancy stopped rolling.

"Remo!" she yelled.

"Yeah?"

"I'm up here in the loft. With King. A prisoner!"

"I'm a little busy right now," Remo said, and men were screaming.

"What's got me? What's got me?" one shrieked.

"I do," said Remo, and the sound of human bones snapping came with a finality that was undeniable.

"What's going on down there?" King yelled.

A man yelled back. "Something is down here! And it ain't the damn dinosaur!"

Then a gurgle came from the vicinity of the yelling man, and when King called back to him, there was no answer.

"Somebody hit the light!" King screamed.

In the darkness, Skip King became aware of a shape looming in the black empty space before him. It was a long shadow amid patterns of shadow, and he sensed eyes on him even though he couldn't see an inch past his sharp nose.

Came a low, interested sound: *Harrooo*.

And a noxious cloud swept over Skip King. It smelled disagreeably of raw mushrooms.

Remo was moving through a twilight that only his eyes and those of Chiun's could discern. To everyone else, the barn interior was pitch dark, except when someone expended a clip of ammo.

Those flashes were growing infrequent now.

Remo came up behind a man, tapped him on his shoulder, and the nervous man brought his weapon around in a chattering semicircle.

Before the bullet track could cross Remo's chest, Remo drove two fingers into the back of the unprotected skull, just under his green beret. They came out clean. The two holes squirted blood and thick matter, but Remo had already moved on.

The Master of Sinanju took hold of a neck in one bird claw hand. He squeezed. The flesh surrendered and then he was holding the hard bones of a man's spine. The bones proved no more resistant than the flesh, and the man struggled briefly then hung limp in the Master of Sinanju's grasp.

Chiun dropped him onto the growing pile of bodies and turned to another foe. This one was walking blindly in the darkness, his eyes so wide they threatened to pop from his fear-struck skull. He was sweeping his weapon around, prepared to execute shadows.

Except that he could not even see shadows.

So the Master of Sinanju gave him a voice to shoot at.

"I know something you don't know," he taunted.

The weapon muzzle shifted and erupted in angry challenge.

But the Master of Sinanju had already stepped behind the man, saying, "You missed. As I knew you would."

The man whirled. His bullets peppered the walls and shook hay down from the rafters.

"Damn!" he cursed, removing an ammunition clip and replacing it with a fresh one. He had drawn close to the great tail that lay uncoiled the length of the floor, unawares.

"You may try again, blind one," Chiun squeaked.

This time the man stopped in his tracks and pivoted, firing.

The Master of Sinanju effortlessly dipped under the stream of crude metal. He came to his full height once more, his voice a strident bell.

"You are defenseless now."

"Says you." And the gunman got off a final shot. One bullet. The round struck the hauler, ricocheted twice, and struck the Apatosaur in the thick meaty part of the tail.

The tail twitched in the darkness, and blood oozed.

Seeing this, the Master of Sinanju gave a cry of anger.

"*Aiieee!*"

His sandled feet left the ground floor in a leaping kick. One foot caught the gunman in the head, imploding his blind, fear-strained face. The Master of Sinanju landed gently on the body as it struck the floor.

Then he stepped off the quivering hulk to examine the injury done to the ugly African dragon whose bones meant long life.

Skip King was staring into a darkness that seemed to be staring back at him. His mouth felt dry.

"Somebody," he croaked. "Anybody. Turn on the lights."

Somebody did. The hauler's headlights blazed suddenly. They made the back of the barn a cauldron of white light and tall shadows.

Skip King stood on the edge of the loft, blinking into the cold reptilian gaze of a backlit serpentine head.

"Oh shit," he said.

Nancy called out, "Remo! Are you all right?"

"Who do you think turned on the lights?"

"Thank God."

"Somebody tell this thing to stop looking at me like that." King said in a voice that was unnaturally low.

"He's all right. Thank God he's all right," Nancy sobbed.

"Uh-oh," said Remo.

Nancy started. "What?"

"Old Jack caught one in the tail."

"Bad?"

"Looks like a scale wound, or something. It doesn't seem to be bothering him. It's just standing here."

"It's looking at King."

"I don't like the way it's looking at me," King said. "It's creepy."

"You'd better get back," Nancy warned.

"Why?"

"Because it's been shot in the tail. It could go berserk at any time."

"Wouldn't it already *be* berserk?" asked King in a dazed voice. He was just standing there, like a jumper on a ledge.

"The Apatosaurus is so long that nerve impulses have to be relayed along the spinal column through an organic relay near the tail," Nancy said. "Like a booster station."

"What does that mean?"

"It's been hit in the tail. But doesn't know it yet. When the pain reaches the brain, there's no telling what will happen."

"Oh," said King, talking a step backward. He took another.

Then the placid goat eyes staring at him flared. The Apatosaur suddenly acted as if it had whiplash. It reared up, a titan of black-and-orange flesh, on its rear legs. The forefeet hanging before it, it thrashed its long neck about the barn, banging its head and snout against the rafters like a snake in a box. Wood splintered and showered down.

Harruunk. Harruuunkk. Harruunkk.

"Oh shit," said King.

The fit of pain was over quickly. Still balanced on its rear legs, the head righted itself, and eyes questing, its crazed gaze fell on one figure.

The head dipped, looming closer, every tooth in its yawning mouth exposed.

Nancy tried to roll out of the way. King stumbled back.

"Don't hurt me! Don't hurt me!" he was screaming, waving the orange snout away.

His heels encountered an obstacle. He looked back and saw Nancy, lying there, all but helpless.

Skip King knew opportunity when he saw it. He pulled Nancy to her feet and got her in front of him, trying to use her as a shield.

"King! Let go, you jerk!"

King cowered behind his prisoner. "Don't let it get me, Mommy! Don't let it get me!"

The head snaked down, a splash of orange with blazing eyes.

Frantic, Nancy brought her heels down on King's feet. They dodged. In her ears was King's voice screaming—inarticulately now.

The scream was cut off as if by a blow. The snap of great teeth coming together sounded over her head.

King's grip suddenly went away, and Nancy knew to duck.

Looking up, she beheld Skip King, arms and legs jittering, being carried away. His head was in the Apatosaur's mouth and it had closed. The rest of him dangled like so much clothed meat.

As she watched, the creature threw its head back, upending it. And Skip King went down the long gullet like so much cabbage.

Nancy watched in blue-eyed horror, then turned her head away at the sight of King's tasseled loafers slipping from sight.

Remo was at her side a moment later, his strong fingers shredding her bonds.

"You okay?" he was asking.

"What about Jack?" Nancy asked in a shaken voice.

"I was hoping you had some ideas."

The Apatosaur was gyrating its long neck, trying to get the too-large morsel down. It wasn't succeeding. It moved its rear legs clumsily, trying to hold on to its precarious balance.

"It's going to choke! Can't we do something?"

Remo called down. "Chiun—any suggestions?"

Chiun's voice floated up. "Do not fear."

And the Master of Sinanju was suddenly a fluttery shape on the creature's great dappled back. He leaped onto the neck with the agility of a monkey seizing a coconut tree bole. And like a monkey, he climbed to a point just under the jaw hinge.

There, Chiun took hold of either side of the reptile's muscular throat and gave a hard twist. The crack of vetebra was audible.

"No!" Nancy screamed.

"Damn," said Remo.

The serpent's head came down, dropped its uneaten meal, and raced it to the floor.

Every rafter and roof shake shook off dust and grit when the monster slammed into the floor.

The Master of Sinanju leaped off the collapsed carcass to land on the floor. He paused, inserted his fingers into the sleeves of his kimono, and regarded the two pairs of horrorstruck eyes—Remo's and Nancy's—with unconcern.

"It is done," he intoned. "The beast has been quelled. I await my deserved reward."

25

"It is not dead," intoned the Master of Sinanju when they climbed down to join him at the Apatosaur's side.

Nancy's eyes, hot with tears of anger, went to the creature's head. She placed a hand in front of its nostrils. They grew instantly moist and warm.

Then she buried her head in its orange forehead and sobbed in immense relief.

"It was only a realigning of the spine, producing unconsciousness," Chiun announced.

Remo blinked. "Chiropractic?"

"Did I ever tell you, Remo, how a Master of Sinanju, penniless and stranded far from his village, divulged certain secrets of Sinanju to a foreigner in return for passage home, and centuries later, a new breed of charlatan became as numerous as cockroaches in Europe?"

"Never mind," said Remo. He examined the hauler. The back was ruined. It looked as if Godzilla had sat on it hard.

"I don't know about you, but I'm not up to moving this thing again," he said to no one in particular. "Never mind where we could put it."

Nancy came up, wiping at red eyes.

"I was taking Punkin to the Zoological Gardens in Philadelphia. I have a friend there. Burger Triumph would have to sue to get it back."

"Good plan. Too bad you didn't make it."

Nancy walked around the beast, which was limned by the hauler headlights. She stood near the back, the belly of the Apatosaur was clearly exposed.

"It's a bull!" she gasped.

The Master of Sinanju looked to his pupil. "The strain is obviously too much for this woman, Remo. She now believes this hideous dragon is a bull."

"I think she means it's a bull Bronto, as in a male."

Frowning, the Master of Sinanju floated over to where Nancy was kneeling to satisfy his curiosity. He returned almost at once, his wrinkled face crimson with embarassment.

"It is definitely male. And that woman is leering at its maleness in a disgusting way."

"Nancy's allowed. She's a cryptozoologist."

The side door opened and Remo and Chiun dropped into tense crouches, ready to attack or defend as the circumstance warranted. A rustic-looking man with an odd fringe of a beard and a quaint round-brimmed hat poked his head in, saw them, and said in a Germanic voice, "Who is in my barn at this hour making such noises?"

"This your barn?" asked Remo.

"Ja."

"We want to rent it for a few days," Remo said.

"Why should I rent you English my barn?"

"Or we can just leave this bull Brontosaurus for you to clean up?" Remo said, cocking a thumb over his shoulder.

The man looked past Remo for the first time, eyes going round as the brim of his hat.

"How many dollars per day vill you pay?" he asked.

"As many as you want if you leave us alone," Remo replied.

"I do this. *Danke.*" He clapped the door shut behind him.

"Who was that?" Nancy asked, coming around to see.

"Some Amish guy," said Remo.

"Amish?"

"We're in Pennsylvania Dutch country. Didn't you know?"

"No. My God! That poor man. What will he tell his family?"

"If he's smart, nothing." Remo was looking at Skip King's broken body lying in the hay. "I thought you said they ate only vegetables."

Nancy refused to look at the body. "They do. Old Jack wasn't trying to eat King, just to punish him. I guess he recognized King from Africa. He was probably the first human being he ever saw."

"Well, he's a used doggy chew-bone now," Remo said.

The Master of Sinanju strode up to Nancy and fixed her with his stern hazel eyes.

"I have twice rescued this ugly beast," he said, his wispy chin held high.

"That's true," said Nancy.

"I claim my reward."

"Little Father—" Remo began.

The Master of Sinanju cut him off with a curt chop of his hand. "When this noble creature expires at the end of its natural span, its bones are mine."

Nancy had been holding her breath. She let it out in surprise. "If I have anything to say about it, it's a deal."

The Master of Sinanju bowed, and with a last forlorn look at the slumbering dragon of Africa, he padded from the barn.

"Remo, you will give this woman our secret telephone number."

"Secret?" Nancy said.

"Actually, this is a 'don't call us, we'll call you' situation."

Nancy followed Remo to the barn door, "You're not leaving me alone to work this out, are you?"

"Don't sweat it. I'll make a call and I guarantee you the Army or Air Force or someone will show up by sunrise."

Nancy followed Remo out into the Pennsylvania

night, but the sight of clumps of curious Amish farmers converging on the barn forced her to double back.

"Damn!" she muttered. "I hope I don't have to
explain the entire Mesozoic to those people."

The next day, Remo listened to Harold Smith explain the aftermath of the night's events.

"The board of directors of Burger Triumph has re-
signed en masse," Smith said.

"They're hamburger any time you say," Remo
suggested.

"Not necessary. The Justice Department will be is-
suing indictments soon for crimes ranging from bringing a wild animal into the country without meeting
the proper quarantine and inoculation requirements to
endangering an endangered species."

"That ought to get them three whole weeks in Leav-
enworth," Remo said.

"The Apatosaur is now safe in the Zoological Gardens in Philadelphia," Smith went on.

"How'd you manage that?"

"A helicopter skycrane and the Army Corps of En-
gineers. It was dangerous, but the only way to move
the creature. Dr. Derringer was very helpful in super-
vising the transfer."

"What's going to happen to it?"

"Unclear," Smith said wearily. "The Burger Triumph people, without admitting any corporate culpa-
bility, have agreed to underwrite the animal's food
and board. Already, protest groups have surfaced demanding the creature be returned to its native habitat."

"Figures."

"The bodies of the so-called Congress for a Green
Africa have been identified. They had no connection
with the real group of that name, which are still operating in Africa. The dead men were known crimi-
nals, apparently hired to create a plausible threat to
the animal so that its death could be faked without
suspicion."

"One thing I don't get," said Remo. "Who were the guys firing blanks in Africa?"

"This is surmise," said Smith, "but if as Dr. Derringer reported, they could not be the U.S. group because they spoke in African accents, and they were not the actual Congress for a Green Africa, they could only be African mercenaries of some sort. It is fairly clear that Burger Triumph must have bribed President Oburu in order to get the dinosaur out of Africa. My guess is they were units of the Gondwanalandian Army pretending to be the ecoterrorist group. The Congress for a Green Africa is tailor-made as a scapegoat, after all"

"Well, I'm glad that's all over with. I've lost all my illusions where dinosaurs are concerned and I'd just as soon forget the whole thing happened."

"It might cheer you up to learn that Doyce Deek had confessed to a total of seven murders and the Utah authorities have begun reviewing the conviction of Roy Shortsleeve. A process from which the ACLU is keeping a conspicuous distance. It seems they are under growing pressure to close their Salt Lake City office. They have not been able to explain the dead convicts in their dumpster."

Remo laughed. "My week will be complete if you have some bad news about Dr. Gregorian."

"That matter is still under review," Smith said. "I will let you know. In the meantime, I have a plane to catch."

"Vacation?"

"A day trip to the Zoological Gardens. I am quite anxious to see this Apatosaur with my own eyes."

"Don't get too close," Remo warned.

"I understand it is quite tame."

"Mushroom breath," Remo said. "It'll get you every time."

After Remo had hung up, he went upstairs to the meditation room, where the Master of Sinanju sat attired in a gold silk kimono, his eyes closed.

Remo settled onto a mat facing Chiun. The Master

of Sinanju did not open his eyes. "Smith says it's a wrap on the Bronto," Remo said.

"I do not care."

"Still burned about losing out on a drumstick?"

"The creature cannot live forever. I will outlive it. I can afford to be patient."

"Glad to hear it. So when are we moving?"

"Never."

"What about all the so-called 'undesirable' neighbors you've been moaning about?"

The Master of Sinanju opened his eyes. "This castle is now my home, small as it is. I will not be driven from it by squatters."

Remo's face fell. Then his dark eyes grew crafty. "You mean you're willing to coexist peacefully with thieving Chinese, greedy Japanese, and slovenly Vietnamese practically pounding at the castle gates?"

"No."

"Good."

"Beginning tomorrow, Remo, you will go from door to door and inform all Vietnamese, Chinese, and other undesirables that they must find a new city in which to dwell. Tell them that this is the wish of the Reigning Master of Sinanju."

"And if they decline your polite request?" Remo asked.

The Master of Sinanju closed his hazel eyes, his face serene. "Drown them in the moat. After you have dug it, of course."

There's an epidemic with 27 million victims. And no visible symptoms.

It's an epidemic of people who can't read.

Believe it or not, 27 million Americans are functionally illiterate, about one adult in five.

The solution to this problem is you... when you join the fight against illiteracy. So call the Coalition for Literacy at toll-free 1-800-228-8813 and volunteer.

Volunteer Against Illiteracy. The only degree you need is a degree of caring.

ROC

WORLDS OF WONDER

☐ **THE HISTORICAL ILLUMINATUS CHRONICLES, Vol. I: THE EARTH WILL SHAKE** by Robert Anton Wilson. The Illuminati were members of an international conspiracy—and their secret war against the dark would transform the future of the world! "The ultimate conspiracy . . . the biggest sci-fi cult novel to come along since *Dune*."—The Village Voice
(450868—$4.95)

☐ **THE HISTORICAL ILLUMINATUS CHRONICLES, Vol. 2: THE WIDOW'S SON** by Robert Anton Wilson. In 1772, Sigismundo Celline, a young exiled Neapolitan aristocrat, is caught up in the intrigues of England's and France's most dangerous forces, and he is about to find out that his own survival and the future of the world revolve around one question: What is the true identity of the widow's son? (450779—$4.99)

☐ **THE HISTORICAL ILLUMINATUS CHRONICLES, Vol. 3: NATURE'S GOD** by Robert Anton Wilson. These are the events which will soon reshape the world . . . (450590—$4.99)

☐ **AGE OF DINOSAURS #1: *Tyrannosaurus Rex*** by J.F. Rivkin. They searched the Brazilian jungles for a long-lost expedition and found a gateway to elsewhen. . . . (451872—$4.50)

☐ **DIRTY WORK by Dan McGirt.** Retirement just wasn't what it was cracked up to be! In this heroically hilarious fantasy novel, can the woodcutter-turned-Champion slay pirates, conquer Demon Lords, and win back the Superwand? Probably not. . . . (452151—$4.50)

☐ **MOONRUNNER: *Under The Shadow* by Jane Toombs.** He was a shapeshifter, part-man/part-beast, seeking both his lost past and the one haven where he could be safe from magic's dark curse. (451716—$4.99)

Prices slightly higher in Canada.

If you and/or a friend would like to receive the *ROC Advance*, a bimonthly newsletter featuring all the newest and hottest ROC books and authors, on a complimentary basis, please fill out this form and return it to:

ROC Books/Penguin USA
375 Hudson Street
New York, NY 10014

Your Address
Name _____
Street _____ Apt. # _____
City _____ State _____ Zip _____

Friend's Address
Name _____
Street _____ Apt. # _____
City _____ State _____ Zip _____